Cyberchicks

Book 1
Cyberchicks in Love:
A Satire for the Star-Struck

Book 2
Cyberchicks go Wild:
What Happens Next May Shock You!

Cyberchicks
IN LOVE

Title: Cyberchicks in love:
a satire for the star-struck / Barb Dwyer
Series: Dwyer, Barb. Cyberchicks ; 1

ISBN: 9780645212976 (hardcover)
ISBN: 9781923212077 (paperback)

BISAC codes:
FIC028120 Science Fiction / Humorous
FIC02725 Romance / Romantic Comedy
FIC027130 Romance / Science Fiction
FIC016000 Humorous / General
FIC009080 Fantasy / Humorous
FIC027030 Romance / Fantasy
FIC052000 Satire

A catalogue record for this book is available from the
National Library of Australia

ABN 67 099 575 078
PO Box 345, Shoreham, 3916, Victoria, Australia
www.leavesofgoldpress.com

Cyberchicks IN LOVE

A Satire for the Star-Struck

Cyberchicks Book 1

Barb Dwyer
(Virtual love-child of Douglas Adams, Nora Roberts,
Terry Pratchett and Jane Austen, though unacknowledged due
to implausible genetic mutations.)

Critical Reviews

"This lavishly told masterpiece is stylish, sophisticated and thrilling, with moments of gut-wrenching realism and intense emotion. The language truly sings. Terrifically satisfying stuff!" ~ A. Lyer, *The Daily Undependable.*

"Let yourself be carried away by the read of a lifetime! Make no mistake, this is a monumental literary experience." ~ V. Gullible, *Sunday Telephone.*

"Reading this story was an indescribable experience." ~ Ophelia Payne, editor of *Tripe Odd's Alien Taxi Service Weakly.*

"They never had anything like this when I was in the Gnus and Loyals." ~ Major Blooper, ex British Army.

"This story is so instructive it ought to be standard military issue!" ~ Private Parts, US Marines.

"What can the publishers these days be thinking of?" ~ Evan Elpus, *Londinium Evening Standup.*

"Cyberchicks" is like a never-ending sailor's yarn. Bring more rum!"
~ Captain Albert Ross, SS Minnow.

"They use just the right number of vowels" ~ S. Johnson, Author of a Most Illustrious Dictionary, Who Does Not Wish To Be Associated With This Book.

"Some of the greatest works of modern fiction have been created by the most seriously deranged minds" ~ S. Freud.

"I have read this book and now I would like to get back into my grave." ~ A. Einstein.

"Name your price for the movie rights" ~ S. Spielberg. "~~No matter how cheap, I'm not interested.~~"

"The punctuation is unusual." ~ L. Tolstoy.

"It may have frayed my sleeve." ~ Moliere.

"Not as good as my books." ~ J. Austen.

"I am very attractive man. Place me in your story upon several alluring women of marriageable age." ~ Borat S.

"Tess is my kind of woman. Please give me her telephone number."
~ Ra Ra Rasputin.
"Could you please forward to me a copy of the TOATS Rule Book on Etiquette?" ~ Secretary-General of the Untied Nations.

"The penmanship in "Cyberchicks" is extraordinary. My husband and I hope ~~never~~ to see more literature of this quality throughout the Commonwealth. Keep calm ~~and please go away~~." ~ E. Windsor.

"I am biggest "Cyberchicks" fan in my country." ~ Terry Bull, editor, *Air Banana In-flight Magazine.*

"If you hate political correctness, this is for you. If you like political correctness, this is for you. If you don't care either way, this is for you. Also, if you don't know what political correctness is, this is for you. Have I missed anybody?" ~ Journal of Plausible Reviews.

"Geheim habe ich meinen fictional Abenteuern in dieser erstaunlichen Geschichte gefolgt. Ich schauen vorwärts zu jedem Kapitel." ~ Siegfried P. Hinkelheimer . . .

(. . . which AltaVista®'s Babelfish online translator rendered as "I followed to mean secret fictional adventures in this amazing history. I look forward to each chapter.")

Proud winner of the 2024 TOATS Literary Award[1]

---

1   "Too Obviously A Total Setup" (Award seal designed by Artifical Fatuity®)

EPISODES

THE GRIPPING PROLOGUE

After adding the finishing touches to the *Cyberchicks* manuscripts, Barb sat in her office thinking up clickbait-ish titles for them and trying to write a Gripping Prologue, while imbibing vast quantities of red wine.

If this gigantic Beer-Moth of a story were ever to be published she would have to do the typesetting herself, using an outdated, pirated copy of SetIt&RegretIt® (which would explain the many errors). She could never present it to a proper publisher; she knew none of them would be daft enough to touch it.

On taking a second look at what she'd just written, she was not sure she'd spelled "Beer-Moth" correctly—shouldn't there be another "h" in there somewhere?—but never mind. It was one of the impressive words she planned to use to dupe Leaves of Gold Press into publishing *Cyberchicks*.

Distractedly, she tapped the end of her pencil on her teeth and quaffed more wine. The half-empty bottle on her desk caught her eye, and she scrutinized the label more closely.

"*Chateau 42*," she read. (What was a chateau, anyway?) "*Velvety notes of compost and chimney entwine with a whisper of shoe polish, woodpecker, and a subtle, spicy hint of thoroughbred racing stables.*"

Barb typed "chat" into the Babelfish French Translator on her computer. Before she'd typed "eau", she decided to finish her glass of wine and pour another.

On the screen, the translator showed that "chat" meant "cat", so she typed in the other half of the word. Apparently "eau" meant "water in French.

So, "Chateau" meant "Catwater"—really? She sniffed at the wine. Oh well, there was no accounting for taste... in any case, now she had an idea for the Gripping Prologue.

She wrote: "Authors are often told that to really grip readers' attention in the opening paragraphs of a book they need to mention 'blood'"and 'death. 'Lust' is also said to be a good drawcard.

"The problem is, although there's quite a bit of blood—not to mention lust—sprinkled throughout this long, sprawling, chaotic, disjointed, slightly bawdy tale, hardly anybody actually dies.

"That's not for want of trying. I mean, one character is actually devoured by a crocodile at one point, and lives to tell the tale (though she's never quite the same).

"The thing is, when you've got a group of passionate fangirls, each with her own agenda, all writing the same story, with no pre-planned plot whatsoever, then as soon as one of them kills off a character someone else figures out a way to resurrect them. After all, one of the joys of writing sci-fi/fantasy fiction is that anything is possible . . .

"So, now we've got the gratuitous "Opening Paragraph Blood and Death (Not to Mention Lust) Mentions" out of the way (tick).

" . . . and since anything is possible, let's start this story somewhere in the middle and then progress to a flashback.

"Here goes . . . "

1

LEGS THAT GO
ALL THE WAY TO
VALHALLA

Comments posted on the Siegfried P. Hinkelheimer fansite:

UNEARTHLY BARB

Wednesday 8 July 1998

I just arrived back from Fiji[1] yesterday and WOW! What a holiday!!!! I couldn't wait to tell you all about it. You SPH fans are not going to believe this. The flight to Nandi[2] Airport went smoothly, but as I was waiting in the queue to pass through customs, I noticed a striking figure standing in the line next to mine.

---

1   Fictitious Fiji. It's a country on UnEarth.
2   Actually "Nearly Nandi" Airport

There was something about that demeanour, something lithe and lean and self-assured, that struck a familiar chord.

He turned around.

Oh my gosh! Could it be? Who else has those arresting blue eyes, that glance that could floor a woman at a hundred paces? Yes—it was none other than Siegfried!!

He caught me staring, and returned a slow smile.

After the customs official scraped me up off the floor, Siegfried had vanished. Feverishly I struggled past the customs desk (why do those guys always take so long checking my documents? Do I look suspicious?) As I hurried through to the baggage collection carousel, my eyes raked the assembled crowd. There he was, waiting for his suitcase, but as luck would have it, his luggage must have resembled mine, for I saw him lean down with his customary feline grace and remove my suitcase from the conveyor belt. Pantherlike, he started to walk away.

"Excuse me, that case is full of my lingerie," I stammered.

He turned upon me the implicit barrage of his gaze. It lanced through me like a sliver of blue ice as his perfect eyebrows shaped a faint interrogation.

"The suitcase is mine," I explained feebly.
Smiling gravely, he replied, "Zen allow me to carry it for you." In one swift movement he had returned to the conveyor and swept up an identical suitcase—his own. I found that the ability to speak had left me. My throat had gone dry. My legs were shaking. My pulse raced. I was a sick woman.

As we walked side by side to the doors of the international arrivals section, he said, quite conversationally, "Vere are you staying?"

"Oh . . . at the Plastic Palm Tree Resort," I managed to whisper.

"Vat a coincidence!" he smiled. "So am I. But, only for a short time. Soon I will be boarding my yacht to go sailing among the islands. Unfortunately I haf a problem—ze crew member who vas to accompany me is now unable to do so. Do you haf any experience with sailing?"

"No . . ." I gasped. Coming to my senses I added, "But I'm a quick learner."

He nodded. "You vill find, I am a goot teacher."

It was all settled, before I had even left Nandi airport—I was to accompany Siegfried on a sailing tour of the islands. If you would like me to post the next instalment of my Fijian holiday, please let me know. It was incredible.

ORIGINAL DONNA
Wednesday 8 July 1998
Barb! You beast!!! Chapter Two! Chapter Two! (I admit you had me going there for a moment!)

ORIGINAL BARB
9 July 1998
Chapter Two will be posted tomorrow, Donna, I promise. I haven't had time to type it all yet. So many adventures!

The following day as Barb sat at her desk typing the next chapter she thought, "Juliana hasn't been visiting the SPH fan site lately. Well, if she's off being red-haired and Icelandic somewhere unknown, I might as well adopt the look myself!

"I started off blonde, looking like Cloudy Chiffon®, but what the heck, I'm a demi-goddess in cyberspace. I can change not only the color of my avatar's hair, but 'my' entire body-shape if I want to ..."

UNEARTHLY BARB

10 July 1998

Chapter Two: The yacht's sails billowed, great white arcs printed against the sapphire of the Fijian skies. Long and lean was this vessel, like her captain. Her bow knifed through the waves, spear-heading a V-shape of fluorescent foam. My heart leaped like the dolphins playing in the bow wave. Could this really be happening?

I looked across the deck at Siegfried. He stood, negligently balanced, one sun-tanned weather-beaten hand on the tiller. His eyes—narrowed in that way we know so well, with the little crinkles at the corners—scanned the horizon.

A thought wandered across the dreamy paths of my brain. I was the only other person on board. Shouldn't there be a larger crew? Should I have contacted Lottie and Tess and Donna? Should I have told them to board the next plane to Fiji so that they could accompany us on this cruise?

Regaining my senses with a jolt I shook my head violently, to clear the dust from my brain. "What, and spoil the whole thing?" I said to myself. "Would they do the same for me? As if!!!"

Softly, against the susurration of wind and waves and the plaintive mewing of gulls, I began to sing a ditty which was practically the only thing I currently remembered from two years of German classes at High School.

"Blau, blau, blau sind alle meine kleider,

Blau, blau, blau ist alles was ich habe.

Darum liebe ich alles was so blau ist

Weil mein Schatz ein—" I broke off, chased a few syllables around in my head and wished there was a handy AltaVista Babelfish[3] translator nearby. Giving up, I lamely finishing with, " . . . sailor ist."

Suddenly I realized that Siegfried was close by. He had roped the tiller into position and left the yacht on auto-pilot.

"Oh!" I stammered shyly, "I didn't intend for you to hear that song!"

"Did you truly mean zem, zose verds you sang?"

"I—er—yes, but I cannot remember the German word for 'sailor' . . ."

He leaned and whispered the translation in my ear. His breath was as sweet and warm as a tropical night. I had known that is how it would be, during all those months when I had sat hour after hour in front of a flickering screen, clutching my shopping bag full of worn-out videos, my fingers aching with the sheer agony of pressing rewind, rewind, rewind, every time he appeared.

"I can hardly believe you chose me to be your crew-member," I stuttered. (I always seemed to be stuttering and stammering around Siegfried.)

---

3   AltaVista Babel Fish was a free Web-based multilingual translation application. On December 9, 1997, it was launched as AltaVista Translation Service, at babelfish.altavista.com. In February 2003, AltaVista was purchased by Overture Services, Inc. Five months later, Overture was taken over by Yahoo!. In May 2012 Yahoo! Babel Fish was replaced by Bing Translator.

"How could I fail to notice a red-haired Icelandic girl mit legs zat go all za way to Valhalla on a goot day?" he said with a shrug. (I wondered if I should feel slightly guilty that the original author of this description was Juliana.)

I held my breath. One question was burning on my lips. WOULD THE SEXY SAXON GET HIS SOX OFF?

At that precise moment, the yacht gave a lurch. A freak wave had hit us and we were thrown off balance. Siegfried tried to catch me but I was thrown overboard, and he along with me . . .

ORIGINAL DONNA
10 July 1998
Barb, what an amazing vacation! I can't wait to hear how you were rescued, and am even more desperate to find out why the heck you ever came back???

ORIGINAL BARB
10 July 1998
Thanks for your feedback Donna. Is there anyone else out there at the moment? Or have they all gone to Fiji?

UNEARTHLY BARB
10 July 1998
Chapter Three: Water came up at me, a green glass wall. It reached up to engulf me like wet cellophane pulling me down. As it closed over my head, I thought I was done for. I sank, flailing my arms wildly. In my panic I had forgotten how to swim. A school of neon fish flashed past, brilliant topaz and burning amethyst.

At least I was drowning in an attractive environment.

But I had underestimated my hero! Just as I was about to pass out, I felt myself rising. A hand had grasped my amazingly long red Icelandic hair and was pulling me up. My head broke the surface. When I had finished coughing and spluttering I discovered that I was being held in my rescuer's arms. His mouth was about an inch from mine.

"Do not fear," he murmured reassuringly. "You are safe now."

Let me tell you—close up, those eyes were like two window-panes of lapis lazuli looking out from some remote desert fastness. Instantly I went as limp as a strand of seaweed.

"Danke schön," I said weakly, the last two words learned in High School German classes returning to mind opportunely.

And then another odd thing happened, because I could think of nothing else to say. There we were in the middle of the ocean, with the yacht drifting away fast, the top of its mast barely visible behind mountains of water, and all I could think of was that Siegfried's heart was beating dangerously close to mine.

"You are very beautiful," I heard him say. I closed my eyes. I just knew he was about to kiss me. But before anything happened, a spear of agony shot through my left foot, as though someone had run a hot wire along the marrow of my bones.

Opening my eyes, I screamed. Through that emerald water the unthinkable was clearly visible—a grey nurse shark was fastened to my foot. Blood swirled through the depths like raspberry cordial. I kicked out desperately, feeling myself dragged from Siegfried's arms.

Bizarrely, it seemed to me that a large swordfish swam right up to me while my foot was being devoured by the shark. The swordfish opened its mouth and said, "Omelette or mixed grill? Omelette or mixed grill?"

Next moment, I woke up on the plane to Fiji with a Thrills & Spoons® novel open in my lap, a pointy-nosed air hostess hovering over me and a really bad cramp in my left foot, probably induced by airline food . . .

THE END

ORIGINAL BARB
10 July 1998
Has anyone else had a similar experience with SPH? All contributions welcome!

But who is Siegfried, and who are these other people? And where are they? And how did this cyber-narrative madness begin?

To explain, we must flash back in time, to the events that led up to The Creation of Unearth . . .

2

THE OBSESSION BEGINS

 On the Original Planet Earth, Original Barb grimaced at her List of Things To Do. Most of it was written in an unintelligible scrawl, all of it was boring, and none of it had been crossed out.

Absent-mindedly she tapped her pencil on the surface of her desk, wondering where she had hidden the last stash of chocolate she wasn't going to eat. A moment later she dismissed the thought from her mind. Looking for it would only delay performing the tasks listed on the List of Things To Do.

She began rummaging amongst the dingy pleats of the filing cabinet. Just as she had reached "F" for Forbidden, Fattening and Fruit 'n' Nut, the phone rang.

She picked up the receiver (only rich people had cellphones in 1998).

"Hi Barb," Original Lottie said, giggling girlishly on the other end of the line. "Tess and I have just come back from the Archival Cinema. We saw a movie called *Das Rat.*"

"Really?" Barb peeled gleaming silver wrappings from several dark brown cubes of chocolatey sweetness. "Another rodent movie?"

The Archival Cinema screened only classic or cult motion pictures, or oldish flicks that had been released several seasons ago, or indie foreign films which never made it to the mainstream venues, like the recent spate of bizarre European movies inexplicably featuring rodents. Tickets were cheap, which is why the cinema was popular with Barb's impecunious friends Lottie and Tess.

"Not 'rat', 'rat'!" Lottie elucidated. "*Das Rat!* It means 'The Council' in German."

"All right! It's not my fault you watch random Euro-flicks."

"I've already seen *The Rat*, anyway," said Lottie. "Saw it ages ago. That really is a rodent movie."

"Good, was it, this latest Rat movie that's not about rodents?" asked Barb, her voice somewhat muffled, as if her mouth were full.

"Oh yes," enthused Lottie. "It's about this German battleship during World War Two."

"Mmm?" Bored, Barb swung around in her chair again. Her foot accidentally knocked over the rubbish bin and several pages of her 1998 desktop calendar spilled across the floor.

"You see, the crew goes through hell," Lottie continued. "They are almost killed when a destroyer depth-charges them, then a storm blows them off course and they nearly collide with a German U-boat, and they're running out of food and fuel when they score a hit on an Allied convoy, but the captain feels sorry for the men on the burning tanker and has to make a moral decision."

"Are you sure you're not reading this?" Barb demanded, wiping chocolate off the corners of her mouth. "You sound so erudite."

"No," Lottie replied injuredly. "I told you, I've been studying how to write movie scripts. And later the battleship is fired on by Allied patrol planes and damaged, so it has to hide in a Norwegian fjord to escape, but the food is running out and they are desperately trying to fix the boat so that they can make a break for freedom. And this man who's the captain, he's very heroic."

"Right," said Barb half-heartedly, doodling with a pen on the back of her arm and ignoring the decaying apple core lying beside the overturned rubbish bin.

Lottie went on in the style of a professional movie critic, "It has a very moving finale. The screenplay depicts the struggle between good and evil in the early twentieth century. The sets were so good, you could almost smell the ocean . . ."

"Cut the crap," interrupted Barb. "There's something simpering about your voice and you keep giggling. It's the movie's hero isn't it? You've got a crush on him, haven't you! Admit it!"

Lottie could bear it no longer. Dropping the erudite tone she said, "Dammit, Barb, he was gorgeous."

"Just as I thought. You've developed yet another fan-girlish obsession."

"Tall," crooned Lottie, ignoring Barb's sardonic tone. "Amazing eyes, like chips of heaven. Lean, athletic frame. High, moulded cheekbones. Tess fell in love with him instantly; I didn't. The way I feel about him right now, this seems astounding to contemplate, but I suppose it's not surprising. The man I've been dreaming about all my life was dark-haired—a cross between Daniel de Licious as Sparrowfoot in *The Last of the Michoacan Pocket Gophers*, and Colin Firth as Mr Darcy, with Nicolas Birdhouse's body thrown in for good measure. The hero of *Das Rat*, with his burnished curls, doesn't really fit the bill.

"But inexplicably, some way into the film I found myself gazing yearningly up at the screen and sighing; 'I love you'. It was probably one of those little smiles—the merest flicker of a cheek muscle—that got to me. It was also, for me, definitely something to do with him being 'Captain'. He is the perfect captain; a strong, quiet, lonely man, somewhat remote, but always accessible, always humane, compassionate; a man to trust implicitly; to love; a captain whose crew would die for him. I would!"

"Are you sure you're not reading this?" asked Barb uncertainly. "Nobody talks like that—"

"Of course not," Lottie averred ambiguously. She continued, "He also loves his ship. That first time we, the audience, see the vessel, the way the captain looks round at his comrades and says, 'That's our ship', with such pride and love in his face; at the end, the way he hangs onto life just long enough to see his ship 'die'; that touched me deeply. But, almost above all, he has that magnetic inner gleam—what is it?—a vast sense of humor?—profound knowledge of the world?— has he perhaps discovered the meaning of life? I tottered from the theatre a changed woman, managing to mumble to Tess: "A captain to die for.

"Honestly, Barb," Lottie's voice now had husky overtones, "I've never seen anyone like him. I go all funny just thinking about him."

"Oh really?" Barb said drily. "Come on, he can't be that good. They've all got some flaw."

Even as she said this she glanced fondly at the huge Daniel de Licious poster adorning her office wall right next to the brightly-colored Fiji Travel poster. "Except you," she mouthed silently, smirking adoringly at her idol's handsomeness. He'd been so absolutely wonderful in his starring role as Sparrowfoot in *The Last of the Michoacan Pocket Gophers*, and he'd been utterly brilliant in the heartrending movie *My Deft Ferret*. Come to think of it, it wasn't just Europeans who were inexplicably producing a glut of rodentish movies . . .

"Hello? Hello!" Lottie was babbling on the other end of the line.

"Oh, yeah," said Barb, recollecting that she was supposed to be holding up her end of the conversation. "You were saying?"

"I was asking you what you are doing this evening."

"Nothing much," Barb said evasively. Secretly, she had planned to relax by "surfing" that new-fangled thing called "the Internet", doting on pictures of Daniel de Licious or languidly researching pointless items like "Mesopotamian pasta sculptures" and "reproduction fourteenth century field armour". She'd probably end up visiting a few desperado rock-band fan sites to read the pathetic fan-fiction poured onto the Internet from aching prepubescent hearts. The stories involving improbable meetings with their idols were always worth a laugh.

"Tess and I are going to see the movie again this evening," Lottie said. "Wanna come?"

"Okay," said Barb brightly, crumpling up her List of Things To Do and the empty chocolate wrapper. "I'll be there. Incidentally, what's the name of this hero captain actor guy?"

"Siegfried," said Lottie. Only she didn't just say the name, she approached it with the diffidence of a love-struck schoolgirl, formed the vowels in a sort of hallowed whisper and pronounced the consonants as though tasting a fine wine. As she exhaled the final syllable her palate seemed to caress it, her vocal chords twanging a counterpoint to the melody she made of the name. She even made it sound as if there were two little dots that looked like beady eyes peering over the first 'e'; some kind of exotic diacritical mark.

"Seegfreed? What kind of name is that?" Barb wanted to know.

"It's German."

"I might as well check him out to see if he's as gorgeous as you say. Seegfreed what?"

"Siegfried P. Hinkelheimer," breathed Lottie.

Little did Barb realize what an impact that appellation would have on her life from that moment.

Later that evening Original Barb, Lottie and Tess, wall-eyed and beetroot-faced, staggered out of the Archival Cinema. Their hair hung dishevelled around their young, not unattractive faces. Their cheap T-shirts and jeans looked crumpled. In their hands they held printed copies of the cinema's forthcoming attractions, with which they were still fanning themselves.

"Hot in there, wasn't it," stated Tess, red-cheeked, trying to catch her breath.

"Mmph," soliloquised curly-haired Lottie, tongue-tied and drooling.

With a robot-like gait the three young women walked down the road silently for several minutes. So intent on their musings were they, that they paid no attention to the traffic swerving, honking its horns and narrowly missing them.

Eventually Tess pushed a lock of her short, pale hair out of her eyes and said, "I think we're heading in the wrong direction."

A yellow taxicab which had been bearing down on them suddenly veered out of their path. Its horn blared, the rude note descending in pitch as it dopplered away. A toxic cloud of carbon monoxide enveloped the three pedestrians like a bluish mist.

Barb said, with unexpected insight, "Let's get off the road."

They skittered out of the trajectory of an oncoming bus and landed on the sidewalk, clustering underneath a street light like three drab moths. Ragged scarves of exhaust gases slowly dissipated from their clothing.

"Movie's showing again tomorrow at seven p.m.," said Tess conversationally.

"Mmph," acknowledged Lottie, whose eyes, vacant and glazed, resembled some of the sparsely-constellated areas of the Crab Nebula.

"We have to wait that long?" trumpeted Barb.

Wearing an anguished look, Tess started chewing nervously on a corner of the forthcoming attractions brochure. "It is a long time," she said worriedly, "Don't know if I can manage it. Is there anywhere around here we could buy a bottle of vodka?"

Barb sighed, assuming a long-suffering air. Tess just hadn't been the same since she and Lottie had sailed across the Atlantic on a tall ship with all those Vulgarian sailors. The holiday had proved to be an exciting adventure, but Tess had developed a worrying penchant for vodka, garlic and good-looking young Vulgarians.

"No there's not," she said firmly. Looking down at her own forthcoming attractions she noticed half a page was missing. There were teeth-marks all along the top of the remaining half.

"Egad! We're in a bad way!" she exclaimed as it came to her that she had just eaten a goodly portion of *The Wizard of Oz*. "I doubt whether we can hold on for twenty-one hours without seeing *Das Rat* again."

"Siegfried," moaned Lottie. "My Captain. Mein Kapitän." She giggled insanely, high-pitched, like a jockey in a pit of feathers. (By now she'd lost the ability to pronounce two fictitious dots in 'Siegfried', but compensated by tacking a spare pair onto 'Kapitän'.)

"No, we definitely can not," agreed Tess, eyeballing Lottie with some alarm, "but what can we do?"

"Video store," blurted Lottie. "We can borrow every movie he's ever been in!" She took off like sleep-walker on speed, her arms stretched out in front of her as if already reaching for video cassettes to grab off the store's shelves. Tess accelerated to keep pace.

"Wait for me!" cried Barb, running along behind.

Where they had been standing, in the sallow pool of lamp-light, a flurry of brochure pages drifted down like flakes of peeling whitewash.

Nineteen hours later, tendrils of grey smoke began curling up from Tess's antique video cassette recorder. Sitting bleary-eyed on the well-worn furniture in Tess's lounge room, the three friends continued to stare at the TV screen. An hour after that, the VCR made a noise that sounded like 'whumph!' and the screen went blank.

No amount of kicking or cursing would coax the machine to life again, and Lottie's brother had been a professional VCR repairman, so Lottie really knew how to curse.

"Drat, drat, drat!" yelled Tess, jumping out of her threadbare armchair. "Look, it's chewed up the tape!"

Glittering coils of magnetic ribbon jumped out from the black box as she repeatedly pressed the silver 'eject' button. Helpfully, Lottie was sobbing into a lumpy cushion. Smoke coagulated along the ceiling like a forgotten genie.

"They just don't make these machines like they used to," shouted Tess. "A little continuous usage, a few thousand four-second rewinds and prolonged pauses on Siegfried's face and next thing the whole shebang overheats and blows up. Now the video of The Heliotrope Parrot is ruined, and it's the only SPH movie we could find! Pass the vodka, Lottie. And stop kissing the tape—you're making me feel ill."

17

"Siegfried's in there somewhere," mourned Lottie, peering through her spectacles at handfuls of shiny brown ribbon as though she might catch a glimpse of his face among the magnetic signals.

"It's six p.m.," said Barb grimly, pacing up and down. "If we hurry we can scour three, maybe four more video stores on the way to the cinema."

"But we don't have a working VCR to play them on," objected Tess.

"True, but we can look at the pictures on the front of the cases," elucidated Barb, waving aloft the case of *The Heliotrope Parrot*, on which Siegfried appeared in one corner.

This suggestion galvanised them all into action.

"I can't believe we could only find one video with him in," repeated Tess bitterly as the three obsessed fans crammed themselves into Lottie's geriatric Valkyrievagon® "bug". "One video!"

"I imagine it's because all his other videos are out on hire," surmised Lottie, feeling for the steering wheel from beneath a frightening tangle of glossy plastic tape. "Some other women are probably watching them right now."

"How dare they!" muttered Tess.

By the time they arrived at the Archival Cinema, stopping at every video rental store along the way, the three companions had managed to obtain a second video.

"What happens when the man with the gavel is even crazier than the psychopaths he sentences?" sensationalised the blurb on the jacket of *Judge Mental*.

Lottie clutched the cassette fiercely to her chest and they staggered to their seats.

"Why are we staggering?" Barb wondered aloud.

"Because we haven't eaten anything except popcorn since this time yesterday," snapped Tess, who was also suffering from a hangover.

"Shut up, both of you," hissed Lottie. "It's starting! *Das Rat!*"

As the house lights dimmed and the wide screen glowed incandescent, three copies of 'Forthcoming Attractions' began flapping back and forth in unison in front of three rapidly over-heating faces, like the wing-beats of hyperactive insects.

For weeks, the three friends scoured cinemas and video rental stores. They had hunted down and watched every existing copy of every Siegfried P. Hinkelheimer movie in the neighbourhood.

"It's no use," Tess said despondently as they wandered out of the Archival Cinema for the twenty-first time, after the evening session, "*Das Rat* has finished its run and we can't find it on video anywhere. In any case, our VCRs have all broken down and we can't afford repairs or new machines. What hope do we have?"

Through swimming eyes, Barb stared down at her friends. They weren't quite as tall as she was, and the neon glare of the suburban night washed the tops of their heads with a ghastly pallor.

Omigosh, they look terrible, she thought in italics—*bags under their eyes, pinched cheeks, haunted miens, their hair*

19

sticking out at odd angles with crushed popcorn caught in the tangles. Plastic shopping bags full of worn-out video cassettes clutched under each arm . . .

Catching sight of her own reflection in a passing wing-mirror she flinched, almost dropping her shopping-bags. What she beheld made her friends look like supermodels. *So,* she thought, again in italics, *this is what going without sleep, crawling around video stores, inhaling the smoke of wrecked VCRs and sitting for hours in cinemas pigging out on ice-cream and chocolate while gasping, sighing, drooling and crying her way through a movie did to a girl.*

"We can't go on like this," she announced decisively.

"But what can we do?" wailed Tess.

Nobody replied. They clustered under the lamp-post again, netted in the frayed gauze of its light. Neon signs glimmered along the rows of nearby store-fronts. Overhead, in the leaden sky, monstrous clouds were eating up the stars.

"Do you think it's going to rain?" quavered Lottie, gazing skywards and experimentally extending her palm. A couple of passers-by dropped some coins into it.

"Wonderful!" sniffed Tess. "Now everyone thinks we're destitute bag ladies."

"Siegfried," Lottie simpered.

"I think we all agree it's time to get a life again," said Barb, secretly calculating whether Lottie had enough coins to hire another video, preferably *The Last of the Michoacan Pocket Gophers*, "and I believe we could do so if only we could get a regular Siegfried fix whenever we needed it."

Thunder rumbled in the distance.

"It's going to rain," said Tess thinly. "A storm's coming. We'd better start for home. Otherwise the videos are going to get wet."

"A regular Siegfried fix," echoed Lottie as they began treading the sombre asphalt of the footpath. "My sister's husband's Mum has a VCR that works."

"Where does she live?" Tess quickly quizzed.

"Only about ten—"

Lottie broke off. With a skull-splitting crash, a jagged blade of pure light clove the night in two. For the duration of a cockroach's heart-beat, the suburban landscape was revealed in garish, ghastly detail, as if a giant flashbulb had exploded.

Then, like a steel curtain, darkness clamped down.

"Ouch," said Barb out of the gloom.

"All the lights have gone out," shrieked Tess, panic-stricken.

"You've got your eyes shut, dimwit," said Lottie. "You all right, Barb?"

"I've been struck by lightning," proclaimed Barb in an evangelistic tone. "Either that or I've had an idea."

"What idea?" asked Tess, opening her eyes.

Lottie said, "Is it about how to get another Siegfried fix?"

In the flickering neon radiance Barb's tangled hair was standing on end like a sunburst. A slow, beatific smile spread across her haggard features.

"Yes," she breathed. "Oh, yes."

Half an hour later, the three desperate fans crowded around Barb's office computer. The monitor screen glowed into life.

This being the year 1998, it was only seven years since the World Wide Web had become publicly available. It was still a novelty.

"This is the 'Internet'," explained Barb, as her computer's screen turned white and displayed a long, horizontal rectangle in the middle. "Or it might be called the World Wide Web, I'm not sure what the difference is." The others had heard of the Internet of course, and Tess even owned a computer, but she hadn't explored the Internet much yet.[4]

"Now," said Barb with a professional air, "I'll just type the name 'Siegfried P. Hinkelheimer' into this search engine box, press 'enter' and see what comes up."

Lottie was looking gloomy. "It's pretty unlikely you'll find anything," she prophesied. "I mean, *Das Rat* has only been showing at crappy old art-house cinemas, it's outdated, it never really succeeded in the mainstream cinemas. Hardly anyone outside Europe has ever heard of—" she paused to lovingly relish the name—"'Siegfried.'"

Light-emitting diodes blinked gaily on the dial-up modem. It emitted a sound like "*pshhhkkkkkkrrrrkakingkakingkak ingtshchchchchchchchchcch*ding*ding*ding . . .* " The hard disk groaned and lines of text suddenly appeared on the computer's monitor.

Three young women screamed.

"Will you look at that!" yipped Tess. "Top of the list of possibilities! 'The Siegfried P. Hinkelheimer Fan Site!'"

"The *only* possibility, in fact," mumbled Barb.

---

4 The Internet was in its infancy. There was no Facebook, TwitterX, Instagram, TikTok, Pinterest, YouTube, Reddit or Google. Not even MySpace.

"Someone else has heard of him after all!" squeaked Lottie happily, "and appreciates him, what's more! There might be pictures! And gossip! Quick, Barb, click there."

Barb's hand reached for the mouse and her index finger moved at speed. On the screen, the cursor metamorphosed into a pointing arrow. Click! went Barb's mouse-button.

The screen whitened out like spilled flour and then a graphic began to unfold in the centre, layer upon layer. Within that graphic, two eyes lanced out like shards of sapphire. Below them appeared rugged ranges of cheekbones, a finely-chiselled countenance, a strong chin and that most charismatic, enigmatic of smiles.

Lottie clutched at a chair-back for support. She gurgled intelligently.

"There it is, girls," chortled Barb, "the Home Page of The Siegfried P. Hinkelheimer Fan Site. 'Built by Donna', it says here. I wonder who she is."

"Home!" Tess murmured happily. "This website feels like home!"

They looked at the website's menu.

"Which link shall we click on first?" asked Barb. "Movies? Images? Links? Feedback? Interviews?"

"Movies," squawked Tess. "We have to find out what else he's been in."

Click.

A list appeared.

"Ooh, look!" said Lottie, wide-eyed. "He's been in lots!"

"Yeah, lots I've never heard of," said Barb. "Probably second-rate crud, but who cares." She clicked on "print". The printer rattled. A rectangle of creamy bond came rolling out of its maw and Barb read aloud the list ink-jetted upon it.

"In addition to *Das Rat*, there is *The Seventh Swine, The Creep, No Go, Sugarcane Jones, Princess Iylbiseeinya, In the Nostrils of Idiocy, Wake Up: it's the End of the Line, Quicksand, Laden with Liars, The Tenderness of Vowels*—"

"Here, that's an odd title," interjected Lottie. "Shouldn't it be T*he Tenderness of Beef*?"

"Or Wolves?" said Tess.

"Nope, it's "vowels", Said Barb.

"Oops, I mixed up the letters," said Tess. "I blame it on lack of sleep. Thought it must be some were-wolf flick, but it looks like a movie about how hard it is to speak English when you're Australian.

They read on.

Sandhill, Fashion and Pallor, Annihilating Motor Vehicles, The British Are So Impatient, Murder: By Reason of Eccentricity, Surface Paradise, LOL, A High Bright Reason, Thrill Schmooze, The Substitute Distillers, The Sherbert Bomb, Judge Mental, Airforce Fun, Interferer, The Water-Pistols of Etiquette . . .

"Well!" exclaimed Tess, glancing over the inventory with satisfaction. "He's had plenty of minor roles, at least. That gives us enough to go on with. Now, click on that menu heading 'Feedback,' and we'll find out what the other fans are gossiping about before we pass out from over-infatuation while looking at 'Images'."

Click.

The recent "Feedback" postings materialised on the computer's screen, preceded by the names of their authors. As the three fans began to read, they realized that they had indeed come 'home'. This was where the nitty was really getting gritty...

3

THE FEEDBACK PAGE
OF THE SPH FANSITE

ORIGINAL AMY

Sunday 18 January 1998

Juliana, you weren't brusque at all. A little cynical, maybe, but not brusque. I'm curious, though, and I'd like to put a question to everyone. What is it about Siegfried that attracts you? Not just physically, but emotionally. Myself, I think of him as a poet and a romantic. That's what appeals to me about him.

ORIGINAL JULIANA

Sunday 18 January 1998

Amy, I'm going to have to be cynical again. Physically and emotionally what attracts me to him? Simple. He looks like a man who could take me to the Seventh Heaven and back in no time.

He looks like a man who need not learn anything more about carnal knowledge (do I make myself clear or need I add, a man who has done every position imaginable from Kama Sutra ...)

This is the overbearing feeling I have had for him since I saw *Das Rat* two years ago and had shivers railing down my spine to such a degree that I am surprised my friends sitting next to me did not catch fire.

I'm going off to the slopes now for a couple of days and shall be missing you all. But I'll be back. Donna, I can't thank you enough for a weird and whacko site. Those new pics in "Images" are to die for, but they have just ruined my day. How am I supposed to get any constructive work done when Hinkelheimer is out here looking all poetic and saccharine? I still haven't made up my mind whether I prefer my Hinkelheimer all sweet and gentle or moodily dangerous.

ORIGINAL SONIA
Tuesday 20 January 1998

A fascinating query—why are we attracted to Siegfried? For me the attraction is an indefinable, spirit-piercing compulsion. It's a mingling of his fluid, agile way of moving, with his flawless vocal qualities. Oh, his voice! The modulation, his ability to infuse his speech with a tender, soothing quality, or to exact esteem by uttering a single command. His Austrian-influenced pronunciation is unique, quite different from that of his fellow countrymen. I have heard his voice described as 'auralgasmic'– the ideal adjective!

He is arrestingly handsome, though not in the traditional sense of the word. And somehow he has the kind of demeanour that is suggestive of secret or private knowledge.

For me, his masculine poise and self-assurance is very seductive. He simultaneously exudes power and tenderness. In any movie scene he outshines all other actors with his charisma, even when he is neither speaking nor moving.

For me, his entire physical and emotional make-up are amazing. I envy anyone fortunate enough to have actually been in Siegfried's presence. I think it would be bliss to meet him in person. Imagine being confronted with all that vigour and masculinity . . .

Oh my! What a lovely thought!

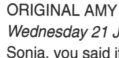

ORIGINAL AMY
Wednesday 21 January 1998
Sonia, you said it in a nutshell. You very eloquently put into words how I feel about this man. It's ineffable; it's a soul thing.

Last night watching *Das Rat* with two people who had never seen the movie, they couldn't quite get why I was so enamoured of the Captain. They thought he was cool and handsome—but it goes way beyond that for us, doesn't it? Feline (or even lupine, like a wolf) describes him so well. It's the way he moves, the hands, the intelligence, the intensity, it's presence and sheer magnetism. How come real guys aren't that intense?

Anyway, thanks for the beautiful description. I couldn't have put it better myself.

ORIGINAL DONNA
Thursday 22 January 1998
Well, I watched *Surface Paradise* last night. I will write a review of it as soon as I've had a chance to watch it again, because I confess I haven't a clue what it's about, yet. The plot struck me as a little odd, but then five o'clock to seven o'clock in the afternoon are not prime TV viewing hours for me and my attention was

almost everywhere else throughout. Siegfried was a main character—actually a good guy for once. Did anyone else catch the movie?

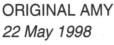

ORIGINAL AMY

22 May 1998

Donna, your attention was almost everywhere else? During a Siegfried P. Hinkelheimer movie? That's it. I'm taking away your official SPH Fan Club Decoder Ring.

P.S. How'd the man look, anyway?

ORIGINAL DONNA

Friday 23 January 1998

LOL, I am properly chastised, Amy. The admission of distraction is a punishable offence. Does it count if I concentrate twice as hard when I watch it next time?

With regard to your last question . . . how does "heavy sigh" sound? He appears as our lean, stubble-jawed romantic— the version we all appear (so far) to favor.

ORIGINAL AMY

Friday 23 January 1998

Donna—well, you're forgiven, seeing as how you were nice enough to build this site and all.

I watched *The Seventh Swine* last night and it is hands down my favorite in terms of which version of Siegfried I like best. I don't know how anyone can have such luminous eyes. The way the film is lit, they are shimmering blue, sometimes turquoise, sometimes shining, like a reflection on water. Quite breathtaking. Sigh.

I wish I could get my hands on *Surface Paradise*—none of my local video stores seem to have it. Maybe I could get it through the Internet. But that would mean I'd have to PAY big bucks for a Siegfried video—and that would be admitting I have a serious obsession with him. Which I don't. Really I don't. Honest. (Lean, stubble-jawed? GROAN. I have to go take a cold shower now.)

Original Juliana **ORIGINAL JULIANA**
Sunday 25 January 1998
Good to be back. Trust me to get mauled by a ski-lift—now I have severe pelvic pain and a job interview to boot tomorrow, so gotta be quick.

Amy, whatever you do, DO NOT BUY that video. It is the first step on the long and slippery road to severe addiction. You'll end up in a home with a sackful of pathetic videos. For all you people out there with a sackful of pathetic videos— my condolences.

One week of Hinkelheimer deprivation has left me cocky and clear-sighted. (I'm trying to quit him, you see.)

After goggling my heart out in the fansite's "Images" section, something occurred to me. Why is his cheek and chin so . . . wobbly . . . is that the right word? Is that the result of the accident on the *Sandhill* set we all read about with sinking hearts? Does anyone know, has his face always been wobbly . . . or is it just me being stupid and shallow again?

Amy, I will email you as soon as I get my job interview done. Have to go and do some hard-core focussing done now . . .

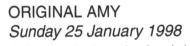

ORIGINAL AMY
Sunday 25 January 1998

Juliana, glad you're back in one piece and I hope the interview goes well. But I have to say, you go away for one lousy week and NOW you're noticing Siegfried's flaws. Oh sure, be all clear-sighted and objective, but I warn you—it won't last. You'll be back here in the gutter with us addicts soon enough.

If by "wobbly" you mean the acne scars, he's always had those. I think it gives him character and the battered look I love. Otherwise, I'm not sure what you mean. I think you're playing up the flaws so you can wean yourself. Give it up, girl.

Oh, and what makes you think I'm not already a severe addict who sits at home watching SPH movies, hmmm?

ORIGINAL JULIANA
Monday 26 January 1998

Hinkelheimer's got a ACHNE[5]? My lord, I must have been wearing rose-tinted glasses in the past. Never noticed that before. No wonder that busky beard suits him so well, covering all those scars up. "Wobbly" was a bad choice of word but I was totally out of it yesterday and offended him badly. Now kiss and make up time.

Just read Sonia's exquisite description of Hinkelheimer and now I remember what I used to see in him. Watched *Das Rat* (again) to really rub it in. He is gorgeous, that smirky half-smile of his drives me mad.

You seen that scene where he sits at his desk writing

---

5   Throughout this series, Juliana's unique spellings and grammar have been preserved for posterity.

and that skeleton-like figure comes lurking to say sorry. Hinkelheimer slowly, sensually looks up from his writing and there is something in his eyes that goes straight to my nerve-centre. After he says his words he slowly and sensually looks down again, with a slight nod. That is a masterpiece of understated acting. And he is the master of it. Now I am all peppered up to go out and kill those employers. Take me or leave me. See ya.

ORIGINAL AMY
Monday 26 January 1998
Yeah, I just BET you'd like to kiss and make up with him, Juliana. Good luck on the interview.

ORIGINAL SONIA
Monday 26 January 1998
Whoa, I am a tad tardy in posting this comment I know, but I was fortunate enough to see *Surface Paradise* on free-to-air TV over the weekend and naturally I recorded it so by now I've watched it several times!

Siegfried is so handsome in it. He still looks like the our favorite hero the battleship captain, but instead of the uniform he is wearing riding pants and a shirt with most of the top buttons undone.

ORIGINAL JULIANA
Monday 26 January 1998
Shirt mostly unbuttoned . . . Sonia, you gotta send me a copy. I pay you anything. P.S. Has he got a hairy chest?

31

ORIGINAL SONIA
Tuesday 27 January 1998

Hi Juliana, you'd get a better view of his body by watching *Annihilating Motor Vehicles*. That movie shows quite a lot of him! His chest is just perfect–not hairless and shiny, not a gorilla-like mat but somewhere in between. As for acne–who cares??? Most people would say it compliments his craggy, masculine look.

So you have returned to SPH fandom, eh? And not before time! I can't understand why you tried to leave in the first place. For my part I am well on the way to the gutter of obsession, which I will inhabit blissfully, devoid of all possessions other than my Siegfried videos.

ORIGINAL NATHANIEL HINKELHEIMER
Friday 30 January 1998

Um, well, hi everybody! This is great! Nathaniel Hinkelheimer is my name and I'm German. I don't know HIM, but it sure would be great to meet him!

ORIGINAL JULIANA
Friday 30 January 1998

Nathaniel Hinkelheimer—that gotta be two of the most sexy names I know of. Could you kindly wrap up in a parcel and fly yourself over to me. What a day this is proving to be. Mr Perfect finally asks me out and here on this site someone is presenting himself by THAT name, sighhhhhhh . . .

ORIGINAL NATHANIEL HINKELHEIMER
Saturday 31 January 1998

Heeeeeeelllp! Hi everybody I'd just like to say thanx for sending me so many emails but honestly I don't know Siegfried!! :)

I'm asking you not to send any more, if u don't mind.

ORIGINAL AMY
Saturday 31 January 1998
What's the deal with this Nathaniel guy?

ORIGINAL ALICE
Saturday January 31st 1998

I have no idea, Amy. Juliana's the one who wants to go out with him.

ORIGINAL NATHANIEL HINKELHEIMER
Saturday 31 January 1998

Darling Juliana I want to reply to your email as I said I would, but by mistake I lost your address. Would you email me again? ;o)

By the way, you have made a grammatical error with your German. After I post feedback to the Siegfried P. Hinkelheimer fan site, a page appears up with the message, 'Vielen Danke fur das Besuch'. The proper way to say it is 'Vielen Danke fur den Besuch'.

ORIGINAL JULIANA
Saturday 31 January 1998

My date went swimmingly, for everyone who wants to know. I am almost in Seventh Heaven. Well, Alice and Amy, I send you the gory details as soon as I can.

Nate, are you talking to me or Donna? I am not in charge of this site and will not be held responsible for any spelling mistakes, you little swot you. There, you had your chance and you blew it, if you deleted my email address. Bad luck for you. I am not in the business of handing it out to all and sundry.

ORIGINAL DONNA
Saturday 31 January 1998

Well hello Nathaniel and thank you for the language lesson. I happily assume responsibility for that German phrase which automatically pops up after anyone submits a message. I'll go and change it :) Juliana, why are most of us being deprived of the gory details of your legendary evening?

ORIGINAL JULIANA
Sunday 1 February 1998

Nate, darling, I did not mean to offend you, calling you swot and everything. I am such a hothead these days, blowing fuses all over the place.

Am in the middle of packing and my new found lover is having the weekend with his kids. Life sucks. Anyway, Nate, how can we be sure you are not the real McCoy using some ridiculous address to wind us chicks up out here?

Donna, you want gory details, you get some, I will mail you.

ORIGINAL AMY
Sunday 1 February 1998
Could it be that Nathaniel IS Siegfried P. Hinkel-heimer, using a false name? Quick, Nathaniel, what color are your eyes? If you answer limpid luminous blue, you blow your cover! I told you Siegfried would lurk here some day.

ORIGINAL JULIANA
Wednesday 4 February 1998
. . . with risk of lowering the tone of this very high brow site I just want to flog a message to Siegfried in case he is lurking out there in cyberspace.

I am a gorgeous red-haired Icelandic person with legs that on a good day reaches Walhalla[6]. On the right toxic mix I'll do anything.

Except handcuffs. Absolutely paranoid about handcuffs. Gives me the creep.

I'll do anything your girlfriend do. At twice the speed. I sing, paint and tap dance. And I do accents. Have a terrific Nigerian one in store.

But please hurry up, let's face it, you are not getting any younger and I am just about to leave puberty.

Really. I am not pulling any legs here. It is all true. Honest to God.

---

6   This is the post from which Barb stole Juliana's red-haired Icelandic persona.

In Barb's office, the three fansite lurkers paused to stare at one another. After a few disbelieving shrugs they turned back to the light-filled rectangle of the screen, a window into one dimension of cyberspace. They resumed reading.

ORIGINAL SONIA
Wednesday 4 February 1998
Handcuffs don't bother me. Cheeky, Juliana!

ORIGINAL AMY
Wednesday 4 February 1998
Me neither.

ORIGINAL JULIANA
Thursday 5 February 1998
So I've blown it now, haven't I. I am such a virgin, still did not realize that handcuffs were in such a widespread use. Anyway, you might not have a problem with handcuffs. But I am real THIN, disgustingly emaciated. So there.

ORIGINAL DONNA
Thursday 5 February 1998
You will notice that Nathaniel seems to have run for cover . . . :)

ORIGINAL ALICE
Saturday 7 February 1998
Maybe he's looking for the keys. . .

ORIGINAL SONIA

Monday 9 February 1998

Well what does anyone expect? The man probably got scared away by all the feral fan-girl hormones.

Managed to catch The Substitute Distillers the other evening. Naturally Siegfried's the villain.

I am always glad when he's landed another role, however since I saw this film I am feeling rather flat. Dunno whether it was the lighting or makeup or what, but he just looked pretty old. And he sometimes does a little nod, like a nervous tic. His neck was kind of wobbly. It makes me feel glum.

I mean, I'm not saying he's not stylish and acting wonderfully knavishly in the part, and he's absolutely fantastic for his age, however it does bug me that his neck is not that firm.

Dejectedly . . .

ORIGINAL SONIA

Monday 9 February 1998

Apologies–I meant to mention that the make-up department had put brown coloring through his hair. This did not detract from his appearance, though.

ORIGINAL JULIANA

Monday 9 February 1998

Does that mean no curls? C'mon, Sonia, give us everything—is there a stubble, perhaps even a beard. What sort of accent does he master in this one, is there a romantic twist (a girl can always wish, can't she) I know I am such a bore, but I live for these tiny details.

ORIGINAL JULIANA

Monday 9 February 1998

Sorry, one more thing. His neck is wobbly...! The guy's face is awash with acne scars and his neck is WOBBLY. Surely the pack of us must be out of our minds. I'm gonna change loyalties to the Ray Fiends fan site. (Have just witnessed his crafty needlework in The British Are So Impatient.)

ORIGINAL AMY

Monday 9 February 1998

Juliana, if you weren't my friend I'd banish you from this site! We are all mad. But Ray Fiends, beautiful as he is, bores the crap out of me. He's too perfect.

ORIGINAL JULIANA

Tuesday 10 February 1998

. . . madness I know. Ray Fiends's beauty is TOO bleading[7] obvious—so much so it insults my intelligence and taste. It was just a cheap pun, that's all. But Siegfried is of course in another league. His beauty is mind-bogglingly interesting, he can be anything to anyone, as we have all noticed by now.

Sorry everyone. It really was just a joke, no way am I going to join forces with those boring types on the Fiends fansite.

ORIGINAL DONNA

June 10 1998

No Juliana, once you're one of us you can't ever leave, we'd have to kill you. I didn't even notice the

---

7   Juliana's unique spellings are not typos!

nervous tic, so guess I'll have to see The Substitute Distillers again just to check it out.

A teensy part of me recognises the appeal of Ray F. while the balance is riveted on the likes of Siegfried. I can't explain it, it might be a brain stem thing? I'm fascinated by him. The cure for all the B-grade films is of course get out one of your copies of *Das Rat.*

ORIGINAL ALICE
Wednesday 11 February 1998
What's the big deal if he's got a small space between his teeth, the odd blemish and grey streak, and an annoying idiosyncrasy, ie. the nod? He's not some airbrushed magazine picture or plastic surgery freak, which is precisely why everyone here is attracted to him!

 ORIGINAL JULIANA
Wednesday 11 February 1998
Wobbly neck, acne scars, gap teeth, annoying nod, grey haired, pasty, smirks . . .the list of quirky sidelines is getting ridiculously long-winded. Anyone else got something to add while we're at it? Keep it coming. . .

 ORIGINAL AMY
Wednesday 11 February 1998
Alice—what annoying nod?

ORIGINAL JULIANA
Wednesday 11 February 1998
AMY, surely you cannot have missed THE NOD. It is most annoying as it happens all the time.

ORIGINAL AMY
Wednesday 11 February 1998
Color me dense but I still say WHAT NOD? You mean like a Parkinson's thing? Or like a sexy, curt 'I'm cool' thing?

I agree with Alice. The guy's still the most interesting man on the planet, flaws and all. Besides, I KNOW Juliana is overcompensating, trying to convince herself she's not as obsessed as she is. Right, Juliana?

ANYWAY, here's a board contest: What do you say when someone asks you what board you're on? Creative answers only, please!

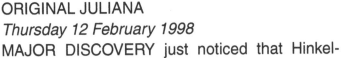 **ORIGINAL JULIANA**
Thursday 12 February 1998
MAJOR DISCOVERY just noticed that Hinkelheimer's ears are in fact POINTED. As the flaw list now stands the man is far beyond human, he has now officially reached the TROLL category. Kill me if you must, but that would explain his sexual magnetism. p.s. which board? I always state The Philosophical Society. A good one that is, people never ask any further questions.

 ORIGINAL AMY
Thursday 12 February 1998
Hey, don't knock trolls until you've tried 'em.

ORIGINAL SONIA
Thursday 12 February 1998
I would really like to see some extra images of Siegfried on this website, Donna! There's a dearth of pix from some of his movies.

His very sparse minor imperfections are the reason he's so unique and intriguing. In fact they make him even more alluring.

Juliana—POINTED EARS? What movies did you spot this in? What scenes? I HAVE to take a look. Amazing.

By the way, I know what 'Nod' you mean. It really appeals to me, I view it as a typical mannerism of a self-assured man who's in complete control.

ORIGINAL AMY
17 February 1998
Here's a funny one. I ran across an old diary last night and the page fatefully fell to this entry:

26 May 1982 "Last night Tom and I went to see *Das Rat*—a film that is moving, unforgettable and very timely because of the Falklands mess. I am still affected by the Captain's death. I feel as if I am in mourning for him. I cried in the theatre and afterward."

Sobbed was more like it. For days. I was 23 in 1982—boy do I feel old! I just think it's funny that a diary I haven't looked at in years should fall to that page.

ORIGINAL JULIANA
17 February 1998
Amy, surely that means YOU are the CHOSEN one. Quick, get into your wedding gear and hike a lift to München. The Troll Master of the Rings Himself have called upon you, thou fairie ladie . . . my advice dress in something virgin like and chuck some ketchup up your . . . (for the uninitiated, faked virginity)
Juliana (not mad but bored. honest).

41

On Barb's computer screen the messages ceased. The last one had been posted that very day. It seemed to Barb that imprints of the fans' powerful yearnings seemed to have escaped through the cyber-window into her office, where they drifted and keened subsonically, like fading ghosts.

Possibly it was just that the fluorescent tube on the ceiling needed replacing.

"So, what is it with these weirdos on the Internet?" Tess wondered. "They're completely freaked out on the guy. They're infatuated neurotics! Fixated, besotted addicts!"

The three friends exchanged glances.

Into the fraught silence Barb blurted, "Who wants to be first?"

Elbowing Barb out of the way, Lottie sat down in front of the monitor. Her fingers flew across the keyboard.

 **ORIGINAL LOTTIE**
17 February 1998
Here we are! The SPH Australian fan club. Thanks for the Web site; it's nice to know to know we're not alone in our obsession…

We've just got back from seeing *The Substitute Distillers* in the cinema; we saw *Air Force Fun* last week; we wonder if other people in the cinema notice the gasps of excitement when some bad guy portrayed by Siegfried is seen for the first time, and then the sobs and moans when he finally gets shot. We get up to leave after that and are surprised that people are still sitting there watching the rest of the movie. We're going to see one of his really old movies soon—"The Lost Car Keys of Gertrude Flower"—we'll let you know what it's like.

The keys rattled away like beetles galloping on biscuit tins. Tess and Barb peered over Lottie's shoulders, the screen's radiance bathing their faces with an unearthly illumination.

Meanwhile, a nanosecond away in cyberspace, something weird was happening. Perhaps it was powered by some unpredicted and unprecedented interactions between the intricate nodes, algorithms and interfaces of the World Wide Web, or by the fickle, garish radiation of neon lights and fluorescent tubes, or by the extreme passions of a motley band of obsessive, hero-worshipping fans. Whatever the reason . . .

Long, long ago, approximately four point six billion years before the instant you are reading this, the Original Universe blinked into existence. In the chaos of its birth pangs, bits of it were torn apart. One sphere of rock, revolving in third position around a certain star, survived. Eventually, having wrapped itself in a comfortable layer of gas and cloud, it cooled to a point at which oceans formed, and awaited further developments.

Three point nine billion years ago a couple of complex, long-chain, carbon-based, organic chemical compounds invented the phrase "get a life" by floating up against each other, snogging, and ending up as the first single-celled organism. The common ancestor of ants, cab drivers, translator-fish and chocolate had appeared.

Life enjoyed a relatively peaceful time being slime and pond scum for the next few millennia until some of the more sociable specks amongst them began gathering together to form larger organisms. Early hominids arose, and Life's first spark of higher intelligence eventually germinated.

Out of chaos, *Homo sapiens* emerged . . .

. . .which goes to show that no matter how much preparation you put into a project the end result is often a bit disappointing.

It also demonstrates that when enough matter is thrown together with enough energy in the right conditions, then sooner or later—somehow, somewhere—something will appear that wasn't there before . . .

4

THE CREATION OF UNEARTH

Around the middle of the twentieth century, some of the pond scum's descendants assembled a tangle of wires and circuits and called their invention a "computer". Over the next few decades the nerdier spawn hooked these computers together to form a larger network called the Internet. Squillions of fragments of virtual matter began whizzing to and fro across the face of the planet, and back and forth from the space junk circling above.

By the end of the so-called second millennium the distinction between organic and inorganic intelligence was blurring. Circuits silently opened and closed their pathways as swiftly as thought, behaving like brain synapses. DNA code and binary code had mysteriously coalesced.

The semi-organised chaos of cyberspace's Virtual Universe bore a striking resemblance to the state of the Original Universe four point six billion years earlier. At the culmination of this process enough virtual matter was thrown together with enough energy, in the right conditions. Somewhere, somehow, something appeared that wasn't there before ...

Which is how it happened that about a nanosecond ago, in a galaxy very, very close by in cyberspace, an unplanet—third from the unsun – popped into existence:

UnEarth.

Its vast, primeval landmass, which might have been called Pseudo-Pangaea, was currently undescribed and thus unpopulated. This was soon to change ...

The fluorescent tube on the office ceiling had developed an ominous hum. By its uncertain light, Barb leaned back in her chair and flipped through a pile of free brochures she had picked up from the travel agent that morning.

It had been months since she and her friends had discovered the Siegfried P. Hinkelheimer fansite. They logged onto it several times a day, but apart from that, the ever-present feeling of love-sickness and the constant video hunting, their lives had pretty well returned to pre-Hinkelheimer normal.

The fansite had seen a few changes. A few new contributors had appeared, including two named Emily and Tammie. Juliana's postings had ceased for some unknown and probably unreliable reason. No doubt she was off being a red-haired Icelandic vixen somewhere, Barb thought idly. Damn, I'm jealous of that hair...

Tapping her pencil on the desk she cast a sidelong glance of disgust at her most recent List of Things To Do For Home and Office, which lay in a smudged and crumpled heap.

"Take out garbage," demanded some of the more legible scrawl. "Go shopping at stupormarket." "Phone bank manager and grovel for leniency." "Trace source of ants infesting cupboards." "Phone B.M. and beg for extended deadline." "Clean mould off bathroom tiles." "Pay phone bill." "Scrape gunge out of kitchen sink plug-hole."

She shuddered.

Munching on a square of Rum 'n' Rhubarb® Barb opened a brochure titled "Fiji: A Palm-Fringed Paradise in Crystal Waters."

A tropical island almost leapt out at her, startlingly emerald green against a sun-drenched sky so cloudless and intensely blue it might have been glazed with cobalt. A sugar-powdering of white sand, a striped deck-chair, hibiscus flowers floating like open hands on limpid wavelets which kissed the shore . . .

Barb was reaching for the phone to call the travel agent when she remembered the current condition of her bank balance. Her hand froze in mid-reach. Sighing, she drew back.

"Ah, Siegfried," she murmured fondly to the lopsided black-and-white photocopy of the cover of *The Heliotrope Parrot*, now pinned up next to the poster of Daniel de Licious, "Ah, Siegfried, if only I could afford a holiday."

It was then that inspiration struck for a second time.

A strange light kindled in Barb's eye. Another strange light kindled in her other eye. Leaving the Rum 'n' Rhubarb® to melt all over the List of Things To Do, she booted up her computer, logged into the Hinkelheimer fan site and began to compose a message for the Fan Feedback page.

It so happened that at this precise instant in Time the energies, complexities and evolutions of the Internet had reached a unique fulcrum in their development. The creative flow now being uploaded from one single P.C. was enough to tip the balance.

Synergy was unleashed.

In cyberspace, on the Virtual Planet of UnEarth, the supercontinent Pseudo-Pangaea suddenly shattered into two vast land masses—Legendary Laurasia and Ghostly Gondwanaland. With inconceivably rapid evolution through the Meretricious Mesozoic Era, several lesser continents broke off and formed.

In the northern hypothetisphere, Legendary Laurasia split into Not-Quite-North America, Ersatz-Europe and Allegorical-Asia. Meanwhile, Ghostly Gondwanaland—the protocontinent of the southern hallucinasphere—broke up into Imitation-India, Artificial-Australia, Simulated-South-America, Almost-Africa and An-Apology-For-Antarctica.

UnEarth was as yet UnPopulated. It would eventually collect its denizens by two distinct methods, one of which was a gradual osmosis of individual existence from Original Space to Cyberspace. This process would involve an Original Person spontaneously dividing into two, with the cloned version migrating to dwell on UnEarth in cyberspace. This virtual version, or avatar, would forever be linked to its original template by way of a kind of cyber-literary quantum entanglement, each entity somewhat mirroring the other. Those Originals who developed UnEarthly cyber-versions of themselves would be oblivious of the phenomenon until it had occurred. And even then, most of them would only be dimly aware of it.

On Original Earth, certain obsessed movie-actor fans, fusing with their alter egos in cyberspace, were about to become demi-godlike creatures. They would possess the power to create a sub-cast of virtual entities on UnEarth by the second method of population, which was known as "description".

Because the descriptive powers of the demi-godlike creators were restricted by their imaginations, the sub-cast of fictitious characters would often be stereotyped, two-dimensional and sadly lacking in credibility. Furthermore the descriptions of various countries would be severely limited by the fact that gaps in authors' geographical knowledge were haphazardly filled in by misrepresentations gleaned from clichéd movies, in which, for example, all deserts are portrayed as nothing but sand dunes. . .

Nevertheless demi-gods can adorn themselves with the looks and hair they want, wear the fashions they like, accessorize like any millionaire . . . and they would all be determined to make the most of their powers.

49

"If you could have the face of any other woman on Earth," someone had once asked Barb, "who would it be?"

"Cloudy Chiffon®[8]," she had replied.

Idly, Barb let her imagination take flight. As she stared into space visualizing her alter-ego, somewhere in virtual reality it commenced to actually take shape.

And what a shape!

Sitting down at the keyboard in front of the computer, she began to type. She described her ideal self, her avatar. . .

 UNEARTHLY BARB'S BIO:

Barb's origins are obscured by the mists of legend and romance. Some say that as an infant, she was discovered, washed up on a lonely island shore, by a lighthouse-keeper.

An arcane tattoo around the ring finger of her left hand was her only distinguishing mark, yet it lent no clue as to her identity.

Raised by the lighthouse-keeper and his wife amongst their own family, Barb grew up to be a young woman of astonishing beauty—some said an exact replica of Cloudy Chiffon®. It was whispered that she had strange powers. Had it not been

_____

8   The "registered trademark" symbol is silent.

for the remoteness of the windswept isle and the treacherous seas incessantly pounding its rugged coastline, she surely would have been sought by hordes of young suitors.

The news of her stunning looks travelled across the ocean, borne by tall ships, their sails unfurling against the grey and stormy skies like the wings of wild swans. The seven handsome sons of the lighthouse-keeper all fell in love with the beautiful girl from the sea, yet she looked upon them only as brothers.

When one evening a tall stranger with long, dark hair arrived at the isle enquiring after the lighthouse-keeper's adopted daughter, Barb mysteriously fled the place of her childhood and ranged out into the world, where she now roams, writing or doing what I wot not what of.

These are the only heretofore known facts about the history of Barb, scribed by the oracle Myopia and subject to change without notice.

As Barb's fingertips jabbed savagely at her keyboard, UnEarth underwent profound changes. Erroneous evolution proceeded through the ensuing geologic eras at a rate of giga-hertz, until a collection of illusory islands began to form at approximately one hundred and eighty degrees East, seventeen degrees South—just to the left of the recently invented international date-line. The name of the island group?

Fictitious Fiji . . .

Later that same day, a message appeared on the "Fan Feedback" page of the Siegfried P. Hinkelheimer fansite. It was not written by Original Barb, but by her avatar, UnEarthly Barb. It was her very first post.

UNEARTHLY BARB

Wednesday 8 July 1998

I just arrived back from Fiji yesterday and WOW! What a holiday!!!! I couldn't wait to tell you all about it . . .

Okay, so now the flashback is out of the way and we can get on with the story.

5

NOW, WHERE WERE WE?

ORIGINAL EMILY
11 July 1998
Barb—I laughed, I cried (actually I laughed so hard I cried!) I'm headed for Europe in August—there's no telling who I might run into. :)

ORIGINAL BARB
11 July 1998
Hi Emily—I'm glad you laughed, I thought everyone would probably just reach for their phones to tell the little men in white coats to come and take me away. I hope you meet someone very interesting in Europe next month—interesting and Germanic and blue-eyed and lean and kinda intriguing.

If you do, I for one would like to hear about it.

And by the way, here's a web site everyone might find useful. It's named after a translator fish in Douglas Adams' "Hitch-hiker's Guide to the Galaxy"®. The software will translate words from any language into any language and back again. Try typing in a few sentences in English. Translate them into German and then re-translate to English. Due to the literalness of computer translation, the results are mind-boggling. Definitely good for a laugh.

The site's address is http://babelfish.altavista.digital.com/cgi-bin/translate?

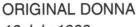

ORIGINAL DONNA

13 July 1998

Well, Barb, your story DOES have a tragic ending despite having kept both your feet ... you never got that kiss! You must have wanted to slap that airline hostess. The babelfish at Alta Vista® is already responsible for some of the more ... er ... interesting translations on this site.

Emily, if anything interesting appears on your vacation, you will share ... won't you? I'll be in Europe at the end of this year ... do you suppose ... ???

ORIGINAL EMILY

13 July 1998

The Greek island I'm going to is a favorite of German tourists. Many vacationers sail between islands while on holiday... so who knows—something (or is it someone?) interesting may turn up! :}

ORIGINAL LOTTIE

15 July 15 1998

I'm logging in from Tess's computer. Barb—you idiot! We'd come and visit you in the place where the men in white coats took you, but they'd be sure to lock us up as well. Thanks for the story—haven't laughed so much in ages—I was chuckling for hours (days!) after I read it.

The tragedy is it's not far removed from some of the foolish thoughts in my own head.

ORIGINAL DONNA

16 July 1998

The babelfish has just given me a good laugh, especially seeing its re-translation of its own translation! Here are the original and the babelized versions.

Donna wanted to say:

"Let's have some fun. Emily, if you find Our Hero bobbing around in the sea between Greek islands, you will need to nurse his poor broken heart since Barb vanished on him so abruptly!"

Which the babelfish rendered as:

"Lassen Sie uns etwas Spaß haben. Emily, wenn Sie unseren Hero finden, in das Meer zwischen griechische Inseln herum ruckartig zu bewegen, müssen Sie sein schlechtes gebrochenes Inneres warten, da Barb auf ihm so unerwartet verschwand!"

Which in turn, turned into:

"Let us something fun have. Emily, if you find our Hero to move into the sea between Greek islands around jerkily must wait you its bad broken inside, since Barb on it disappeared so unexpectedly!"

So, Em, don't forget your binoculars!

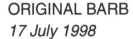 ## ORIGINAL BARB
17 July 1998

Interesting re-translated translation, Donna. I just love that Babelfish site! I think Babelfish was put there simply to brighten our lives and cause those around us to scratch their heads as we fall from our office-type comput-er-desk chairs and roll about on the floor in hysterics.

And I would like to add that by now Siegfried may have been rescued, or have rescued himself. I somehow feel that the sea is his element and would obey his commands—that he might have been borne back to the yacht on the crest of a foaming wave, and swept up back onto the deck.

The prevailing wind would then swing around to fill the sails, speeding him straight to the shores of—THE U.S.A.? FINLAND? And then, who knows? Maybe one day Donna or Emily or anyone might be walking down the street to buy the daily paper when a tall stranger, who had been consulting a map on the street corner, might look up and say, "Excuse me, I am new in town. Can you direct me to someplace vere I can find a bed for ze night?"

And what would your reply be, hmm???

Triggered by ethernet signals, weird lighting, seething hormones and ancient modems faultily transferring data, a cyber-version of a fan named Tammie evolved on UnEarth...

Original Barb

UnEarthly Barb

UNEARTHLY TAMMIE

17 July 1998

Barb, perhaps the weather and currents might drive the boat towards Malibu Beach in California. A freak wave could overturn the boat one morning, and he would float to land, reaching it just as I arrived on the beach to do some sunbathing. As he lay sprawled on the sand completely worn out, he would gaze beseechingly at me from those sky-colored eyes!

ORIGINAL BARB

20 July 1998

Tammie, you would then be presented with the problem of figuring out whether Siegfried (having dragged his gorgeous body from the sea, exhausted and barely able to whisper his plea for help) needed mouth-to-mouth resuscitation or not. From a medical point of view, taking into account the symptoms, I would say yes most definitely. In fact you would owe this to him, to save his life.

Hey—what am I saying? Just don't go playing Florence Nightingale TOO enthusiastically Tammie, or my long red Icelandic hair will be going green with envy back here in Australia. Oh, where did I go wrong? Once I was in his arms and now he's in California . . .

After you have saved his life he will of course be most grateful to you. He might even ask if there is any way he can repay you for your kindness. You of course, with only his welfare at heart, might recommend that he takes a holiday in Australia to recover . . . ?

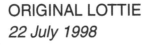

ORIGINAL LOTTIE

22 July 1998

Oh Tammie—lucky woman; mouth to mouth! Remember the lip-balm; you might need it after three hours of resuscitation. Please tell us all about it!

UNEARTHLY TAMMIE

25 July 1998

There he was prostrate and semi-conscious on the sand, that handsome guy who had been carried to the beach on the crest of a wave. The sea had been rough on him. Salt infused his hair and his mouth was parched, peeling. To my dismay he seemed to be having trouble breathing, so remembering my first aid lessons I swiftly pressed my lips against his and proceeded to revive him with my own breath.

Four hours later I noticed that his mouth was no longer parched and peeling, and that was without the help of store-bought moisturisers! Coming to his senses, Siegfried groggily whispered a couple of names. Leaning closer I interpreted them—"Lottie!" he said, and "Barb!"

Alas—I suspect it is in Australia that Siegfried's true loves dwell…

Additional gossip to come afterwards…

ORIGINAL BARB

26 July 1998

More AFTERWARDS??? Tammie, how can you expect us to survive that long without knowing what happened next, there on the sunlit, golden beaches of California under a cornflower sky filled with clotted cream clouds???

6

OF BABES AND BABELFISH

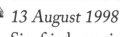

ORIGINAL EMILY
13 August 1998
Picking up from Donna . . . but we're still left with a dazed and basically helpless Skipper lying around on the beach with only an angry, jealous girlfriend to look after him. What'll we do?

UNEARTHLY EMILY
13 August 1998
Siegfried regained his enough of his faculties to crawl over to a nearby call box. He picked up the receiver.

"Get me my agent!"

Cut to the interior of Athens Airport. Time: later on. Siegfried is waiting at Gate #3 to hop a plane to Santorini. His mind keeps wandering over the events of the last few weeks. So often when his eyes are closed he sees the image of Lottie being ripped out of his arms and the distinct echoes of an ominous voice repeating "Omelette or mixed grill? Omelette or mixed grill?" over and over. What could it possibly mean?

Meanwhile Emily, sitting on her suitcase, is totally engrossed in her book and fails to notice that a man is standing in front of her.

"Excuse me," he says. Startled, she looks up to see a very stunning German man in blue jeans, black t-shirt and sunglasses. She wrinkles her brow trying to figure out why he looks so familiar ...

ORIGINAL EMILY
13 August 1998
Barb—I thought it was Lottie who was torn from his arms. Upon further investigation it was you! I should just put in (Insert your name here) from now on! :)

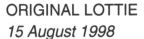

ORIGINAL LOTTIE
15 August 1998
No, it wasn't me ... NOTHING would tear me from his arms! You SPH fans seem to be spread pretty thinly across the U.S.A. and the rest of the world. Strange that all us Aussie fans seem to live in Melbourne and we all know each other!

In my spare time I'm writing a script for a film about a sailing ship. If I had my choice, Siegfried would play the main role. After his riveting performance in *Das Rat*, it seems natural to expect Siegfried to be the hero in all nautical films.

"Hmm," Barb thought as she read Emily's last post. "Insert Your Name Here, eh?" And even as she dwelled on this thought, yet another virtual character was born on UnEarth.

Meanwhile, it was too late to save Emily—she had been drawn in. Her UnEarthly avatar had been cloned into existence. As she sat in front of her computer dreaming up a chapter, her gorgeous alter-ego, UnEarthly Emily, commenced to evolve in cyberspace, as follows:

UnEarthly-Emily

UNEARTHLY EMILY'S BIO:

Emily, a well-endowed lass with a fiery spirit, was born in the Forests of Southern Europe. Raised by a band of roving circus performers, she learned the art of juggling and knife throwing. Due to a slight miscalculation while blindfolded, she missed her target by inches and wounded an innocent spectator (who actually wasn't so innocent, but that's another story).

Deciding it was time to take her vivacious personality on the road, she left the troupe and headed for the high seas.

Emily became an expert with pistol and cutlass and was considered as dangerous as any male pirate. She was fearless in her exploits and the life of any boarding party.

Her last confirmed sighting was as a fire-eater in the Virgin Islands. Rumour has it she has since settled down, preferring to write novels about her exploits in a great, oak-panelled library with the scent of almond blossoms and frangipani wafting in from outside.

ORIGINAL EMILY
15 August 1998
Lottie—I'm also a writer (hobby) and was curious enough to take a screenwriting class recently. I'm working on three. Maybe we should collaborate!

UNEARTHLY EMILY
15 August 1998
Back at Athens Airport—Emily realizes the man in front of her looks remarkably like Siegfried.

"You look a lot like Siegfried P. Hinkelheimer," she twitters.

He smiles. "I am Siegfried P. Hinkelheimer."

"Oh." she says casually while all her insides melt down to her toes. "Is this the right gate for Santorini?"

"Yes it is."

"Thank you."

"Don't mention it." Siegfried walks away. Unfortunately Emily is in Economy Class and Siegfried is in First Class. During the entire flight she is staring at the back of his head.

Cut to balcony of cliff-side apartment: Emily throws her bags on the bed and opens the French doors to the balcony. She walks out to see the spectacular sapphire blue sea and the blazing white city of Thera on the cliffs. Closing her eyes, she inhales the Mediterranean air.

"Hello again."

Startled, Emily turns to see Siegfried standing on the adjoining balcony . . . what an amazing coincidence! :) He looks at her over the top of his sunglasses. Her heart skips a beat as she gazes into those magnificent eyes.

"Hello." She walks over to where his balcony meets hers. He takes off his sunglasses and studies her face. Emily wonders if he can hear her heart beating—because to her it sounds like it's going to explode . . .

ORIGINAL BARB
19 August 1998

Omigosh, Emily. This is just getting too exciting for words. I'm really glad the SPH Saga is continuing. It's turning into a Work Of Supreme Art. I can hardly wait to find out what happens after he studies your face so earnestly.

All I can hope for is that the balcony doesn't collapse, its structure stressed by the violent tremors of your heart. Do you think it's possible he might leap lightly and athletically over his balcony to yours? Oh and is he still wearing the deliciously figure-hugging jeans and black T-shirt or has he changed into something a little more, or maybe *less* comfortable?

UNEARTHLY BARB
19 August 1998

If you are unclear on these points please let me know and I will use my binoculars. By an astonishing coincidence I am staying in the hotel opposite and I think I might just be able to glimpse your balcony from my window.

Osmosis was taking place. Already, without any inkling of what was happening, Barb was simultaneously in two places. On Earth, she sat staring stupidly at a screen. On UnEarth, she stood staring stupidly through a pair of binoculars.

Others, sucked in by the virtual vacuum of cyberspace, were beginning to follow closely at her hypothetical heels. Donna was next to be cloned. Her avatar's description is as follows:

UNEARTHLY DONNA'S BIO:

Donna was kidnapped in childhood and raised by Tibetan Monks in the belief that she was the true Dalai Lama, until the arrival of puberty when her incomparable beauty and stunning femininity revealed the depth of their error. Striking out across Asia alone on horseback, she conquered kingdoms and plundered hearts in search of her true destiny. Her youthful exploits are the subject of the biographical best-selling epic, "Magnificent" by J. Michener.

UNEARTHLY DONNA

19 August 1998

Barb you're correct, you are in the room opposite, because I'm in the one directly above yours and I do have my spyglasses handy. Siegfried obviously came to the hotel by a more direct route than our own Emily, cuz he's apparently had time to shower. He's in his bathrobe . . .

UNEARTHLY EMILY

19 August 1998

"Nice robe," Emily managed to squeak out. Just then the phone rang.

"The phone is ringing," Siegfried said.

"Yes."

After a pause, Emily blurted, "Oh, the phone! Be right back."
Dashing back inside she answered, "Parakalo?"

Donna, able to pry herself away from the binoculars, excitedly replied "Emily! Is he wearing anything underneath?"

"What! Who is this?"

"It's me Donna, and if I'm not mistaken, Barb is next door."

Emily walked over and peered carefully through the curtain. To the right, she could see Siegfried smoking a cigarette. He was leaning on the balcony, talking to someone. Looking to the right she saw Barb straining so hard to lean inwards that she was in danger of breaking the small separator between the balconies.

With all hopes of an encounter for two dashed to tiny bits on the Aegean floor, Emily spoke into the telephone receiver again. "Come on over Donna, the door is unloc—"

Before she could finish, she heard Donna's footsteps running down the stairs. Returning to the balcony, Emily announced to Siegfried, "What a coincidence! It seems that two of my friends are staying in Thera as well! Hi Barb, you may want to be careful. That might break, you know."

Just then the balcony's rail on which Barb was leaning, started to give way . . .

Siegfried, thinking quickly, leaped over the railing separating the balconies. He ripped off his robe and threw one end of the belt to Barb, saving her from certain death.

Hmmm . . . how come she always ends up in his arms?

UNEARTHLY BARB

20 August 1998

Meanwhile, back in Thera—YES! It finally happened! Barb was back in his arms after having been so tragically ripped from them by a shark. Wait a minute—she was not actually IN them yet. She was hanging off the end of his bathrobe belt, dangling from a hotel balcony on the fortieth floor—a situation which was almost as exciting and a lot less desirable.

The wind whistled past with an eerie sound. The ground below looked dizzyingly far away. Slowly she started to climb up, urged on by the encouraging cries of Emily, Donna and—could it be? That was Lottie's voice. Barb had not known she was staying here too . . .

She thought to herself, "That's jolly decent of them, they might have just let me drop and that would be one less contender for dinner for two with Siegfried."

Then she realized that their cries were not of encouragement. They were shrieks of admiration—after all, Siegfried had just ripped off his bathrobe. "What am I missing?" she wondered.

Just as she reached the balcony, she looked up. Her hands instantly become nerveless, her jaw dropped. Before she comprehended what was happening she had let go of the belt.

Oh no, not again! The wind rushed upwards past her ears. Counting down from forty, she closed her eyes and waited for the end.

But no! Fortunately she landed in the hotel swimming pool. There was a terrific splash and babelfish were tossed in all directions, shouting incoherently in German.

By the time Barb had crawled out of the pool and recovered, Siegfried was nowhere to be found. All that she could discover was a broken balcony and a discarded bathrobe. What's more, Donna and Emily and Lottie were missing too. Still dripping wet, she searched the entire hotel, to no avail.

Where could they all be?

ORIGINAL EMILY
20 August 1998
I'd love to answer that but I'll leave that up to you girls! I'm REALLY off to Greece in the morning. Be back in two weeks!

Emily was trying to make one final effort to remain a unified human being dwelling on Original Earth. Little did she know that her cyber-persona was already leading an autonomous existence on UnEarth. Cyberspace had claimed her, too, in the end.

Meanwhile, Lottie's alter ego was beginning to coalesce as she envisaged...

UNEARTHLY LOTTIE'S BIO:
An (almost) descendant from King Edward I, Lottie was born in a magnificent castle on the banks of the river Nore in Ireland. At her birth, the church bell rang joyously for five minutes (before it cracked).

Original Emily

UnEarthly Emily

Two days later her family were turned out of the castle, bankrupt and destitute. They stowed away in the hold of a three-masted barque, bound to Chile for nitrates. But the ship foundered in mountainous seas off Cape Horn with the loss of all hands. Lottie and her family swam across the Pacific Ocean to Australia, where she has lived ever since.

Stunningly beautiful and dazzlingly intelligent, Lottie almost gained three university degrees, and would have achieved international fame as an artist, if they had only printed her name on the catalog. She just missed out on being the first woman to sail solo around the world, and she gave back her Olympic Gold Medal for showjumping after she realized she'd accidentally ridden someone else's horse.

She went on to write what would have been a best-selling novel, but the only copy of the manuscript was stolen from the back seat of her car. She is presently at work on a film script which will star Siegfried P. Hinkelheimer, in a truly heroic role. Needless to say she is sure to make millions and win numerous awards…

UNEARTHLY LOTTIE
22 August 1998

How nice, Lottie thought, to find herself so suddenly and unexpectedly transported to sunny "Gratuitous Greece" when she thought she was in the midst of a miserable Melbourne winter!

She watched Barb plummet into the pool but didn't hang around long enough to see if she surfaced. She rushed off to where she thought Siegfried's room was located, but after a long and desperate search she finally stumbled across him sipping drinks in the bar with Donna and Emily. Thank goodness he had some clothes on again. Lottie's delicate sensibilities were easily embarrassed.

Soft music was being piped from speakers hidden behind the potted palms. Subtle lighting gleamed from polished surfaces and uniformed hotel staff flitted back and forth like motorised ladybugs.

A quick glance in the gold-tinted mirror behind the bar confirmed Lottie's visualisation of her appearance. There was no doubt; she was some hot babe—lean and athletic, tawny muscles rippling like a tigress, waist length tresses of auburn curls and 'loser' stamped unmistakably across her face.

Plucking up courage she approached Siegfried, her pathetic little heart pounding against her ribs.

"Excuse me, Mr. Hinkelheimer," she said (hoping she had the pronunciation right), "but would you like to read my script?"

"Why not?" he replied with a little smile. Her head spun at the sound of that "auralgasmic" voice.

"It's back in my hotel room," she yodelled.

Lottie couldn't help a discreet triumphal wave to Donna and Emily as she exited with Siegfried. She was aware of him walking by her side with that decisive, quick walk—graceful and fluid as a panther.

"You ridiculous female," she said to herself. "You've climbed 180 ft masts without raising your pulse rate—why now is your heart about to exit through your mouth and why do your knees knock together so violently that they're turning black and blue? Is this a life-threatening situation? Is he likely to kill you if you say something stupid?"

She made the mistake of glancing up at his face. The light caught his curls and cast interesting shadows beneath his cheekbones. He was regarding with a slight smile. His eyes; extraordinary— "like catching sight of a piece of blue sky or a stretch of open water" —were gleaming with amusement.

Well . . . Emily, Donna, half-drowned Barb dragging yourself out of the swimming pool with a few babelfish clinging to your toes . . . you're back in with a chance. Lottie has swooned in a wretched heap at his feet—which she would kiss if she was still conscious—Siegfried looks slightly anxious—he wanted to read that script—but Donna and Emily are quickly on the scene.

"Don't worry about her," they say, dragging Lottie out of the room by her feet and throwing her into some prickly bushes; "You've still got us."

UNEARTHLY DONNA
24 August 1998

Donna and Emily exercised their herding instincts and indiscreetly manoeuvred Siegfried back to their table. Unfortunately no one could hear him mumbling, "What a lot of brazen women!" over the loud squishing of Barb's soaking wet shoes.

"Don't mind our friend Lottie, she hasn't had her medication in several hours." said Barb, flicking a babelfish out of her eye. "She normally isn't the least bit shy."

Meanwhile, Donna was giving Emily a decidedly calculating glare and wondering just how many lives Barb had.

"Well!" she blurted, eyeing the bar, "I'll just run and get us a round of drinks . . . and a towel . . ."

Noting the insufferable fact that Tammie appeared to be disentangling her self from UnEarth, Original Barb, driven by forces she did not understand, endeavoured to ensnare Tammie's pseudo-self.

She had also perceived that aside from some long red Icelandic hair, her own avatar's appearance was somewhat amorphous. It was time to perform a little overt describing . . .

UNEARTHLY BARB
25 August 1998

Long, lean and clad in a slinky wet dress which clung to every taut curve of her flawless body, Barb strutted into the hotel bar. She tossed her head, flinging back lengthy locks of hair the rich hue of an autumnal sunset. All the men in the place ceased their conversations, pausing with their drinks raised half-way to their lips. They watched her, their eyes raking her svelte and slender form from head to toe.

Barb was oblivious of the effect of her charms.

I wonder how long it will take for Donna to get the drinks, and for Lottie to extricate herself from those rather thorny bushes, she thought deviously to herself as she poured the water out of her squishy shoes and cleaned yet another babelfish out of her ear. From the corner of her eye she saw someone who looked like Tammie entering through one of the far doors. Barb knew she would have to act fast.

"Gosh, Donna's taking such a long time," she said loudly, producing a hip flask. "Fortunately I have a little medicinal brandy right here!" She poured a large nip each for Emily, Siegfried and herself. Tammie was about to burst on the scene. Would she notice her hero? The competition was getting serious.

"Look over there!" said Barb suddenly, and while Emily and Siegfried were peering blankly in the other direction, Barb tipped a sleeping potion into Emily's drink and a love potion into Siegfried's.

"Was betrachteten Sie?" asked Siegfried.

"Huh?" said Barb, blank-faced. "Oh that's right, he's German, isn't he."

She whipped out her phrase book and started madly flipping through it. Meanwhile, Emily began cosily chatting to Siegfried in fluent German, which set Barb's teeth on edge. What's more, they raised their glasses, linked their arms through each other's and proposed a toast.

"Hang on," shrieked Barb, "I think you've got the wrong drinks!"

At that moment Tammie accidentally bumped into their table. The three glasses went sliding everywhere, hopelessly mixed up. Miraculously, none of them spilled.

"Hi Tammie, won't you join us in a drink?" said Emily brightly.

"Have mine," groaned Barb, defeated.

"Ist hier zu Ihrer guten Gesundheit!" exclaimed Siegfried with surprisingly babelfishish grammar. As everyone quaffed brandy, Barb squeezed her eyes shut. Belatedly realising that if Siegfried got the love potion he would fall in love with the first person he saw, she quickly opened them again and leaned across the table, staring straight into his gorgeous blue irises.

"I'm drowning again," she thought ecstatically, fervently hoping that by chance he might have picked the love potion. Siegfried put down his glass. He took a deep breath and . . .

Just then who should come rushing up to the table but Lottie, covered in scratches, Donna carrying a large tray of drinks, Tess with a bottle of vodka and (Insert Your Name Here) wearing a very sexy outfit.

Barb almost fell off her chair. They looked like porn stars, the lot of them—Tess with her long-lashed blue eyes, her mane of blonde hair and her voluptuous body clad in a slim sheath-dress of black lace; dark-haired Donna, tall and willowy in a backless, low-cut cocktail gown, (Insert Your Name Here) in a mini skirt and thigh boots.

"Dammit," Barb muttered under her breath. "I see they've been up to a bit of serious self-describing—"

"Oops," interrupted Donna, surreptitiously whisking away a bottle labelled "Love Potion" Barb had inadvertently left on the tray, and hiding it behind her back.

Siegfried surveyed the whole scene—seven deliriously beautiful women, one with a babelfish in her pocket, one with a few prickles still stuck in her hair, all anxiously staring at him. He looked straight into Barb's eyes.

"I really must tell you," he began.

"Yes?" she squeaked, scarcely daring to breathe.

He smiled and continued, "I've always loved y—"

At that very instant a passing waiter dropped a tray. Down crashed twenty wine-glasses and a flagon of Zorba's Explosive Green Wine®. The cacophony drowned out the last few words of Siegfried's sentence. Ignoring the waiter, the shattered glass and the profusion of exploding green bubbles, seven incredibly luscious women craned forward to hear.

"What did you say?" tremulously murmured (Insert Your Name Here) on behalf of them all.

"I said," stammered Siegfried, "I've always loved y—yu—unique situations like this."

Aghast, they all stepped back.

Abruptly, Tammie fell asleep on her bar-stool.

Gazing at Siegfried, Emily said indistinctly, "I love you."

"We know that already," her companions said, elbowing her out of the way before Siegfried realized what she was blathering on about.

"Guten abend," said Siegfried, suddenly seeing Lottie. "Don't you have a script you want to show me?"

Just who was this "Insert Your Name Here" woman? Barb wondered distractedly as she stared at the paragraphs she had just uploaded through the ether to the feedback page. Surely she had not meant to type in an extra rival for Siegfried's affections? This story was taking on a life of its own. Why had she been stupid enough to describe the other women in such glowing terms? And why did she continually sabotage her own chances with Siegfried?

Quickly she recalculated, counting on her fingers. "Me, Emily, Donna, Lottie, Tammie, Tess and that "Insert Your Name Here" person. Yes, that's seven.

Hitting the "reload" button she craned forward to see if anyone else had contributed a chapter yet.

UNEARTHLY DONNA

25 August 1998

"Script?" cried Donna, rapidly distributing glasses everywhere. "We've seen it!! It's a bit of whimsy, all about several crazy women who first meet on a web site dedicated to a gorgeous international film star and soon find themselves ... BOTTOMS UP!!"

After a startled moment, everyone realized what she meant and gulped their drinks. Donna continued, "—swept up in a globetrotting adventure with the very object of their desire!"

"Whaa??" moaned Tammie, adjusting admirably to the twin shocks of suddenly finding herself in Greece and (quite accidentally) nearly in Siegfried's lap. Under the influence of the sleeping potion, she collapsed onto the floor and began to snore loudly.

UNEARTHLY TAMMIE

26 August 1998

Luckily Siegfried had been fraternising with the beautiful women at the table, and he noticed what had happened to Tammie. Without hesitation he jumped up and ran to help her. Reaching down his muscular arms he gently raised her lovely shoulders and rested her upon his lap.

"Himmel!" he exclaimed in sudden shock. "Is she all right?

Original Lottie

UnEarthly Lottie

This is the young woman who rescued me on the beach!"

Murmuring "Does this bring back memories, schatzi?" he placed his mouth against hers with wondrous tenderness.

Hoping for some reaction he drew back, but Tammie remained wrapped in slumber...

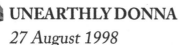

UNEARTHLY DONNA

27 August 1998

And Tammie woke up. Groggily she looked around and discovered the kiss may have been just a dream, as she had somehow been transported to a comfy chaise longue with a pillow and a "Do Not Disturb" placard.

The shock was enough to dissipate the effects of the sleeping draught. Brushing past the crowd of ogling male patrons, she rushed back to the lounge to regain her place at Siegfried's side! The table was getting quite crowded but she wedged into place between Siegfried and the mysterious stranger.

"Mmf lff ynnn," said Emily, so absorbed in staring adoringly at Siegfried she didn't notice that Donna's hand was clapped over her mouth.

"Could everyone spread out a little bit?" begged Lottie from inside the press of bodies. "I can't breathe."

No one moved.

A look of confusion appeared on Siegfried's face as he tried to stand up and found himself wedged in by beautiful feisty females.

"Bitte, benötige ich . . ." he began to babble, but actually he was thinking, *Ich muß der glücklichste Mann auf Masse sein*[9].

UNEARTHLY BARB

28 August 1998

Next he thought, *I wonder why I thought that?* After more than fifty years of being gorgeous, he was completely accustomed to having beautiful women throw themselves at him everywhere he went. He was so used to it that he did not even notice it any more.

He directed his burning blue gaze across the table at (Insert Your Name Here), who had just offered him another drink. Politely, he declined.

"May I have a word with you in private?" Barb whispered to him. He nodded.

After a quick trip to the men's room, he detoured to meet her behind a potted palm. "We have to get out of here," Barb said urgently.

"Why?" asked Siegfried.

"Too much competi—I mean, it's getting too crowded in here. We should go to someplace with more space to breathe."

The gorgeous cyberchick glanced over her shoulder. Donna was administering a love potion antidote to Emily. Tammie, (Insert Your Name Here), Tess and Lottie were frantically swivelling their heads in all directions, searching for Siegfried.

"Oh? Where did you have in mind?" asked the Sexy Saxon.

---

9   I have to be the luckiest man on Earth.

"Australia," said Barb, suddenly fanning out a set of tickets. "I have everything right here. The limo is waiting outside and the valet has your bags already packed."

"But how have you arranged this?" Siegfried was astonished.

"No time to explain—we must hurry before the other—I mean, before the private jet leaves. Let it suffice to say, that I am not only ravishingly beautiful, I am also incredibly rich."

Taking Siegfried's arm she hurried him out the door, into the limo, straight to the private landing strip, into the private jet and off to Australia. They landed in Australia without any incidents or accidents along the way, and there they were, alone together in Barb's mansion in the outback desert. Nostalgically, as she counted the diamonds on her necklace, Barb thought of her beloved friends back in Greece, wondering briefly what they were doing now.

But only briefly.

ORIGINAL DONNA
August 28 1998
hahaha! Bitch! :)

On original Earth, Lottie phoned Barb.

"What do you mean by taking Siegfried off to some so-called mansion?" Lottie demanded. "He has a woman, you know. I read about her somewhere. Her name's Brunhilde. I bet she'd be pretty stirred up if she found out what you've done. Just wait'll you see what happens to you next!"

For Lottie, reality had become a little blurred.

"Oh yeah?" sneered Barb, who was suffering from similar delusions, "See if I care. Do your worst."

She banged down the receiver.

UNEARTHLY LOTTIE
29 August 1998

Meanwhile, back in Greece ...

"Where's he gone? Doesn't he wanna see m'script?" slurred Lottie, her eyelids starting to droop. Bang! Her head hit the table and she was asleep with her nose squashed against the Formoleum®.

"Beautiful, balmy evening," commented Emily happily. "Nice for a stroll in the sunset—but where's he gone?"

"Yes, where is he?" chorused the bevy of gorgeous girls, panic rising in their voices. They all leaped up and headed for the door to go in search their idol.

Crash!

They glanced round, but it was only Lottie falling off her chair. But was it accidental?

Tess, who had gone back inside to retrieve her vodka, was tottered towards them wearing a sly smirk. Somehow she missed the door and careered off towards the bar. She'd spotted a Vulgarian sailor—got a penchant for them—with another bottle of vodka.

Barb had mysteriously disappeared, so it was just the Americans now, hot on the trail. But what was this? The phone at the bar was ringing.

"Anyone here called Donna?" shouted the barman. "Some guy—Lance something—for you. Says it's urgent."

Wow, could Donna run! Now she was flying through the air—it was a pity she hadn't noticed Tess and the Vulgarian sailor on the floor.

The other women exited in a crowd of jabbing elbows, emerging into a glorious Grecian pink and gold sunset. But suddenly a dark shadow blotted out the sun. Could it be a pirate ship looming on the horizon? No, it was Brunhilde, striding in from the west on those incredibly long legs, her blonde tresses flying behind her and a look of fury on her gorgeous face.

"He's gone to Australia!" she shouted, "with that ... that ... trollop!! I'm on the next plane to Australia! Wait till I catch up with ... " Her voice faded as she strode off towards the airport, followed by a gaggle of desperate women, all pulling out their credit cards.

See you in Australia, Barb.

Original Barb phoned Original Lottie.

"Who's that Lance person?" she shouted into the mouthpiece.

"Didn't you know?" Lottie's tinnified voice sounded prim. "I found out that Donna is the Webmaster of many sites, not just the SPH one. One of them is a Lance Boyle fan site."

"What? Never heard of him."

"Where have you been? Lance Boyle is quite famous, not to mention gorgeous as well. He stars in that TV series—*Centurium®*, I think it's called. A detective show. You know the kind of thing, they use electronic devices to track down people, stuff like that."

"Hmph," Barb disparaged. "Well, I don't think you'll get rid of Donna that easily. And stop fainting whenever Siegfried is around, you coward!"

Lottie mumbled a noncommittal reply.

"By the way," Barb added, "You've got the wrong name. It's not even Brunhilde. And if you think you're planning some kind of revenge on me for my brilliant abduction of Siegfried, think again!"

She slammed down the phone.

7

TRIPE ODD'S ALIEN TAXI SERVICE

UNEARTHLY BARB

1 September 1998

It just goes to show that Emily, Tammie and (Insert Your Name Here) had been drinking far too much. As soon as the setting sun glared brilliantly into their glazed eyes, they began to hallucinate. First they saw a pirate ship, next, a Wife. Everyone knows Wives simply do not exist in these kinds of narratives. Every character is both unutterably beautiful and SINGLE, especially the hero, who is even more Single than anybody else.

Being nothing but a figment of sozzled imaginations, the so-called Brunhilde incarnation turned as translucent as fog on a windscreen and proceeded to evaporate like splashed wine on a barbecue hotplate.

"Didja see that?" gasped (Insert Your Name Here), dropping her credit card in astonishment. The others gurgled knowledgeably by way of reply.

Three hundred Vulgarian sailors arrived and entered the bar the girls had just quitted. Paying no attention to the hot-blooded sailors, the luscious heroines piled into a taxi and made a dash for the airport.

"Americans call taxis 'cabs' you know!" the driver pedanted.

"That's okay. It does them good to learn a new language," replied Tammie.

As they reached the airport, the sound of aero-blades chopping the air filled the evening air and the hotel helicopter landed on the tarmac. Lottie leapt out, looking remarkably sober.

"I finally caught up with you!" she said triumphantly.

"Where's Donna?" shouted Emily.

"A strikingly handsome man called Lance turned up and asked her to marry him," replied Lottie.

"Where's Tess?" yelled Tammie.

"Er—" said Lottie, remembering the arrival of the three hundred Vulgarian sailors, "I'll tell you when we reach thirty thousand feet. Everyone's ears will be popping then, and they won't be able to overhear what may be considered an—" she coughed politely, "X-rated topic."

Tammie, Lottie, Emily and (Insert Your Name Here) climbed aboard a big QUAINTAZ® 747 which took off and, seemingly moments later, landed smoothly somewhere in the mysterious Australian outback. . .

UNEARTHLY BARB

1 September 1998

At her outback mansion, Barb sank into her deck-chair under a palm tree by the salt-water lagoon-pool, sipping an ice-cold Croc-on-the-Rocks.

Beside her, Siegfried was dozing.

As she reclined, nostalgically counting the diamonds on her necklace, she savoured the prospect of the romantic moments she would spend alone with this gorgeous German film star, now that she had shaken off the other cyberchicks.

She woke from her reverie as the butler Peeves, in his immaculately pressed livery, appeared noiselessly and bowed with the precision of a robot.

"Visitors at the front door, Ma'am," he enunciated with the flawless accent of a BBC radio announcer.

"What?" Nervously, Barb sprang from her chair, knocking over her drink. "I thought we eluded them ... I mean ... have you activated the automatic defence shield?"

"Ma'am might wish to know the visitors' names before we blast them backwards into the desert at high speed."

"Oh, all right. Who are they? It's not a gaggle of women who look like supermodels is it?"

"It appears to be a Mr. de Licious, ma'am, with his producer and location manager. They are looking for an outback mansion as a setting for Mr. de Licious's next film."

What a relief! "Well, don't just stand there!" shrieked Barb, waking Siegfried from his nap. "Let them in!"

"At once, ma'am."

Barb was aware this wouldn't be the real DDL of course. On Unearth it would be a "DDL as Sparrowfoot in *The Last of the Michoacan Pocket Gophers*" lookalike, with a totally different personality, if he had a personality at all. (She couldn't be bothered describing one for him.)

"We were lost in a sudden and inexplicable sandstorm," explained the location manager as the three visitors entered the spacious entrance hall of the mansion. "We are fortunate to be alive—"

"Yes, yes, of course. Welcome!" gabbled Barb, batting her eyelashes at the gorgeous Daniel lookalike and flicking her hair coquettishly. The "famous actor" regarded her with a puzzled expression.

Just then, through the still-open doors Barb heard the faint roar of aero engines in the distance. With catlike proficiency she sensed danger.

"Allow me to show you around the property," she invited quickly. The nape of her neck was tingling. Every nerve in her body was pointing in the direction of the local airstrip, now that she heard the drone of the landing plane.

"Perhaps a drink, first?" the DDL-lookalike suggested.

"Of course, what was I thinking? Peeves—drinks, pronto! And activate the you-know-what!"

As Peeves returned with a tray of glistening drinks he murmured to his employer, "The automatic defence shield appears to be malfunctioning, ma'am."

"Right," she murmured back. "Take care of the other two dudes." More loudly, Barb added, "Well, drink up everyone, time's getting away from us. Daniel, come with me!"

Moving fast, she exited with "DDL" just before four extraordinarily lovely women burst on the scene, carrying luggage marked with QUAINTAZ® labels.

"Guten tag!" A familiar voice welcomed the ladies. The newcomers discovered Siegfried still seated under a palm tree by the salt-water lagoon-pool. He rose to his feet, upsetting the caviar, and held out his arms. "Gute Himmel! It is you, mein liebling!"

But to whom was he referring??

On Original Earth, Lottie phoned Barb.

"I finally saw *In the Nostrils of Idiocy* for the first time," she gabbled excitedly. "It's a one hour and forty-five minute video, which turned into five hours for me. I couldn't keep my fingers off the pause button. Dammit, Siegfried looked good! I think I'll have to purchase a copy. Then maybe I can find a way of editing out the supporting actresses."

"Great idea—and editing members of SPH's fan club INTO it in their place," Barb suggested with more enthusiasm than she felt. Lately, she had not been looking for SPH movies. Her fascination—never very strong to begin with—was wearing off.

"It's a great plot," enthused Lottie. "Siegfried plays a twisted maniac called Justin Sain. Everything Justin Sain writes comes true, and he writes some pretty gruesome stories, I can tell you."

"That's right, go ahead and reveal all the surprises when I haven't seen the movie yet," seethed Barb.

"And I've thought of a name for our online SPH saga!" Lottie burbled, barely pausing for breath.

"What?"

"'The Old and the Senseless. Get it? It's a parody of daytime soaps—'The Bold And The Beautiful', 'The Young And The Restless' . . .'"

"Yeah, I get it, but who are you calling old?"

"Oh, um, right," said Lottie. "Certainly not us. It must be him. He's old and we're senseless."

"Sounds good. Let's roll with it. Anyway, I gotta go. Gotta, um, go read some emails . . . "

"Speaking of the Internet, what's with that (Insert Your Name Here) interloper?" Lottie said crossly. "As if we need yet another female vying for his affections!"

"She isn't my fault!" Barb said hotly. "Emily invented her at Apocryphal-Athens Airport on 13 August!"

"At where?"

"Oh, I don't know why I said that," stuttered Barb, "I meant, you know, at Athens Airport in the story . . . " Her voice petered out weakly. "Anyway, I'm not in the SPH fan fiction any more. I just wrote myself out with "Daniel de Licious". I'm going back to my first love."

"Yeah, right. See you on the site," Lottie said.

She thumped down the telephone receiver.

UNEARTHLY LOTTIE
September 04 1998
"The Old And The Senseless" Part 32 (He's old, we're senseless—none of US are old, are we?).

The story so far, in case you're getting confused (I am!)—

Barb has been carried off by "Daniel de Licious" or vice versa, Donna has leapt into the long, lean arms of "Lance Boyle," and Tess has sailed off into the sunset with three hundred Vulgarian sailors and several crates of vodka.

Beside the salt-water lagoon at Barb's outback mansion in Australia, Siegfried was holding out his arms—"It is you, mein liebling!" But before Emily, Tammie, Lottie and (Insert Your Name Here) could rush into his embrace, a crocodile suddenly leaped out of the water behind Siegfried, its fearsome jaws agape.

Without hesitation (Insert Your Name Here) threw herself at the croc. It dragged her back into the stinking lagoon in a death roll. Thank goodness we've got rid of (Insert Your Name Here)!

Siegfried and the Americans (Emily and Tammie) stood horrified! The wire doors of the "mansion" (some mansion, Barb!) banged in the wind, blowflies buzzed around an emaciated kangaroo and ravens croaked as a dust storm approached rapidly through the lightning-streaked sky.

Lottie was first off the mark. Being Australian she had seen this sort of thing lots of times. She ran towards Siegfried, waving some dog-eared documents. "Would you like to read my . . ." Emily pushed Lottie in the back and sent her flying.

"Forget about that crap, gorgeous," Emily said smarmily to Siegfried, "I've got THREE scripts for you." She put a seductive arm through Siegfried's. "Let's go back to Greece. Look, there's a taxi-cab coming to take us to the airport."

And indeed, a taxi could be seen approaching in a cloud of red dust. For a remote outback mansion, this one attracted a surprising amount of traffic.

Just then Siegfried's mobile phone rang. It was Barb.

"Lovely man," she sobbed, "please come and rescue me. Daniel's so mean and nasty. He's made me dye my hair black and talk in a French accent, now he ignores me. I thought he'd be Sparrowfoot, but instead I find he's in training for the sequel to '*My Deft Rat*'—I mean '*Ferret*'! Please, please help me!"

"Thanks a lot, Lottie!" Barb yelled into the phone. "Blowflies and an emaciated kangaroo, eh? How dare you try to ruin my outback mansion! Daniel's mean and nasty, eh? You're trying to ruin my boyfriend too! You'll never get away with it!"

The phone's receiver suffered a stress fracture from being so violently hung up.

Notwithstanding the tempests of outrage flying back and forth along the telephone network, it had finally happened – the saga was officially named, and the acronym was 'TOATS'. There was no stopping it now. . .

UNEARTHLY EMILY
Monday, September 07, 1998
Emily, overhearing the conversation due to the mobile's volume control being turned way up, thought to herself: "*My Deft Rat* . . . over my dead body!

"Siegfried darling, on second thought, Greece can wait. We have to rescue Barb. Being trapped in a bad sequel is a fate worse than death!!"

Siegfried looked deeply into her eyes and admired her loyalty to her friend. (An admirable trait if it were true but Emily would rather keep a close eye on Barb since she still had at least six lives to go . . .)

Lottie, brushing herself off, had a very perturbed look on her face. "Well, two can play that game," she thought. Aloud, she said, "I agree. Let's all help Barb."

Siegfried returned to his telephone conversation with Barb. "Vere are you?" Silence on the other end . . . Hallo? Hallo? Barb? Hallo?"

A very pleasant recorded female voice answered, "If you would like to place a call please hang up and dial again . . . "

"She is gone! Zomezing must haf happened!"

Emily, thinking quickly, called Donna from her cell phone. "Donna? Hi, it's Emily. We need your help. Actually, I need Lance's help. I'll do anything! Do you think the Centurium Group® can run a trace on a mobile phone call placed to Siegfried? Oh . . . you'll be happy to repay him, well, uh I won't go there . . . His number? Hold on. Siegfried, what's your mobile phone number?"

Siegfried replied, "555-1234."

ORIGINAL BARB

7 September 1998

Where is Barb? Will Daniel's sequel be *My Clumsy Ferret* or even *Rat*? What's with all the rodent movies? How will Donna ever repay Lance for tracking down the phone call? Will Tess learn to speak Vulgarian before the vodka runs out? Will Siegfried ever read Lottie or Emily's scripts? Will the taxi-cab driver charge them extra for long distance transportation? Stay tuned . . .

UNEARTHLY BARB

September 08 1998

As soon as one's back is turned the whole scenario falls apart!!! Observing from a distant and mysterious location via my notebook computer I have now discovered (thanks to this site) that the servants at my mansion have forgotten to feed my pets.

"What pets?" I hear you cry. And I reply, "The kangaroo of course, and the rest of the menagerie—the ravens, the blowflies and the crocodile." Well, not the crocodile, obviously my friends did feed THAT while my back was turned. Thanks guys, I would hate to imagine Nigel the Croc wasting away. Pity about (Insert Your Name Here). But wait—have we in fact got rid of her, or does she have as many lives as Barb????

(And ???? just for good measure.)

Shock, horror—(Insert Your Name Here) is in fact phoning on her cell phone, from inside Nigel's stomach, pretending to be Barb. The real Barb, still with long red Icelandic hair, is in the arms of the real Daniel de Licious-lookalike, who has waist-length black locks straight out of The Last of the Michoacan Pocket Gophers. The spectacular couple is landing in his private helicopter at Daniel's palace in (Implausible) Ireland where they will get married and live happily ever after, secure in the knowledge that any other Barbs mentioned are not the real ones.

Meanwhile Siegfried is stranded in Australia with some diabolical characters, waiting for a dust storm and an ominous taxi-cab, battered and much modified, which looks like one of the vehicles from the *Mad Max*® movies crossed with a 1959 Carripac Coop Devil®, the Spookzappers'® Ectomobile®, a classic Lemon Cab® and the Frugal Earth® street-view® camera car, the whole thing sprinkled with ® symbols, and topped with a radar dish and a compact but extremely bizarre crashed spaceship welded to the roof.

Barb sat back in her office chair and sighed with satisfaction. She thought: It doesn't matter what Lottie tries—I have written myself out of the saga and that's that. My adorable cyber-persona is happily existing in virtuality with DDL's handsome avatar. And there's nothing Lottie can do about it.

How wrong she was. . .

ORIGINAL LOTTIE

Friday 11 September 1998

Haven't written my next instalment of "TOATS" yet—been too busy writing my movie script!! (Wanna read it? Anyone?) Had to laugh when I read Tammie's method of watching "Thrill Schmooze" (Sep 2); sounds tragically like me with my overused pause and rewind buttons. I can make a few meagre minutes of Siegfried turn into a whole evening's viewing.

We had our "ladies' night" to see *Das Rat* (6th time we've seen it in a cinema). At intermission we looked round to find we were almost the only women in the place—wall to wall men, most of them young and quite a few good looking. Good God, why was I looking at them when my head was full of the Captain?!

One of them came up to us and started chatting (I'd sailed with him in the past but hadn't seen him for ages). Barely got over the formalities—hadn't even introduced him to anyone, when I said, in a panic; "Aah! The movie's started!" and we all ran away up the stairs leaving him standing there thinking he'd got halitosis.

Tess and I have just bought our copies of *Das Rat*—Director's Cut: Limited Collector's Edition, includes behind the scenes interviews with cast and crew. (Tess bought two just in case hers gets worn out.) The (all too brief) few words of interview with Siegfried are interesting, if only because it's the first time we've seen him as himself.

ORIGINAL LOTTIE

11 September 1998

Back again with a bit more of "TOATS".

UNEARTHLY LOTTIE

11 September 1998

Who are you trying to fool, Barb? Being slowly dissolved by Nigel's digestive juices would seem to be enough of a problem for (Insert Your Name Here), without her phoning Siegfried to pretend she's you!! Come on; we may be senseless, but we're not stupid! You just don't want to admit that you've made a big mistake and that life with "DDL" is hell. But too bad, 'cos Lance has come up with your number. (Thanks Lance.)

Siegfried phoned Barb. Much to the joyous astonishment of Emily, Tammie and Lottie, he said something like this: "Bad luck, you two-timing tart. You said you loved me—all that stuff on the yacht in Fiji—schamlos! Wish I'd left you to the sharks".

The weird alien taxi awaited, its V8 engine growling hungrily. Siegfried tossed his phone into the lagoon and looked around at the senseless ones with a smile.

"Well ladies—where to next?"

Before anyone could answer, the dust storm hit. The tin roof of Barb's mansion exploded into the red sky and the air turned to dust. The pedestrians ran, coughing, towards the taxi. Tammie and Emily, with an arm each, looked as though they were trying to tear Siegfried in half. He, blinded with dust, suddenly halted. Lottie cannoned into him and ricocheted off, falling flat on her back, gasping for air.

After extricating himself from the tentacles of Tammie and Emily and blinking back a bit of sight, Siegfried made it to the taxi and dived in, Tammie and Emily hot on his heels.

The taxi roared off and was swallowed up by the swirling storm. Lottie tottered after it for a few steps.

"Wait for me!" she wailed, "Don't you want to read my . . ." But her voice was lost in the howling moan of the wind.

Barb phoned Lottie.

"Coward!" she shrieked into the receiver.

Simultaneously they hung up on each other.

UNEARTHLY BARB

11 September 1998

Continuing on from where Lottie left off—Lance and the Centurium Group® having successfully traced the source of the mobile phone call to the belly of Nigel the Crocodile who dwelleth in the murky saltwater lagoon of Barb's so-called "flyblown" outback mansion, everyone is now aware that (Insert Your Name Here) still lives within Nigel's innards but languishes in a state of delusion, believing herself to be Barb.

How long (Insert Your Name Here) will last among those stomach acids and half-digested marsupials is open to conjecture. Nobody seems to be about to rescue her.

Siegfried, being a natural-born hero of course, would like to help—however he is unable to do so, being currently wedged in a surrealistic taxi between Emily and Tammie, the only two remaining fans from the Grecian Idyll.

At the moment the heart of the dust storm struck in all its roaring majesty, the taxi windows blanked out in a haze of ochre powder. Undeterred, the driver planted his foot on the accelerator. The speedometer performed several rapid circuits of the dial as the taxi hurtled through the obliterating storm.

"But you cannot see vere ve are going!" shouted Siegfried over the savage howling of the dusty winds.

The driver looked back over his shoulder with an evil grin. "No worries, mate!" he yelled, "I could find me way around here with me eyes shut!"

The passengers gasped. The eye-sockets of the driver glowed empty and white. He was obviously either blind or some kind of alien.

Emily and Tammie, who were crushed closely against Siegfried in the cramped seats, took hold of his arms.

"Save us!" they whispered. At that moment the vehicle clipped one of those huge outback ant-hills that resemble red concrete pillars. Jolted, one of the doors flew open. The inflatable automatic co-pilot was thrown out, but the heinous-looking character at the wheel merely laughed. The taxi raced on . . .

Against a background of peeling paint, the colors in the poster of Daniel de Licious glowed like fields of tulips lit by the morning sun. Barb leaned back in her chair and admired it.

Sparrowfoot raced towards her, permanently held in the stasis of print. Strands of his torn-shadow hair were being blown across that lean, handsome face. Beneath dark brows his eyes were lit by fires of passion. The gathered linen of his eighteenth-century shirt caressed his wide shoulders.

There was something about the way those long, midnight flames of hair softly fell across masculine musculature— which surely must possess the hardness of polished wood— something which awoke a deep, primeval yearning . . .

She glanced at the black-and-white photocopy of Siegfried P. Hinkelheimer. Yeah, he had great eyes. She could understand why Lottie and Tess almost expired every time they watched "This Rat" or whatever it was called. But Daniel—Daniel had been her first obsession. Why change?

ORIGINAL TAMMIE
11 September 1998

Barb, you're a big fan of Daniel de Licious? I think he's cool too, and Ray Fiends also, however Siegfried is the one who really does it for me. His role as the Skipper in *Thrill Schmooze* in particular! Wow, my pulse is STILL racing!

ORIGINAL BARB
12 September 1998

Tammie, I thought it was about time I wrote myself out of this crazy saga and got a life. And what better way to live happily ever after than with "DDL", whose portrayal of Sparrowfoot in *The Last of the Michoacan Pocket Gophers* does for me what Siegfried in *Thrill Schmooze* does for you!!!

102

I have seen the devastating effect Siegfried has on some people—namely, Lottie and Tess, who blush, stammer and go weak at the knees at the mere mention of his name. The words "Besotted" and "Obsessed" do not begin to do justice to their affliction, and I suspect that you and Emily and Donna and several thousand others are in the same "battleship", so to speak. Therefore I thought I would leave Siegfried to those who, by virtue of their passion, deserve him most.

At the local cinema it is quite fascinating to watch Lottie and Tess as we are viewing *Das Rat* for the twenty-sixth time or whatever. As soon as a certain person appears on the screen they have to start fanning themselves with bits of paper so that they will not expire from overheating. They appear to the casual observer to be melting into their chairs like wax against a flame, and I always hope there's a doctor in the audience.

Original Emily

ORIGINAL EMILY/INCHES
13 September 1998
Has the story spun wildly out of control or what?! Barb—I too have a thing for Irishmen and that wonderful Irish actor Gabriel Yearn is right up there ... wasn't he in "The Creep" alongside Siegfried? Haven't seen it but I think he was ...

Original Lottie

ORIGINAL LOTTIE
13 September 1998
Emily, if you like Gabriel Yearn, you'd better not watch "The Creep"—his character is horrible in it—not only does he shoot Siegfried, but he's got a haircut that Hitler would be proud of! (But Siegfried's lovely, so you'd better see it anyway.)

103

UNEARTHLY LOTTIE

13 September 1998

Back in Australia, Lottie sheltered from the dust storm under a camel. The next morning, she and the camel went their separate ways without a backward glance. Lottie wandered in the desert for days, forlorn and desolate. Hunger and thirst took their toll, but she suffered most terribly from having lost Siegfried...

UNEARTHLY BARB

14 September 1998

...Clogged sand turned Lottie's long curls into dreadlocks. Her leopard-print dress was torn to tatters by thorn-bushes. Her dainty Italian shoes fell apart and her nose was so badly sunburned it made Rudolph the Reindeer's look like a scoop of vanilla ice-cream.

UNEARTHLY LOTTIE

14 September 1998

Lottie carried a Survival Kit, but as it consisted of a battered bag full of worn-out video favorites, it was not much use to her in a place with no televisions. When a wandering aboriginal tribe found her exhausted and half dead, she managed to sob; "TV...I need a TV...and a VCR". (Video Cassette Recorder: an artefact of 1998.)

Fortunately for Lottie, the tribe had both these appurtenances in their bark humpies, so hours and hours later, after watching *Das Rat, Thrill Schmooze, The Seventh Swine, The Constable and the Young Lady, Surface Paradise'* etc, (with much use of the rewind button) she emerged fortified and ready to search the world for Siegfried.

But what had happened to him? Had he been carried off to another planet as the supreme male example of the Human Race? Had he been rescued from the alien cab-driver by Emily and Tammie, or had he rescued them? Maybe they all need Donna and Lance to save them.

Donna, we haven't seen you for a while—how's life with Lance? You can always get a divorce, you know.

ORIGINAL DONNA
14 September 1998
The latest chapters of TOATS left me weak with laughter. A blessing on whoever got this started, and I second Barb's motion that it continue ad infinitum. "Lance" has attached himself to me like a barnacle—I think he seems to be having some kind of separation anxiety—but if I can peel him off I'll write myself back into the story.

UNEARTHLY DONNA
14 September 1998
At twilight Lottie emerged from the humpy of the tribe's most handsome warrior, coldly ignoring his pleas for her to return. She stared unblinking into the waning sunset.

"Just how many days have I been wearing this pair of underwear?" she pondered. Her reverie was rudely interrupted by the unmistakable pounding thump of chopper blades, as a Kickapoo AH-64® rose from behind the dune, flinging a blinding cloud of red sand and camel dung into the air. Lottie reached to cover her face against the maelstrom, but at that moment she spied a rope ladder dangling from the belly of the chopper. Having become something of a reckless adventurer, Lottie seized her chance for escape and grasped the rungs, callously leaving the incredibly buff warrior behind to pine away for her forever.

Fearing the worst, she bravely ascended the ladder and peered into the darkened interior as the chopper veered away, carrying her into the night.

"Who are these people?" wondered Lottie . . . "Terrorists? Guerillas? American tourists?" At this last thought Lottie almost bailed out and took her chances with the desert, when she suddenly heard a familiar voice from within.

Could it be?! Was it possible?! After all this time, and halfway around the world—it couldn't be—yet it was, and there could only be one explanation . . .

"Donna!" cried Lottie, flinging herself into the chopper, eliciting screams and other panicked outbursts from the occupants—"It's really you!! And Lance! You're HERE, the Centurium Group®—you made them track me down!? You came all this way to SAVE me!!?"

"What on Earth are you talking about?!" exclaimed "Lance", the first to recover some composure. "We came all the way to Australia on the path of our pal Peter What?, whom we've just now sent away by ambulance, gibbering hysterically about the Wrath of the Almighty, dust storms, and white-eyed alien invaders bent on enslaving the earth."

He continued, shouting over the noise of the aero-engines, "Now we've got to go home, get married, and live happily ever after under a pall of dread and apprehension, suffering the grim realities of my Gift, which is also my Curse. Who are you, anyway?"

"On second thoughts, I think I'll stay here and see if I can wrestle any trace of (Insert Your Name Here) out of that crocodile," mumbled Donna, inching casually away and reaching for the handle of the emergency exit.

"Donnnaaaaa . . . ! Noooooo! But I painted the house YELLOW . . . !!" wailed "Lance", as he found himself about to be abandoned by yet another woman who didn't know a good thing when she saw it.

"Goodbye my love," yelled Donna, over her shoulder. "Don't wait for me—our fates are in the hands of .." and her voice trailed off into the dark.

Lottie was forced to think fast, weighing the options of a trip to the relative safety of America in the hands of the Centurium Group®, or a fall to almost certain death on the hard sands of the desert, where her bleached bones would one day become shelter for scorpions and dung beetles.

At the last moment she grabbed what looked a bit like a parachute out of some nearby webbing and leaped after Donna into the night, thinking that maybe it was a good thing she hadn't just changed into fresh undies after all . . .

ORIGINAL BARB
Tuesday 15 September 1998
Donna, you're hilarious! Great chapter! I have no idea who Peter What? is, or what Lance's Curse might be but am intrigued. Can you shed light? And thank you for your praise—"A blessing on whoever got this started".

TOATS was born on 8 July and is still going strong, getting older and more senseless by the minute. Aufwiedersehen.

Barb

P.S. Tammie and Emily, what's it like sitting so close to Siegfried in a taxi? I hope two parachuting figures don't suddenly crash through the roof . . .

ORIGINAL DONNA
15 September 1998

Barb—My bad; Peter What? is Lance's sidekick (or was) in the first two seasons of Centurium®. Lance's Gift/Curse is his psychic-but-not-psychic insight into the mind of evil, as it were. Make sense? Nobody here quite gets it either, which is of course part of the show's mystique. :)

As for those parachuting women, why, of COURSE fate should steer them into the path of the madly careening taxi—shouldn't it? Only the next chapter's author knows for sure . . . !

Blessings on your next seven generations for instigating so much fun. I pray Seegums doesn't mind. :)

UNEARTHLY BARB
15 September 1998

Back in the arid wastes of Central Australia, the bizarre taxi (crowned with radar apparatus, satellite dishes, antennae, lucky rabbits' feet and similar paraphernalia) was still careening around aimlessly at high speed. Days had passed. It was dark inside the vehicle. The dust storm had subsided but the taxi's windows remained opaque all around, blanketed with the powdered bones of ancient Australian mountains ground down to dust by eons of scouring winds.

Three figures were slumped on the back seat.

"How far is it to the airport?" mumbled Emily.

"Haven't we run out of gas yet?" groaned Tammie.

Siegfried was asleep. He looked gorgeous, despite the layers of sand smudging those incredible cheekbones. Tammie and Emily could not understand how he still looked gorgeous after days without food or water.

"This momma never runs outta gas," snickered the sidereal cab driver, eyeing Tammie and Emily via the rear-view mirror. His beetling eyebrows jumped up and down disconcertingly. "She runs on nuke power," he explained, flashing another evil grin to display his pointed teeth.

Just then, Siegfried woke up.

He stared at Tammie. An expression of recognition dawned across his face.

"Gut Himmel," he said, "I did not know you at first. You are the one who saved me!" His sapphire eyes rested tenderly upon Tammie.

"Yes," breathed Tammie as hope awakened in her heart, "I am the one."

"No kissing allowed in this bus!" squawked the driver, speeding up. The interior of the cab was invaded by the ascending whine of turbines winding up to full power. The passengers found themselves with involuntary grins on their faces as G-force vectors took hold, scraping the very skin back from their teeth.

"This baby's got some grunt, eh?" shouted the driver gleefully, pushing the throttle all the way to the "light speed" indicator.

UNEARTHLY LOTTIE

15 September 1998

Tripe Odd's Alien Taxi® hurtled through the dust storm at an unbelievable velocity, then suddenly flew out into a clear black night full of stars. Siegfried, Emily and Tammie found that what they feared was true; they were in an intergalactic craft rising towards the Mothership and there was UnEarth far, far below and receding rapidly.

As the taxi docked in the belly of the Mothership, the crazed-looking alien mission leader peered in at the windows. Emily and Tammie shrieked in terror, but Siegfried held them close; he was cool, calm and magnificent (of course).

Bruce, the white-eyed taxi-driver from planet Splinge, gloated. He had succeeded brilliantly in his mission to collect the supreme male specimen of the Human Race.

"With all those drooling female humans following him round the globe, this must be the man!" he chortled happily to himself.

But Trixie, the fearsome mission leader was not so sure. His eyes bulged like two table-tennis balls. Jets of steam shot from the nostrils of his long muzzle and his horns shaded to neon purple.

"Xbtyx obt!" he yelled; "Txtabyc cyx? Botxy obyob obt . . . Obxt boty xycy?" etc.

Just as well for Siegfried that he doesn't understand Splingeish. I don't either, but here's a babelfish translation:

"Fool you! Supreme male? Blind are or stupid only you? Eye you at him! Good tcyccyt!! (untranslatable) Flaws not to be counted with and very far not famous is he! Throw out the females senseless clinging and him with him! To Earth planet resume and be again trying!"

Bruce, being a tidy alien, did not just throw our hero and his women out into space as instructed. He took them back to Earth with the intention of throwing them out there.

Not long after, Trixie located the perfect specimen of human masculinity living in a castle in Implausible Ireland with a woman named Barb. This ideal man was abducted and carried off to live the rest of his life as a zoo exhibit on the planet Splinge.

Sorry, Barb!

In cyberspace something went 'zing!' Within a nearby spurious solar system, a greenish-blue planet popped into existence and immediately backdated itself so that it had first appeared at exactly the same time as UnEarth. A painted sign stuck at a rakish angle into its North Pole proclaimed its name—"Splinge".

UNEARTHLY BARB

15 September 1998

"Oi! No kissing, I said!" the cab driver bawled, after a quick glance in the rear vision mirror. He was in the process of opening his drooling maw to add another comment when something hurtled down through the roof, straight into the passenger's seat beside him.

"Omigosh, it's Donna!" screamed Emily.

Bruce yelled incoherently, but was cut off once more when a second object plummeted through the roof directly above his head. It landed on top of him, squashing him flat.

Lottie, wearing some sort of parachute harness, lay draped over the steering wheel. The taxi spun out of control. Fortunately, unknown to the occupants, two parachutes were being dragged along behind it. They filled with air, billowing out like two white chrysanthemums, and dragged the vehicle to a shuddering halt.

"Saved" croaked Tammie through a dry mouth. "Now—what were you saying, Siegfried liebling?"

But even as she spoke, the car door was flung open from outside. The five surviving occupants stared in surprise at the figure who stood in a disgusting state before them. It was none other than (Insert Your Name Here), slightly shredded and dripping with semi-digested marsupials.

"Welcome back," she said soothingly. There was a dangerous edge to her voice. Was it possible she had not forgiven her friends for failing to save her from Nigel the Croc?

"Wha—what do you mean?" quavered Lottie. "Where exactly are we?"

"Right back at Barb's mansion," smirked (Insert Your Name Here).

Everyone stepped out of the taxi. There before them stood Barb's REAL mansion, which all this time had been hidden behind a foliate screen of mulga, wattles and eucalyptus.

What they had previously thought was the mansion was actually an old shed. The real mansion was built of Connemara marble and studded with diamonds. Over the ten-foot-high front doors, a shining bronze plaque displayed the name of the sumptuous estate: 'SANE'. A forest of gold chimneys poked up from the rooves, and the window-panes were translucent insets of topaz. It was set in park-like surroundings and there was a tennis court out the back.

"Won't you come in and refresh yourselves,?" smoothly said (Insert Your Name Here). Siegfried took Tammie's arm and they entered the palatial edifice.

The interior was magnificent. From the marble-floored hallway, sweeping staircases led to the many luxurious suites. Servants bustled hither and thither, filling sunken baths and strewing fragrant petals on the limpid waters.

Soon the weary travellers had bathed away all the dust. Beside one of the indoor fountains of the jewelled mansion they reclined on satin couches, eating and drinking while the servants offered around laden trays of sweetmeats. Peeves the butler poured another splash of Mowit and Showit® into Siegfried's crystal goblet. Undiplomatically, Siegfried kept smiling fondly at Tammie.

(Insert Your Name Here), who was pacing back and forth leading Nigel the Croc on a ruby-studded leash, narrowed her eyes. She looked sideways at Tammie.

What can (Insert Your Name Here) be thinking? Surely she's not jealous?

8

RETURN TO BARB'S OUTBACK MANSION

ORIGINAL TAMMIE

Saturday 19 September 1998

Haha, you girls crack me up! It's been ages since I had such a good laugh! I'm grateful to you for keeping me as a character in the story. I haven't been posting any chapters because I'm not that great at writing.

Hey Barb, I got a buzz out of being made Siegfried's favorite! Can't figure out what made me worthy of such an honor! Truly, I intend to contribute something in the near future – however of course it would not be polite for a lady to divulge her love-life gossip TOO promptly. . .

ORIGINAL EMILY
Saturday 19 September 1998
Yeah, and in a mansion!

Hmmm . . . Lottie, I prefer the way Gabriel looked in *The Predictable Lineup* and *Short Ladies*. Like Siegfried in *Das Rat* and *The Seventh Swine*. I hate to be disillusioned by bad hair days.

Thank goodness we are FINALLY out of that horrible taxi at Barb's mansion (but not the real Barb . . . since the real one is happily engaged in recreational activities with "DDL" in Ireland). Unless we've been through a Quasargate® in the dust storm and we were transported to Ireland . . . In which case Barb will be miffed at all these uninvited guests since she has had no time to go buy food.

ORIGINAL BARB
Saturday 19 September 19, 1998
Tammie—in my opinion, anyone who ever contributes a chapter ought to continue to be written in until she writes herself out or disappears inexplicably from the site. Emily—my fellow Appreciater of Dark-Haired Irishmen! Donna—thanks for putting up with this madness on your pages!

UNEARTHLY BARB
19 September 1998
MEMO: Lottie keeps trying to rip Barb from the arms of "DDL" but so far has been unsuccessful. QUOTE FROM ARCHIVES: "The real Barb, still with long red Icelandic hair, is in the arms of the real Daniel de Licious-lookalike with waist-length black hair straight out of

The Last of the Michoacan Pocket Gophers, landing in his private helicopter at Daniel's palace in Ireland where they will get married and live happily ever after, secure in the knowledge that any other Barbs mentioned are not the real ones."

So that's how it is, Lottie. I don't know who that other Barb was living with in Ireland but it wasn't the real DDL avatar. Actually, as you were sprawling senseless in the sand in Australia, "DDL" and the real Barb were making passionate love in Ireland, for the umpteenth time.

Back to the story . . .

UNEARTHLY BARB
19 September 1998

Servants hovered obsequiously. Siegfried raised his crystal goblet and drank a toast to Tammie, gazing profoundly into her eyes.

"I am so glad I recognised you!" he said.

Reclining on the same chaise longue, they whispered together about the time she found him lying half-drowned on the beach and restored him to health with mouth-to-mouth resuscitation. Everyone else in the lofty hall stared balefully at them with eyes as sharp as stiletto heels and as green as those bits of unidentifiable food you find at the back of the refrigerator. (This was Nigel the Croc's normal facial expression.)

(Insert Your Name Here) was wearing a knock-out gown of scintillating gold lame, stolen from Barb's wardrobe. She could not take her gaze from Tammie's face. The woman was acting rather strangely—and had been doing so, ever since she was swallowed and regurgitated by Nigel (which everyone thought was not sufficient reason).

(Insert Your Name Here) said casually, "Did you know Barb's mansion has a private gym? And a private helipad? And a private plastic surgery clinic with its own theatre?"

She held up her hand. A scalpel's blade glittered wickedly. "Come, Tammie, let me show you around."

Ignoring Tammie's protests, (Insert Your Name Here) dragged her off the chaise longue and out of the hall of fountains.

"Wait!" called Siegfried, but he was too late. The door slammed. Tammie was in (Insert Your Name Here)'s clutches.

Is (Insert Your Name Here) completely out of her mind? What will happen to Tammie if they ever reach the plastic surgery clinic?

UNEARTHLY BARB
19 September 1998

"I must find Tammie!" shouted Siegfried, heading for the door. As one, Donna, Emily, Lottie and Nigel the Croc followed him.

A rapid whirring sound approached, clattering against the blue porcelain of the southern sky. Through the windows, the occupants of the mansion could see a helicopter the size of the *Titanic* and equally unsinkable, approaching the helipad. Out of its windows leaned three hundred and one Vulgarian sailors, cheerily waving bottles of vodka.

Paying no attention to this minor disruption, Siegfried thrust his shoulder against the door and broke it down. Just as he was about to rush through, a strange event occurred. Yes, a strange event! At last! Just when you thought the story was getting too predictable.

Siegfried froze. His eyes took on the yearning look of a man stranded in a remote desert fastness. Slowly he turned his head towards his entourage of women. Lottie happened to be the closest. Siegfried smiled at her in wonder and delight.

"Ich liebe dich!" he said to Lottie.

"Damn!" shouted Donna and Emily, throwing their bottles of love potion on the floor where they smashed into tiny pieces. "Foiled again!"

As Siegfried took Lottie in his arms, Nigel the Croc was busy licking up the spilled love potion, while three hundred and one Vulgarian sailors were hammering at the emerald-studded portico. Sinisterly, there was no sign of the abducted Tammie . . .

Hey Lottie, I dare you NOT to be ripped from Siegfried's side for at least three chapters!!!

ORIGINAL EMILY
20 September 1998
Barb—Too funny! I'm wiping the tears away as I type! As an official member of the ADHI (Appreciater of Dark-Haired Irishmen) I could be happily in my beloved's arms but this is AGOG (Appreciaters of Gorgeous Older German) so I will try to be faithful for the moment :) I will add a chapter later. Now where did I put the box full of videos . . .

UNEARTHLY LOTTIE

22 September 1998

Before plunging into the next thrilling chapter of "The Obsession and the Story," as Emily wisely calls it, I'll just let you know what happened to the REAL Barb and the REAL DDL-lookalike. Yes, he was transported to the zoo on planet Splinge; the good news is—they took Barb too. She clung so piteously to Daniel as they carried him off that, try as they might, they couldn't dislodge her. But after taking a good look at her they decided she wasn't a bad female specimen after all. So now Barb and DDL are both in the zoo; warm, well fed and much admired in their replica diamond-studded palace/cage.

Now for the next instalment of TOATS: Siegfried enfolded Lottie in his strong, lean arms (thank goodness she'd showered and changed her underwear!) She was wearing a strapless, slinky little black dress (from Barb's wardrobe of course). He held her close so that her wildly thudding heart beat next to his. He leaned forward to kiss her, she looked into those eyes, blue and deep as the ocean; thought; Gosh, he's old with acne scars, but ooooh . . . and turned as limp as a wet dish rag.

Yes, she'd passed out again.

She slithered from his arms and her head hit the marble floor with a loud crack. Hopeless. (Yes, I know I'm a coward, Barb.)

Suddenly into the room burst three hundred and one Vulgarian sailors, with Tess tottering along behind them.

"Captain Hinkelheimer," their spokesman addressed Siegfried.

"Hic," interjected Tess.

The spokesman, Sergei, continued, "Our ship svings at her moorings in ze harbour, eager as a hound. Ze vind is fresh from ze vest and she vishes to be gone. Our old Captain Kolomensky and his replacement Captain Sedov have just killed each other and ve vould wery like you to be our captain. You vill wery like our ship—she is most beaudiful in ze vorld!"

Siegfried looked from Sergei to Lottie, senseless on the floor, glanced round at the other quivering women, then turned back to Sergei.

"Sounds good," he said. "Let's go!"

"No!!" shouted Donna and Emily, running after him; "That's an AIR BANANA helicopter, for crynoutloud! Don't go in that!"

But he climbed aboard; so did three hundred and one Vulgarian sailors and a few more crates of vodka—found in Barb's cellars.

Though it was little more than a heap of rust, held together with bits of string, the helicopter managed to lift laboriously into the air, with Tess giggling, hiccupping and hanging from a strut by one hand. Siegfried leaned out and deftly pulled her in as the ancient machine climbed a few extra inches and chugged ponderously towards the coast.

Emily and Donna fell sobbing into each others arms. "Oh Lance, what have I done? moaned Donna. "Please come back!"

Meanwhile, inside the mansion, Nigel the Croc had found Lottie on the floor and stared lovingly at her senseless form, while salivating all over that slinky little dress. Suddenly, the door flew open and in came a triumphant Tammie, holding high a dripping scalpel, spattered with blood and shredded pieces of gold lame gown.

"Oh, my beloved, I'm back!" she cried, then stopped when she saw the almost deserted room. She ran frantically out into the sunset in time to see the helicopter, silhouetted like a bloated blowfly, struggle across the darkening horizon and disappear.

Will Tammie see her beloved again? Will Siegfried survive the Air Banana helicopter? Will Tess ever sober up enough to write her own chapter? Has Lottie found true love with Nigel? (and will he read her script?) And is (Insert Your Name Here) really dead????

ORIGINAL REBECCA
25 September 1998

What a joy it is to discover the cyber-shrine to SPH. Before this I believed I was alone in my admiration for him!

It was last week when I first looked in on these fan pages and saw all the gorgeous images of Siegfried, the information about his movies etc. That very night he featured in my dreams! In my sleeping imagination we kissed—well who wouldn't kiss him? It felt amazingly real. A darn fine way to spend the night, I can tell you! Bravo for this site, everyone —please continue your excellent efforts!

ORIGINAL BARB

25 September 1998

Brilliant chapter Liz!!! I loved it. Rebecca, please write down any further dreams you have and contribute them as a chapter in our long-running Siegfried Fantasy Saga.

ORIGINAL TAMMIE

28 September 1998

Donna, I'm hugely grateful to you for letting us know that an extra-long version of *Sandhill* would be shown on pay-TV last weekend. The great thing is you were right – they did include extra scenes with Siegfried! There were several that had escaped my eyes previously, in which he looked simply delicious. Normally I'm not a fan of Science Fiction, however I taped the whole thing.

UNEARTHLY TAMMIE

28 September 1998

Regarding the SPH Saga—if that helicopter flew past me I would snag it with my supernaturally strong lariat (my best cowgirl move) and bring it crashing safely down!

The Vulgarian crew would pour out and rush at me angrily, but in a move of superb diplomacy I would simply hand out free drinks. My generosity and excellent taste in liquor would overwhelm the crew with admiration, whereupon they would drink many toasts to my good health, start singing and dancing, and soon lose all recollection of both my deed and their gorgeous German passenger.

ORIGINAL GWYNN

5 October 1998

I'm a 'newbie' on this web page and in my opinion it's extremely entertaining. Nonetheless ladies, with all due respect, I feel it my duty to recall you to reality! I feel bound to support the cause of the flesh-and-blood guys of my acquaintance.

You fan-girls ignore the poor things in favor of imaginary blokes in movies, portrayed by handsome thespians!

Go out there and get yourself a male who actually exists!

ORIGINAL REBECCA

9 October 1998

This message is for you, Gwynn. On the Internet there are literally hundreds of thousands of websites dedicated to celebrities and if you look at just a few of them for comparison, you'll realize that the contributors here on the SPH site are NOT like so many other fans who shun the outside world and sit at a computer all day mooning over fictitious heroes and worshipping every hair on their heads.

On the contrary, the SPH fans seem quick-witted and full of fun, as you'll see if you read back through their posts.

Their collaborative 'Fanfic' story is nothing more than light-hearted tongue-in-cheek entertainment.

Seriously, if you go and look at the literary efforts of Fanfic creators on other sites, you'll be amazed at how earnestly they treat their subject. There's no sign of the cheerful self-deprecation or satire that we enjoy here. On other sites, if anyone dares to point out even a minor flaw in their idol, the fans fly into a foul-mouthed rage and start flinging swear words in all directions. In my opinion, it's people like that who are in need of a reality check.

One gets the feeling that Siegfried P. Hinkelheimer fans don't live their lives dominated by some kind of crazy obsession for him. Instead they merely find it entertaining to swap ideas and laughs with fellow admirers of his looks and acting skills.

ORIGINAL GWYNN
11 October 1998
It was only meant as a joke!

ORIGINAL FRANCES
11 October 1998
Bravo, Rebecca. Gwynn's words did not sound like a joke to me! Siegfried is without doubt the tastiest dish I could ever imagine!

Original Donna

ORIGINAL DONNA
13 October 1998
With Siegfried I've had this slow (deliciously so) burn for going on 20 years now. Hey, that's real, isn't it? Having a "thing" for a guy for 20 years—must mean it's real, right?

But as for getting lives, the humor and intelligence here in this little corner of the web provides a brief respite FROM our lives, which are all no doubt equally hectic (and far removed our fantasizings. Sigh.)

If I may speak for everyone that is, pardon my presumptuousness. I had to read your message a second time before my brain registered it as sarcasm. After all, everyone knows that no real man on the planet could measure up to our Captain.

125

ORIGINAL LOTTIE
14 October 1998

Oh, Gwynn, you're a brave woman (or just very naughty) to venture into the SPH shrine with a message like that! (BTW I'm also mulling over a future instalment of TOATS.)

ORIGINAL BARB
Oz-Traylia, Tuesday 20 October 1998

Mulling over a future instalment of TOATS, eh Lottie? You'd better make sure you send it on an even-numbered day of the month. I am also mulling over a possible chapter, but I am honor bound by a strange and ancient Australian ritual, to wait until an odd day to send it. Come to think of it, that's most days . . .

ORIGINAL DONNA
Wednesday 21 October 1998

I'm also mulling over TOATS but I can't figure out when to post, being bound to avoid odd & even days. I'm a liar, I just can't figure out where to go next . . .

UNEARTHLY LOTTIE
22 October 1998

"The Obsession and the Story" returns to our screens! All new episodes! In case you've forgotten, here's the story so far:

Back at Barb's mansion, bereft Donna and Emily weep in each other's arms, while a lustful crocodile dribbles over Lottie as she lies senseless on the floor. Tammie, still spattered with bits of (Insert Your Name Here) has rushed frantically

126

in pursuit of their beloved, who has exited over the horizon in a decrepit Air Banana helicopter, weighed down with four hundred and three Vulgarian sailors, Tess and a rapidly diminishing supply of vodka.

Tammie, having found Barb's Ground Crawler® in the garage, hurtled through the twilight, foot flat to the floor, following a glittering trail of empty vodka bottles. After overtaking the laden chopper and finding a coiled rope in the back of the vehicle (previously used by Barb to capture wild camels), she unleashed never-suspected skills, whirling her lasso to bring the chopper down! What a woman! (Actually, with the engine sputtering its last, it was about to crash anyway.)

A dozen dazed Vulgarians tottered forth, followed by Tess smiling and hiccupping happily, then—looking a little bewildered—our hero.

"My love! You're mine again!" cried Tammie, rushing towards him.

"But my ship ... how will I reach ... aagh," gasped Siegfried, noticing Tammie's state for the first time.

"What's wrong? Oh, that—just a spot of self-defence. It's me—remember? I saved your life in Episode 19 and I can't live without you!" She flung herself into his arms.

"Look Donna," Siegfried said, holding her off—"no, zat's not right ... Ell ... no ... vat's your name again? Forgive me, but I've been feeling razzer confused of late. Now, first things first; ve'd better get you cleaned up."

Tammie looked down at her (borrowed from Barb) tattered and blood-spattered gown. "Ugh yes; I'll get rid of this!"

She pushed the straps from her shoulders and the gown fell with a satiny susurration to her feet. She stood triumphant, her naked perfection bathed in silver as the moon peered up over the vast rim of the world.

"Hmm, zat's a good start," said Siegfried, plucking a piece of shredded gold lame from her dishevelled hair. "But even better, look over zere." He pointed south and, lo and behold, what luck! The chopper had been brought down not a hundred yards from a billabong, whose still waters gleamed tranquil in the velvet night.

As the huge, pale disc of the moon climbed the star-spangled eternity of the desert sky, Tammie and Siegfried swam together in the clear cool water, washing away the outback dust (and the last remnants of (Insert Your Name Here)).

Afterwards they lay arm in arm on the banks, gazing up at the Southern Cross, while in the background a few Vulgarians (on leave from the Red Army Chorus) strummed their balalaikas and softly sang *Ochi Chornye*.

Tammie looked deeply into Siegfried's extraordinary eyes and thought she may as well die right now.

"What's that stuck between your teeth?" he suddenly asked.

"Oh, it's just a bit of (Insert Your Name Here)'s earring", said Tammie, fishing it out and tossing it nonchalantly aside.

"What became of her ear?" asked Siegfried.

"Sadly, I believe I left it attached to her head . . . but we don't have to think about her. It's just you and me now."

"Um, what about her?" asked Siegfried, as Tess's sozzled face suddenly appeared, leering at them over the top of some shrubbery.

"She hasn't got a word to say for herself,' said Tammie, giving Tess a poke in the eye, "so she doesn't count. It's just you and me, dearest love, forever!"

As they kissed tenderly, passionately, a dingo howled at the moon and nearby some bushes rustled ominously.

It can't be Tess—she fell into the billabong. Could it be . . . oh no, is it possible that (Insert Your Name Here) has risen from the dead again, and clinging to the bottom of the Land Cruiser as it bounced over the dust and rocks, come to wreak a terrifying revenge??

UNEARTHLY BARB

Planet Splinge—22 October 1998

Yes it's possible. There is such a thing as CLONING, you know. I used to do a lot of that in my secret laboratory back in the Outback Mansion—when I lived there, of course. I only needed one microscopic cell—and that's about all that was left of (Insert Your Name Here). Not that I can recall what happened to her. The "real world" seems so far away since I started having so much fun here on Planet Splinge, creating a super-race with "DDL" . . . Love these alien tropical nights—wish you were all here . . . (Not really—more like "wish you were all beer.")

ORIGINAL LOTTIE

22 October 1998

WANTED: A few more idiots to write themselves into our soap opera . . . just think; you can do whatever you like with "Siegfried"—drop in by hot-air balloon or gallop up on your Arabian stallion and carry him off to . . . anywhere you like. Get him out of Australia for a start—he's getting very bored with Barb's mansion and all that outback heat, dust and crocodile stuff!

9

THE LOONY
ICELANDIC WENCH
IS BACK

ORIGINAL JULIANA
5 November 1998
I was momentarily sane. Some very long months went by, following the stars, came round of everywhere into neither here nor there. But I had to be damned. Of course. In medias res.

Sunday morning 3.30 am. Dull party drawing to its close. Five diehards slouching on beanbags. Desperate for fags or snogs. No fags. No snogs. Let's watch a video. Absolutely. What's on? Lars van Quish's *Zooropa*. For the culturally aspiring. *Airforce Fun*. For the dimheads. *Le Foin*. Too French. For the subtitled-weaned. None of them left. Vote. Boys wants *Airforce Fun*. Girls wants *Airforce Fun*. No brain cells to spare.

Somewhere in deepest Karrotstan a fearsome ruler is abducted in the middle of the night by paratroopers. Siegfried clad in velvety jimjams emerges out of the shadows for about one and a half seconds.

Pure Bliss.

2 hours later. My hero. Looks fabulous. Walks out of Moscow prison. This moment lasts not much longer, but like dripfeeding opium to a dying cancerian I am hooked.

I am really starting to take a liking to these blissfully short bittersweet snippets of Siegfried in various films. Goddammit. It keeps up the suspense and concentrates the mind beautifully.

A shot. Siegfried is dying for all his worth. In the words of Saki. "He is one of those people enormously improved by death."

ORIGINAL DONNA
6 November 1998
The loony Icelandic Wench is back!!!!! :)
Nice to hear from you again, Juliana. (Insert evil laughter) You can't escape!

ORIGINAL JULIANA
Underneath the Stella Polaris, 7 November 1998
Ha-ha-ha-ha Donna. Yeah I am back in Fanclub Mayhem and there is so much to catch up on this site. All those new fruity, juicy, yummy pics in "Images" for a start, had me crawling floors and carpets. . . nice ones . . . And that long running soap The Obsession and the Story . . . I shall rescue poor ol' Siegfried out of Barb's greedy hands for starters and place him in some geyser or something but I am totally out of synch with the zeitgeist of the story since I am unable to download the July and August archives.

Is there something amiss in the technical department? I have missed out on the start and I can't plunge in without knowing the finer details.

I also note that Benevolent Brunhilde, the beloved of Siegfried seems to have the same chameleon like qualities as her beau. I am referring again to the pics in "Images". On the first pic in dancing mode she looks like a complete trollop (disconcertingly a lot like me when I was 17. All tousled hair and no dress sense or other sense whatever).

On the other pic she has suddenly turned into Grace flamin' Kelly. Which I never manage to do. Jealous. Jealous. A lot.

ORIGINAL ALICE
10 November 1998

Hey Juliana! Great to have you here again! It looks as if your remedy didn't work – you're back with us. Accept the facts, my dear – you're just as addicted as we are.

I know what you mean about that "Brunhilde" in the photos. She seems to have a split personality or something. Very odd.

Original Juliana ORIGINAL JULIANA
11 November 1998

Ciao Alice. Nice to hear from you again. Well, the aversion therapy DID work for about six-seven months or so but like any serious addiction (alcohol, drugs, tobacco, sex or Siegfried P. Hinkelheimer) you are always, always gonna be a recovering addict in danger of slipping back if you don't watch yourself. In my case it was serious lapse of judgement that led to me watching *Airforce Fun* without due precaution and now I am back in the gutter

133

again. But as always . . . I have still not given it up. I have seen the light so to speak.

Yeah I think you are right Alice, there seems to be two Brunhildes. One classy one for award ceremonies and the like, and one spare trollop for late night hangouts in dimly lit nightclubs in Berlin. She does look a bit, well, manufactured.

Enough bitching. I am just jealous like hell and it is the first time I have seen the competition after all these years and I am a sad twisted little thing.

UNEARTHLY EMILY

12 November 1998

Pour yourselves a double latte cappuccino with whipped cream and sprinkles because its time for the next instalment of TOATS! And it's a LONG one! . . .

Tess was happily paddling around in the billabong singing, "Row, row, row your boat, gently down the stream. Merrily, merrily, merrily Siegfried's just a dream . . ."

Tammie's lip lock on Siegfried was interrupted as (Insert Your Name Here) emerged from the bushes battered, bruised and gasping for breath.

Tammie was horrified. "You!" she said.

"Yes, it is me or to be more accurate (Inse)!!!"10

"(Inse)?" Tammie questioned. "Short for 'Insert Your Name Here'? What do you want, (Inse)?" she added suspiciously.

"You didn't think I'd let you get away with my genuine imitation Cloudy Chiffon® Shangri-La® collection earrings did you!" (Inse) shrieked.

Siegfried rubbed his eyes, making sure he hadn't lost what

---

10 Prounounced "Ee-nah"

was left of his senses. Tammie stood up defiantly. Suddenly realizing she was still naked, she reached for Siegfried's hat (not much coverage but it gave her a distinct air of authority).

"Is that all?" Tammie replied as she placed his hat on her head. (A few drunken Vulgarians saluted her.)

"As a matter of fact, there is one more thing . . . "

Tammie held her breath as (Inse) opened up her tattered knapsack and pulled out a brown paper package all tied up with strings (not one of Tammie's favorite things.)

"Siegfried, would you autograph my 4th draft 2nd revision shooting script with director's notes from The British Are So Impatient? Right here, above the line where William Dafriend's toes are about to be chopped off."

Siegfried tentatively reached for the script and the pen (Inse) held out.

"How . . . do you vant me to sign?" he asked.

Meanwhile, Tammie hastily dressed, due to the fact that the romantic mood had been shattered and one of the Vulgarians was looking too interested in her.

She noticed a cloud of dust In the distance, and squinted to try to make out what type of vehicle was approaching. (Inse), for the moment, was dictating the longest inscription for an autograph in history.

Much to Tammie's dismay, the billabong was getting more and more crowded. A few moments later a car . . . no it was a boat...no it was a car/boat? screeched to a halt in front of the bewildered crowd.

As the dust settled the top came down, revealing Emily at the wheel. She smiled at Tammie. "Helllloooo Tammie."

Stunned, Tammie couldn't believe her eyes. "How did you find us?" she asked.

Emily raised her hand. In it was what appeared to be a small tracking device.

"It's a small tracking device linked to a receiver on Siegfried's hat. I picked it up along with the car/boat from SpyTech. James was using the BOMB11 Z3.®"

Emily (wearing Trulie Fang®) disembarked the vehicle followed close by Donna (in Verbose®) and Lottie (in Wulf Lowrent®, accessorized with crocodile boots, belt and handbag). (Inse), who had finally finished her dictation, was sitting on a rock reading and re-reading her newly autographed script.

Siegfried noticed the women. "Emily! Donna! Lottie!!" he exclaimed, then noticing Lottie's boots, "Are those new?"

"You could say that." Lottie replied with a knowing smile.

Suddenly the entire billabong was lit up with blinding bright white lights. A roaring sound deafened them all.

Unable to see they stumbled around trying to find one another . . . (or is it they all stumbled around trying to find a still naked Siegfried?) They shielded their eyes but still couldn't see anything.

"What's going on?!" Tammie yelled.

"I don't know!" everyone yelled back in unison.

"Aliens?" someone shouted.

"Don't be ridiculous! We already did that!" Lottie yelled back.

Then—just as suddenly—the noise stopped and once again everyone was plunged into darkness . . .

---

11 "Böhmisches Ölablassschraube und Motor Bauherrinnen," i.e. "Bohemian Oil-drain-plug and Motor Builders," a posh car brand.

Darkness, then grey, then hints of color seeped into Siegfried's mind. He stirred back into consciousness. Next to him Emily lay, still unconscious. He tried to get up and realized that he was tied with rope.

"Emily . . . Emily. . . vake up."

Emily slowly awoke and was startled to see Siegfried facing her, because she was dreaming about an Irishman (but that's another story).

"Did I miss something?" she said.

"We're tied up together," Siegfried replied quietly. Emily surveyed the situation. Sure enough. One minute they were in the desert and the next she and Siegfried were tied together facing each other on a bed. (Did you honestly think I would have said tied to chairs?)

"Great. Now what do we do?" she asked.

"Ve have to get out of zese ropes before whoever did zis comes back. Here let me try zis..." Siegfried tried to manoeuvre. They squirmed for a few minutes, then stopped.

"Could you—could you move your knee just a little bit, Siegfried?" Emily asked.

"Zat's not my knee."

"Oh my gosh!" she replied.

Siegfried laughed. "Just kidding."

"You are this close to being . . ."

"Being what?" he said, still smiling.

Emily scowled at him. "I lost my train of thought. It's easy to do in this type of situation." She tried to get comfortable. "Listen, we're going to have to switch positions or something. My arm is falling asleep. And I'm really getting hot. Here . . . roll over," she said.

137

"I'm hot too. Must be ze friction, I guess." Siegfried replied as he started to roll.

"Ow! Ow! Ow! Not that way! I think my arm just fell off!" Emily struggled to free her trapped arm.

"I can't roll over ze ozer way, we might fall off ze bed."

Emily gritted her teeth. "Now . . . the rope . . . is digging into my thigh . . . roll . . . over."

Siegfried sighed. "Fine."

Using teamwork, they both rolled and . . . fell off the bed with a THUD! Emily landed on top of Siegfried.

"Not that zis position doesn't have its advantages," he said, "but, could you get off of me? My chest is caving in."

She slid off and they faced each other, once again . . .

. . . One hour later . . .

"You know I think this bed is made of oak," Emily said,

"Actually, it's made of cedar," Siegfried nonchalantly replied.

"How do you know?"

"Because every piece of vood furniture in my home is made of cedar. Even ze tree-house. Notice the texture and darker color. . .see? Did you know that oak is quite flammable?"

. . . One hour later . . .

"Hey," said Emily, "if you squint your eyes, that spot on the wall looks like Marlon Brando."

"Really? Where?" asked Siegfried squinting.

"Over there."

"You're right!"

... One hour later ...

"Siegfried, Siegfried-bo Beegfreed, banana-fana-fo Feegfreed, fee-fi-mo meegen ... Siegfried."

"Emily please, it was funny for the first half hour but ... "

... One hour later ...

"Siegfried? Are you awake?"

"Hmmm?"

"Do you realize by that clock on the dresser we've been tied up for over five hours? Good thing we're dehydrated from the desert ... yawn ... "

... One hour later ...

... the sun has set and night is upon them once again ...

ORIGINAL LOTTIE

13 November 1998

You're back with a vengeance, Emily! And you've left me totally baffled!

I'm going to have to think hard about this, thinks Lottie as she scratches her head and paces up and down in her Nigel-skin boots—pretty snazzy, but what a sad state of affairs that Lottie has become so ruthless in her Siegfried quest that she's now wearing her most ardent admirer on her feet!

And now there's another rival ... the original long-legged Icelandic red-head is back!

Hi Juliana! I read your witty comments back in the archives and thought you must fallen all the way into a computerless gutter somewhere (still yearningly clutching some worn-out videos), or, even more tragic, GONE OFF HIM! Instead, you plead sanity—what sort of an excuse is that? Be grateful

139

you failed to take the necessary precautions, were caught off-guard by *Airforce Fun* and hurled back into the gutter—because it's nice down here . . . who would want to be anywhere else?? And we've got such good company!

Actually, *Airforce Fun* helped to make me insane (not difficult). The first time I saw it in the cinema my little heart thudded wildly with the excitement and I nearly fell off my seat in a swoon. It wasn't all that tedious terrorist stuff in the plane, or even Harrison Prefect doing the same old things he always does; it was just a very short scene of a guy walking through a prison wearing baggy prison clothes and a smirk.

Since then I've worn a couple of holes in my video. Who else could walk into a film for a few seconds and, without saying a word, immediately convince us as a man thousands of Vulgarians would die for? But, come to think of it, not that convincing—because how many Vulgarian generals look as gorgeous as this??

Looking forward to some TOATS from you, Juliana, and from Barb when she returns from Splinge (has she returned? is that perhaps what the white light was?) Rival Icelandic red-heads! Perhaps Barb will dye her hair blonde and grow her legs even longer. Siegfried should like that.

ORIGINAL DONNA
14 November 1998

Hahaha, Emily's BACK! Welcome back Emily, mymymy what an instalment you've left us! Whew . . . scratching my noggin . . . (but maybe Lottie will beat me to the next chapter . . .) Juliana, I fixed the June/July technical difficulty, now you can catch up on TOATS in its fascinating entirety.

ORIGINAL EMILY

14 November 1998

Hi Donna! Well if I'm getting back in the gutter might as well make it interesting! (Insert evil grin here) ;)

ORIGINAL BARB

17 November 1998

Welcome back Juliana. In case you are not aware, your contributions to the archives were the inspiration for my red-haired Icelandic persona. Which I would have liked to hang on to, but unfortunately Lottie seems to think that since you have returned to the fold I'm not allowed to be either red-haired or Icelandic any more.

As you will soon see from her next episode of TOATS. Yes, I have had a sneak preview of the next exciting, not-to-be-missed chapter, written by Lottie, soon to explode across your silver screen.

Barb—who demands to remain red-haired and Icelandic for Siegfried.

UNEARTHLY LOTTIE

17 November 1998

"The Obsession and the Story" continues . . .

Suddenly the door flew open and Barb strode into the room followed by an entourage of scuttling aliens.

"My God . . . you!!" cried Emily.

"What have you done?" gasps Siegfried. For Barb has a New Look; long gleaming raven hair with a wicked white streak, skin pale as alabaster, a figure-hugging, glittering black gown, its long train slithering like a snake behind her.

141

"Yes, it's me . . . back on UnEarth. I've left 'Daniel' minding the children and my lovely little friends here have brought me back for a holiday. I mean to have some fun."

She laughed wickedly. "Untie them!" she ordered and the aliens scuttled to obey.

"But I loved you, Barb," whispered Siegfried as he climbed stiffly to his feet. "Remember Fiji . . . remember the yacht?"

"Yes, I remember," said Barb, gliding across to him and with a slender white hand gently brushing his hair from his face; "I loved you too . . . under southern skies, with the deep blue expanse of the Pacific cradling us . . . yes, I loved you—for a little while." She touched his mouth briefly with her luscious black lips then abruptly turned away with another wicked laugh. "Ooh, I can't wait to get my hands on the original Icelandic red-head when she shows up, but in the meantime—" she lowered her voice ominously—"I've got you, Emily, and I've got Donna, and I've got that nincompoop Lottie, and sweet little Tammie, and mangled '(Inse)', and I've got Tess, sozzled as always . . . Bring them in!"

Some aliens herded the senseless troupe into the room. They clung together and trembled. Instantly their eyes were drawn to their hero as if to a magnet, and they briefly forgot their fears as they gazed at him with stars twinkling in their eyes and foolish smiles on their lips.

"Would you like to read my script?" asked Lottie in a yodel; "I've made you such a hero . . . ohh, but you are so lovely . . ." Her voice trailed off as she swooned again and fell in the usual heap.

"You're sho shtupid," said Tess, giving Lottie a mis-aimed kick, somersaulting and falling on top of her.

"You're ridiculous, the lot of you!" snapped Barb. "Look at you—all squeezed into my beautiful clothes—poor seams all bursting with the strain . . . but you're going to entertain us—my hundred-eyed friends here seriously need some entertaining. You've had your turn, Emily, and I'm afraid my little friends all went to sleep. Though . . . " She walked over to peer closely at the wall. "Yes, ha ha, come and have a look at this, fellas! It does look like Marlon Brando, doesn't it?" She straightened up abruptly and pointed a cruel finger at Emily. "Take her away; throw her in the dungeon! Now . . . who next?"

Siegfried bravely faced her. "Barb, be reasonable", he pleaded. "Emily didn't know she vas supposed to be entertaining you and your ugly buddies. If she'd known . . . if we'd known, I'm sure we could have . . . done somesing much more exciting. Please don't hurt her!"

Barb ignored him; "Donna next!"

Donna leaped forward; "Oooh, something exciting with Seegums? Yes, please!!"

"Not so eager, dear girl", said Barb with a cruel smile; "You've got no idea what's in store for you . . . "

UNEARTHLY BARB

17 November 1998

"Heh heh!" laughed Barb again.

"What's with the evil laughter?" demanded (Insert Your name Here) testily, "Can't you be a bit more original? Twisted megalomaniacs always laugh like that. Get out of the rut."

Immobilising instantly, like a hunting leopard, Barb coolly rested her emerald cat's eyes on (Insert Your Name Here). After a couple of minutes, (Insert Your Name Here) began to squirm uncomfortably and wish she hadn't spoken.

"You seem to forget," said Barb cloyingly, toying with a lock of (Inse)'s bedraggled hair, "That I am no longer the mild-mannered blonde untimely deported to the planet Splinge. On Splinge there's something—something in the water maybe, or the air—something that makes people . . ."

"What?" Siegfried asked with interest.

"Appallingly wicked!" screamed Barb, now going cross-eyed and foaming slightly at the mouth. "Cruel, callous and inhuman!"

Everyone recoiled. Barb's hair had just spontaneously combusted and flames were leaping from her silver skull like a solar eclipse, like the searing gases from a jet engine, like the ignition of fish and chips left for too long in the microwave.

"Ha ha, back to being a red-head," the evil Barb spat venomously. "You think this is the finish of me? Not at all. I have powers now, strange alien powers, and I intend to use them."

Her incandescent hair settled down to a glowing simmer. She patted it back into place with a quick sidelong glance in a nearby mirror and a sickeningly ingratiating wink at Siegfried.

"Now, where was I? Oh yes." Everyone suddenly noticed that Barb had been holding in her hand a bizarre weapon. She raised it, started to laugh evilly, abruptly choked in mid-laugh and finished off with a cough, remembering to be a bit more original.

"I recollect now—I was going to do something drastic, wasn't I?" said Barb.

"No!" everyone responded hopefully.

"You lie!" snarled Barb. "Do you realize what I do to those who cross me? You see what I did to Marlon?" Everyone looked in horror towards the murky spot on the oak wall. "Yes, that's all that remains of him," crooned Barb with relish. "A mere smear on the wainscot."

Everyone trembled, except Siegfried, ever courageous as usual.

"And now," continued Barb, "before my violent demonstration of malignant power, I hereby change the name of this saga. TOATS you say? Ha! As Juliana said, 'speak for yourselves, ladies.' You say TOATS, I say TOAST. Watch this!"

With those words she trained her weapon on her accompanying hundred-eyed aliens and zapped the lot of them.

There was a mild explosion. The aliens burst up into the air. As blackened slices of hi-tin loaf sprinkled with caraway and sesame seeds floated slowly to the floor, Barb crowed, "Forthwith I name this saga TRASH; 'Totally Redundant and Serially Hopeless.' Take it or leave it! And now for your punishment, ladies."

Tossing back her simmering hair of fire, she dexterously altered a setting on her gun. The weapon was now trained on Donna. But the weapon-brandishing hand of Barb faltered, trembled. Her wrist swivelled. The alien gun pointed to Siegfried. Lottie woke up. Tess sobered rapidly.

Everyone screamed, throwing themselves forward to save Siegfried, but it was too late. Barb had pulled the trigger.

A ray of brilliant blue-white dazzle stabbed the air. For a moment, the world seemed to dissolve into an ethereal pinkish mist. As it cleared, everyone held their breath. They stared at the place where Siegfried was once standing . . .

UNEARTHLY BARB
17 November 1998

Barb lowered the gun with a self-satisfied smirk resting lightly on her incredibly beautiful features. She blew the last of the smoke from the gun's nozzle.

"There!" She purred triumphantly, "I've done it! Now there are enough Siegfrieds for everyone. But aye, here's the rub girls—you'll never be truly happy, because YOU'LL NEVER KNOW WHICH OF THEM IS THE REAL ONE!!!"

With a sweep of her black and glittering skirts, she glided from the room on the arms of two of the TEN Siegfrieds she had created with the clone-setting on her alien gun!!!!

Ten Siegfrieds—which is the real one? Will the truth ever be revealed?

UNEARTHLY DONNA
18 November 1998

At the precisely the same instant everyone thinks: "Who cares!?" and all begin moving at once, the entire horde scrambling madly to get their hands on their own cop(y/ies) of Siegfried!

Tess belched wetly. Wearing a foolish grin she fell spread-eagled across the legs of a newly minted Siegfried. While Lottie and Emily argued over a cluster of four apparent Siegfrieds, Tammie and Donna each deftly herded a dazed new clone out of the fray, greed and doubt shining in their eyes as they gaze back at the small crowd of Siegfriedses remaining.

Only a single Siegfried which remained slumped against the wall escaped notice. The seething (Inse), clearly irrevocably deranged, ignored the crowd of Siegfrieds and surged after Barb, bent on destruction and revenge.

The new Siegfried's heads were clearing rapidly, so by then the two initially whisked away by Barb had gained a chance to register her cortisone-injected sagging flesh (we all know time passes more rapidly on Splinge—and hasn't it been merciless with ol' B—) and thrust her away grimacing in disgust. Clearly they've inherited their taste in women from the original.

They ducked into the mass of their brethren just as (Inse) reached Barb and lunged for her throat, her hands tightening vice-like around it.

Emily and Lottie were temporarily overwhelmed at the addition of the two returning Siegfrieds into their immediate vicinity and for a moment stopped arguing. Donna and Tammie, who had suddenly seen the beautiful logic in the numbers, each dragged their copies over to join them. Together they all propped up the sodden Tess and attempted to nudge the lone still-senseless Siegfried out of its stupor.

As Barb and (Inse) thrashed about in mortal combat, a small metallic object escaped the wreckage of Barb's shimmering gown and skittered across the floor, stopping at Lottie's feet.

"It's Barb's magic Splingian personal transportation device!" shouted Lottie, snatching the object up off the floor.

"MMggLLsshppfutllldB!" said Barb, eyes bulging out of her purple face and riveted on the device.

"Wellbeamusthehellouttahere!" cried Emily, grabbing the thing and recklessly stabbing its buttons.

"Wait!" screamed Donna. "Where will it take u—?!"

As the entire group of ten Siegfrieds and five unimaginably lucky women vanished, leaving wicked Barb and (Inse) behind Siegfried-less and bleeding on the floor.

ORIGINAL JULIANA

18 November 1998

Hiya Again, been out of the woods for a few days. Completely disconnected. Have lots to catch up. The Obsession and the Story (still deprived of the beginnings. No access to the archives or so this 'puter keeps telling me) for a start.

Now I have to rethink my instalment set in some very gloomy surroundings in Reykjavik. Siegfried is gonna suffer I am afraid. That much I can tell. And there is gonna be blood letting and mayhem and misery and hell fire and pain and gruesome special effects.

He is gonna feel right at home.

Anyhoot, thanks to everyone for welcoming me back in the gutter. I do think there is space in Siegfried's very accommodating heart for two redheaded Icelandic nymphomaniacs. Boy is he a lucky guy or what. I demand recognition for this. I should be out there hanging around gorgeous godlike swooners with smooth wrinklefree complexions and muscular buttocks. Not tirelessly smooching for some unattainable smug movie star with a smirk. I need a medal.

Barb should therefore not bleach her hair. That is almost tantamount to treason. Personally I think Siegfried should go for redheads or hazels. Blondes doesn't suit him at all. I still can't get over the fact that Brunhilde is such a stereotypical Blonde.

I was really over him you know. Can't believe I am back here downloading those pics of him where he looks really crazy and stodgy and horrific. And then there are the sexy pics that my 'puter lovingly store for me. Well.

The stubbled curly hazeled Siegfried is the best. Shorthaired he looks plain stupid. And he should talk very quietly. Almost whisper. When he shouts (like he did in *Judge Mental* and *Corpse of Clues*) or say something more dmeanding and chewy, I cringe and goes blind. He is at his utmost best when completely quiet. As in *Airforce Fun*.

Enough of that. Gonna have to read The Obsession and the Story now.

ORIGINAL LOTTIE
18 November 1998
I've drawn and uploaded a jacket cover for TOATS. I hope the illustration arrived okay. Have you got it, Donna?[12]

---

12 Note that Lottie's picture is the frontispiece of this book.

ORIGINAL DONNA

18 November 1998

Lottie's phenomenal TOATS cover is up! it's on the last cover page, so use the left arrow to go right there from page one. You can click the picture to get a full size image, which you need to do so you can see it in full glory!

ORIGINAL EMILY

18 November 1998

Lottie it's MARVELOUS! You have captured the essence of TOATS!!! I love it! A request, would another maniacal female please write a chapter! . . . Tess when you stop hiccupping long enough to hold a pencil steady write a chapter!!!

On Original Earth, Juliana stared at Lottie's illustration, which glowed spellbindingly on her computer's monitor. Indeed, this image said it all. Far off in cyberspace, with a sudden explosion her UnEarthly persona was born in its finished state. Feverishly, as if possessed by some literary daemon, Juliana began to type.

150

UNEARTHLY JULIANA'S BIO:

18 November 1998

The Oracle representing Juliana says. I think that picture says it all. No bio needed in this case. What magnificent hair, what beastly horns! That IS Juliana, born of unborn souls, drenched at birth in herring skin and the tousled hair of elkhorn maidens! She is lost in timewarps for eons at a time and is the most inconsistent in devotion to the Object of Desire, she might be off chasing the Man in the Moon tonight, never mind the aforementioned.

And oh yeah, she was born in Walhalla by some unborn souls. Came to earth to get her little horns in a little twist. Which happens now and again, well that is destiny for you!

ORIGINAL JULIANA

18 November 1998

Okeydokey Donna. I have now managed to reach the archives. Thanks. The story may begin . . .

UNEARTHLY JULIANA

18 November 1998

Another TOATS instalment! —

"You stupid cow! You stupid, stupid cow!"

Juliana emerged out of the shrubbery, clasping a bottle of vodka, accompanied by two Vulgarian sailors. She looked splendid. All legs and red tousled hair in the style of a Botticellian angel (well . . . why not?)

151

Barb's beauty had faded after all the battering and her thighs had somewhat fattened. (Inse) kept on hitting her, for some reason, at her noble nose that had by now turned into a bloody mesh of flesh and blood matter.

"Please take that lady away," Juliana commanded her sailors who happily proceeded to carry the screeching (Inse) away, far beyond the billabong (what IS a billabong?)

"Five minutes! Five minutes! I have been five minutes late all my life," muttered Juliana, cursing her disorganisation as she passed heaps of Swabbex® tissues (Extra Soft and Embalmed. For ALL Your Family's Needs!) to the bleeding and whimpering Barb.

It dawned upon her that had she turned up five minutes earlier she could have had them all. All ten of them. And the thought sort of paralysed her slightly. Where did those old(ish) chicks take all those Siegfrieds? Siegfried belongs to our world. A world where nobody can spell the words cellouilithe and Viaegra. The last thing that man needs reminding of is wrinkles, sogging chins and nasal hair. He needs us Barb, he needs youth as desperately as a vampire needs a fresh supply of blood every night. If he spends too much time with those old(ish) chicks he will decay rapidly and die in front of their very eyes.

By now Barb was shaking. She had not understood the enormity of it all. As it all dawned upon her, she let out a weak whimpering and her blooded nosewings were shaking as a mare's would.

"Juliana. What can we do?"

"We will have to get him back, the original, that is. Before those old(ish) bore him to death. We need another of those beamer thingies. You will have to sort one out and quick!"

Gripping her bar of Bradbury®'s Dairy Milk Roast Almond so tightly that it imploded, Barb stared indignantly at the screen.

" . . . thighs had somewhat fattened?" "Blooded nosewings shaking as a mare's would?" Granted, the wording was original and entertaining, (she thought, pencil-bitingly envious of Juliana's literary skills) – but if anyone was going to take an original and entertaining shot at deriding someone else's cyber-character, by rights it should be the prototype herself!

Cyberspace, she thought, *is the one place we can be gorgeous without plucking, waxing, bleaching, coloring, working out, tanning or squeezing our feet into high heels. It's the one place we are in charge of our own description. Some boundaries must not be crossed!*

After she finished having that idea she thought, *I wonder what's going to happen in the next chapter. So many questions are waiting to be answered . . .*

Heedless of the chocolate fragments sprayed across the keyboard she madly began to type.

UNEARTHLY BARB

19 November 1998

How did Emily escape from the dismal dungeon of the strange House of Cedar? (Or possibly oak?) Will Marlon Brando continue to be nibbled by woodworm?

What are the sailors doing with (Insert Your Name Here) far beyond the billabong, and is she enjoying it?

Will Juliana find out what a billabong is?

Will Tess eventually become a teetotaller? Will Siegfried—will any of the Siegfrieds—ever read Lottie's script?

What are Donna, Emily and Tammie doing with all those Siegfrieds and where have they gone?

How does Siegfried feel about seeing himself repeated nine times over?

Will Juliana realize (before it's too late and her physical features get re-described) that there is an unwritten agreement among TOATS authors to insult only one's own persona?

Where are Alice, Frances and Rebecca?

Are there enough Siegfrieds to go around?

Is Lance still pining for Donna?

Will Lottie ever find the cure for fainting whenever she sets eyes on Siegfried?

Have I asked enough questions?

Should I should ask a few more?

Why should I?

Why not?

Why can't I think of any?

10

THE TOATS RULE BOOK ON ETIQUETTE

 ORIGINAL EMILY

Friday 20 November 1998

Gone for a few days and look what you've done! This is so much fun, it's hysterical! Donna, have you thought of cutting and pasting all the back episodes in chapters? We can call it "TOATS—The Early Episodes" . . . It could be a link all its own!

UNEARTHLY EMILY

20 November 1998

This universe is a vortex of tiny components, which lack any parallel in human understanding.

These are characteristics, in a sense, without anything to be characteristic of; they are adverbs without verbs, adjectives without nouns. It is their progression, which makes up time; it is their existence which is matter. Neutrons, protons, and electrons become atoms and atoms become molecules, by locking together and blowing apart they go dancing in their own vortex ...

... Which is exactly how the multiple Siegfrieds, Donna, Tess, Tammie, Lottie and Emily felt as they hurtled through the void.

"If anyone starts to feel motion sickness let me know. I have Bananamine®!" Emily yelled.

Below, the shapes of recognizable topography were starting to form. Siegfried studied the land mass over which they were flying ... a small fishing town with its busy harbour on the south shore. He vaguely remembered stopping there once for lunch before continuing along the coast past a tall lighthouse. The winds there were strong and the sea piled up and broke in spectacular splashes of foam. Siegfried thought he'd rather veer more inland...

Suddenly the strange vortex shifted and they headed towards a spectacular waterfall.

"The Gullfoss!" he shouted. "I know vere ve are!"

As soon as he spoke the vortex shifted again and they flew through the picturesque town of Hafnarfjörður and over the continuous lava fields of the Reykjanes Peninsula to the Blue Lagoon in its otherworldly lava surroundings.

They all landed with a HUGE splash!

"After all that molecular breaking apart and reforming I could use a bath!" Donna commented.

They all agree to a swim in the refreshing, pleasantly warm mineral-rich water, famed for its healing properties.

Donna, Tammie, and Lottie climbed up on their respective Siegfrieds' shoulders to play a game of chicken. The other Siegfrieds joined in a game of Marco Polo. Tess, now incredibly sober, wondered where on UnEarth were they.

"Where on UnEarth, if we are on UnEarth, are we?" she asked.

Emily, who was sitting next to a very quiet Siegfried, turned to him. "Yes, where are we?"

Siegfried smiled and spoke in a seductive whisper. "Inauthentic Iceland."

"Inauthentic Iceland!" Tess and Emily exclaimed in unison.

"It's all Emily's fault for not reading the directions on Barb's magic Splingian personal transport thingy!" Donna lamented.

"Go ahead, blame me . . . Do any of you want to go back?!" Emily questioned them.

Donna, Tammie, Lottie and Tess looked around in the winter-evening darkness, not seeing much now because of the steam rising from the water. They were there with not one, but ten Siegfrieds. And that wasn't a bad thing!

Suddenly, the Siegfrieds started to look kinda funny.

Lottie was the first to notice. "Gee, when I stay in the water too long I just get pruny, but you can start to see through some of them!" She pointed excitedly at the Siegfried holding up Tammie.

157

Tess's eyes widened "Oh my gosh! It must be the high mineral content in the water! It's upsetting their delicate physiological balance and as we all know according to 'Duke's Conclusions on Intergalactic Replicator Guns': 1) The more complicated the technology, the less likely it is to work. 2) The more unstable the technology, the more likely it is to fail in remarkable ways, and 3) Magic is not worthless, but it might as well be."

Everyone turned towards Tess in astonishment. The Siegfried sitting next to Emily smiled . . .

Scene: . . . Someplace else . . .

Juliana wasn't ready yet, she was busily brushing up on the TOATS Rule Book on Etiquette. Barb sat serene and silent on horseback with the handles of the Intergalactic Replicator and a Splingian Personal Transportation Device Locator as well as a brand new Transportation device digging into her waist. She was thinking how lucky she was that she bought all pieces of equipment with her VIZOR® card. They were automatically insured.

Her Splingian mentors had taught her to maintain an emotional distance from her conquests; it helped maintain discipline and allowed her to preserve her mind when faced with a challenge. But this time—this time was different.

Nearby, two people were talking . . .
"What's your name?"
"Tinfingers."
"Tinfingers what? Is that a first name or a last name?"
"It's a name. Like 'Madonna' or 'Sting.'"

158

Original Juliana

UnEarthly Juliana

"Yeah, right. Do you know anything about Inauthentic Iceland?"

"A little. The Icelandic language is still very close to how the Vikings used to talk, and the Icelanders are still Vikings deep inside. This can cause problems, mostly because they feel a need to occupy England and tear down French cathedrals. Nowadays they mostly find an outlet for this by shooting at anyone that tries to fish in their territories," Tinfingers replied.

"Okay, you're hired. Report to Barb."

ORIGINAL BARB
20 November 1998

Thank you Emily! I get to sit serene and silent and heavily armed on horseback at last! Dreams do come true! I am hoping—no, DEMANDING that my new employee Tinfingers looks identical to Daniel de Licious in The Last of the Michoacan Pocket Gophers. Also that I have had a decent nose job since my close and extremely violent encounter with (Inse).

By the way, I do have the entirety of TOATS on my word processing software, as well as several NON-TOATS postings which relate to the narrative. Such as when Emily invented (Inse). Looking forward to visiting Iceland . . .

ORIGINAL DONNA
20 November 1998

Barb I am SO glad someone is archiving this creative effort. It's sure to be a best-seller, translated into every known human language (and Splingian, of course!)

ORIGINAL EMILY
20 November 1998

Thanks Barb! I'm glad you liked the episode. I was delirious with sleep deprivation and I kept writing and writing and writing . . . Thank God someone is capturing all this for posterity! If Tinfingers is looking like DDL you better post fast because I'm sitting back to watch what the heck is gonna happen next!

UNEARTHLY JULIANA
21 November 1998

Hahaha—This is truly great. Another Instalment of TOATS.

Where is the foul-mouthed Juliana?. Where is Insert Your Name Here? Where is the original Siegfried P. Hinkelheimer?

Thump. Thummmmpppp. Juliana landed with a bang. When she dared to open her eyes she found herself on a fishing trawler, linked together with a hundred other trawlers, in the harbour of some very placid-looking fishing village in some very mountainous surrounds. The whole package looked very familiar. Not too familiar. She could not quite place it. She recognised the smell. The smell of the sea—the smell anyone raised by the sea could sense in a nano second. The rotten fish, rotten herring and newly catched cod and salmon. The sounds of the seagulls!

161

Could you actually believe it? The foul-mouthed Juliana's neutrons and particles had been dumped during the journey by a very shrewd Barb. She of course wanted Siegfried all by herself. Barb had landed safely in Röjkvika whereas Juliana had been dumped on some dump somewhere off Norway. She could tell that by the name of the trawler she was sluching on. "Anne-Mette Karesen". If this was not Norway she would eat her knickers.

And when she saw the shady looking crew emerging lazily out of the inner sanctum of the trawler to see what caused the bump, she knew she was right. The true descendents of Vikings. Oh yeah. Right. They had measly thing moustaches and lanky long blonde hair. They also had pink faces and discolored teeth. And they stank. A bit cod. Mostly Baksmälla® Vodka and the bittery moonshine stuff they deftly and illegally manufactured themselves because of the extortionate prices their government was charging for a bit of booze.

"Var i helvete är jag?" (Where am I?) Juliana spoke the panscandinavian lingo everyone from Icelanders to Finnish Swedes can communicate in roughly. The Danish included.

"Svolvaer" said one of them in a slow, disinterested tone. So typical of a latter day Vikinger. She queried them whether she could get quickly to Iceland from here. Barb of course having the beamer thingy and Juliana had no money for the air fare—in her quest to find the love and hate of her life she had squandered her modest inheritance (made mostly out of herring and cods).

The genes of a thousand years of fishermen and their wenches preceded the modern day Juliana. Swearing and foulmouthering was part of her very being. In fact she was made up of it. Not a single count or baron was to be hanging in her family tree.

The Vikingers suggested she go to Trondheim or Bergen and hitch a hike with some boats heading for Iceland. As a freeloader.

"You might get lucky," they sneered.

But then suddenly another fisherman crept up from the inner sanctum and he was scratching his hair dizzily. Juliana´s heart started to thump violently. He was the spitting bloody image of Siegfried P. bloody Hinkelheimer! Only blanker looking. Dirtier. Covered in a fisherman´s apron and cod´s blood. He was quite young. Twenty-five the most. But very Siegfriedish. Complete with stubble.

Stammering he said "Ha-Ha-Hasses Che-cheri-e is he-heading for Re-re-reyk . . . to-to-to-night."

Their eyes met. He had been busy slicing cod.

Heard the word Reykjavik. Hasse is going there.

"Would you come with me" said Juliana as gently as she possibly could. No mean task in itself.

He dropped his huge carving knife and said "Ja." He even had the blue eyes of his master—was he perhaps one of the clones that had been dropped by accident in the same time vacuum as Juliana? It would explain his blank expression and nano personality. He would do for now, thought Juliana.

His name, he said, was Jörgen Petersen. He and Juliana jumped out in the shimmering springlight of Lofoten to look for the salmon trawler Cherie and Captain Hasse.

I´ll be in Iceland soon enough. Barb is gonna have to pay for this, smirked Juliana, tightly holding Jörgen´s hand . . .

ORIGINAL JULIANA

21 November 1998

I dare say anyone unfamiliar with TOATS dropping in on these pages would think we are a bunch of loonies altogether. All newcomers, ignore all the TOATS instalments. At least try to read them from the beginning of the page or in the archives. Then make sense of them. Do not adjust your sets.

ORIGINAL BARB

22 November 1998

Julianachen, please, please, never change. And I don't mean your underwear. You are a one-girl riot, The Red-Haired Rager from Reykjavik. You are never allowed to leave the SPH Fan Club!!!!!!!!!!!!!!!!!!!

UNEARTHLY JULIANA

22 November 1998

On board the trawler Cherie which took seven days to reach Reykjavik was the famous author and travel chronicler Paul Thorough on his last stretch of his journey from Archangelsk to Husavik. This is what he scribbled in his notebook later to be included in his book "Riding the Polar Wind".

"I shared berth with two newly-weds (or so I thought). On their way back to her native country. She was terrifying. Had that focused manic look of an obsessive. A mentally unstable creature. She had piercing yellowish eyes that made me unsettled. She spoke in short sentences and uttered guttural noises that had her husband on his toes all the time—fetching cups of coffee, tidying up and so on. And she stank of cod and dirt and sweat. Do these people ever wash?

"Mind your own business you old fool, had she sneered when I had gently queried. He was pleasant. Very handsome. Throughout the journey I found myself wondering who the hell he was resembling. I had seen his face, somewhere, someplace, a long time ago. Perhaps a movie. Anyway his handsome features, the high cheekbones and the well sculpted full lips made me yearn for civilisation again.

"We made conversation whilst the wench was asleep on the top berth. Straggling English. He said he was Norwegian. Love at first sight. No they weren't married. My question made him blush. I took to him. We became good friends. I yearned to ask him why he put up with the abuse from the top berth.

"On the last day of the trip there was some commotion on the deck. Skipper Hasse and his crew spoke in agitated voices. They had found three stowaways! Jörgen Petersen went to investigate. He was immediately bogged down and sat upon by an hysterical looking female holding a bizarre looking weapon. Two Vulgarians clad in marine uniforms slumped half dazed of too much drink beside her.

"Siegfried. Siegfried. Siegfried . . . It's you . . ." screeched the female.

"'(Inse)!' the mad bitch from top berth shouted as she emerged and set eyes on the screeching stowaway.

"I was not at all surprised they seemed to know each other. Probably escaped from the same looney bin!"

johanna-cum-paul-thorough

ORIGINAL BARB
23 November 1998

Donna, what do you think of Emily's idea about giving this preposterous saga a place of its own, with a link?

ORIGINAL DONNA
23 November 1998

Barb, I think that TOATS demands its own page, screams for it even. Now what we need is an illustrator to provide ..well, illustrations.

ORIGINAL EMILY
23 November 1998

Donna, That's my specialty! I'll work up a couple of graphics!

UNEARTHLY BARB
23 November 1998

So anyway, who's on the trawler *Cherie* which has just berthed at Reykjavik? Correct me if I'm wrong, but I think it's the Wacky Wench JULIANA whose Icelandic computer keyboard can type those funny little umlaut thingys that look like beady eyes peering out over the top of various vowels, plus JORGEN PETERSEN, a younger Siegfried clone who thinks he's Norwegian and who was dropped by accident into the same time vacuum as Juliana, plus (INSERT YOUR NAME HERE), hysterical, yellow-eyed and wielding a bizarre-looking weapon, plus a crew of MODERN-DAY VIKINGS led by CAPTAIN HASSE, plus two Vulgarian SAILORS, plus the author

PAUL THOROUGH, cleverly disguised as Juliana, who is cleverly disguised as him.

According to my calculations, that's one clone too many, since lucky Donna, Lottie, Tess, Emily and Tammie are, as we speak, cavorting in the warm waters of Reykjavik with ten Siegfrieds, nine of whom are slowly dissolving. Obviously there is something wrong with the clone-setting on Barb's Splingian all-Purpose Weapon, Molecular-Replicator and Daily Organiser.

This saga's getting too crowded. Maybe it's time to prune a little dead wood. Hmmm . . .

ORIGINAL EMILY
23 November 1998
Barb . . . how about you fire off an episode whilst I draw our cover . . .

UNEARTHLY BARB
23 November 1998
Meanwhile, back at the Blue Lagoon of Reykjavik (or wherever), wild consternation has erupted amongst the five svelte, slender and superbly-tanned damsels who look as though they are all in their early twenties and ought to be super-models. Yes, we are talking about Donna, Lottie, Tess, Emily and Tammie, looking sensational in gold bikinis (which they fortuitously found floating in the lagoon, coincidentally in the right sizes).

All save one of the Siegfriedses had thinned to the translucency of rice-paper, before developing a web of serious hair-line cracks and shredding to become a gently-falling snow on the water, melting with the soft sigh of steam.

For one ghastly second, the gorgeous babes stared at each other, transfixed with horror. Then, all reaching the same conclusion at the same moment, they lunged simultaneously towards the last Siegfried. The currents of the Blue Lagoon churned and thrashed like a crowd of crocodiles in a feeding frenzy. The waters transmuted from blue to vermilion.

Folk from the nearby town gathered on the shore to gawk in astonishment.

"Vat iss happenink?" housewives with fringed shawls on their heads mumbled in broken English.

"Tourists," croaked an aged and withered grandfather.

The townsfolk nodded wisely, turned and limped back to their fish-stinking cottages. Just as the last villager had closed her door, the thunder of hoofbeats came drumming out of the west, where the sun was sinking in a bath of blood and lava. Two riders were approaching, and the wind began to howl©[13]. The riders pulled up on the lake shores, silhouetted darkly by the magnificent sunset backdrop of curdled colors, garnet, ruby and topaz slashed with carnelian. Who could these two strangers be?

"Stop!" the taller of the two riders called out in a muffled voice.

At this command, the lake waters subsided. Five heads emerged. One of them was Siegfried's. He struck out for the shore, swimming strongly. Behind his back, an unconscious female was being borne away towards the sea by a rogue current. A note attached to the female read, "This exit is only temporary, but to get back into the story you must personally write yourself in."

---

13 © Bob Dylan

The four remaining females strained their eyes to see who the departing one was, their hearts beating wildly in case it was them.

"It's Tammie!" screamed Tess. She looked down and saw a similar note pinned to her gold bikini top. "Warning: write an episode soon . . ." the note declared ominously. Hurriedly, Tess searched for a pencil.

The sunset reflected on the lake waters and now Lottie, Tess, Donna and Emily could see the two riders clearly. The tallest was clad in a tight-fitting cat-suit of black leather, which accentuated the perfectly proportioned curves of her athletic yet sensuous body. Serene and silent she sat, a multiplicity of weapons and gadgets hanging from her narrow waist.

From the neck down she looked great, however the large paper bag she was wearing on her head spoiled the effect.

"It's Barb!" gasped Lottie. "(Insert Your Name Here) must have given her a dreadful beating—she cannot even show her face!"

"Yes, it is I" sonorously proclaimed Barb. "I have returned, and with me is Tinfingers." Through the eye-slits in the paper bag she glanced sourly towards the rider at her side, a misshapen gnome with a hunched back and a dripping nose. "This," she barked contemptuously, "Is Tinfingers. He was meant to look like Daniel de Licious as Sparrowfoot. Ha! Foiled again!" Bitterly, she added, "Someone will pay for this, and I don't care who."

"So you are still evil, I take it?" enquired Donna.

"Aye," said Barb with a slow smile, "and so is Tinfingers, as you will all learn, to your regret."

169

Darkness fell with a thump.

Just then, a party of people carrying flaming torches appeared on the scene, led by a fire-eyed young red-head.

"It's Juliana!" gasped Emily.

Juliana, who thought she looked like a Botticelli angel, had shed her Paul Thorough disguise and was wearing a pair of fake wings which were meant to look as though they were sprouting from her shoulder-blades. One was hanging askew.

At her back followed a huge company of Modern-Day Vikings, amongst which were mingled (Inse), hysterically waving a bizarre weapon which did not work, and a young-looking Siegfried clone.

A Siegfried clone!

The four soggy damsels in the lake suddenly realized that they had lost the "real" Siegfried. He was nowhere to be seen. He must have climbed out when they weren't looking.

As one, they plunged desperately towards the dazed clone Juliana had brought with her from the Reykjavik docks.

"He's mine!" screamed Juliana, "and so is the real one when I can find him!"

"That's what you think," boomed the muffled voice of Barb, as she threw a TOATS Rule Book on Etiquette at Juliana and spurred her horse towards the melee, "Advance, Tinfingers!"

The nearby villagers popped their heads out of their fish-stinking cottages. Tinfingers blew the attack signal on his war-trumpet as Barb galloped forth, yelling, "God for Merrye England and Saint George!"

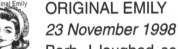

ORIGINAL EMILY
23 November 1998

Barb, I laughed so hard I cried! Brilliant! Cover image option #1 is ready . . . I'll e-mail them to Donna so we can vote for our favorite cover. I'll do three more of varying seriousness. I gave it a subtitle, so now it's "The Obsession And The Story (A Continuing Saga . . .)" Any other suggestions?

ORIGINAL BARB
23 November 1998

Quick work, Emily! Incidentally, if you want to include me in any pix with Siegfried, just substitute a portrait of Cloudy Chiffon®. The resemblance is close, except for the hair color . . . (Yeah, in my dreams.)

That's a good name for the TOATS page—anyone else out there have any other ideas? The more the better, and maybe we can vote on them too, if that's OK with Donna. Epilogue to last episode follows.

UNEARTHLY BARB
23 November 1998

The evil Barb, having distracted everyone by starting a battle, left Tinfingers to do the dirty work. After plunging straight through the fracas and out the other side she galloped far beyond the battlefield, leaving behind the Vikings hacking at the sailors, the crazed women trying to strangle the misshapen gnomes etc. She appeared to be in pursuit of something . . . what could it be?

Who is that lean, suave, running figure she is swooping on? Leaning gracefully from her saddle, Barb scoops up the escaping Siegfried and rides off with him into the darkness of the Icelandic night, just as the Northern Lights begin to flare their delicate rainbow veils dramatically across the sky . . .

 ORIGINAL EMILY
24 November 1998 at 00:00:57 (PST)
You and I have nothing better to do tonight do we? :) Almost done with cover 2!

 ORIGINAL BARB
24 November 1998 at 01:16:10 (PST)
Despite the time printed below, it's just gone quarter past eight on Tuesday evening here in Melbourne Australia!

 ORIGINAL DONNA
24 November 1998
Wow, you are FAST both of you, two covers already, and a gigantic new chapter! I can hardly wait to see the newer, bigger, better, more complete version of TOATS in its fully illustrated glory!

Since my character hasn't yet drifted away on the tide I can take a breather, thank goodness.

 ORIGINAL DONNA
24 November 1998
First run of TOATS on its own web site. Here's the link—have a gander and send suggestions . . . Barb how does the text look, it may be missing parts etc. because I did a quickie on it . . . isn't this fun . . .

ORIGINAL BARB
24 November 1998
Oh yay, Donna, this IS fun, and addictive too! What a great first run. Well done! I don't know how you do all that technological stuff.

Suggestion: that you publish the author's name, date and time as written with each episode. It's interesting to see how much time has elapsed between chapters, how the theme evolves over time etc. Can I email my hoarded TOATS files to you at your Oakland address? Just so's you can compare notes, if you want. Excuse me, the addiction is chipping in and I feel another chapter coming on.

ORIGINAL CONNIE
24 November 1998
Perhaps you should call the site "PINOPH" which stands for People In Need Of Professional Help" . . .

By the way, you may be wondering why Lottie has not contributed to this site for so long . . . I believe that Tess's Internet isn't working . . . my suggestion Tess is FIX IT!!

I am not in love with Siegfried like the rest of you loons, but I go into the website every few days because I love reading your very silly story, especially Barb's episodes, and Lottie's WHICH ARE A LITTLE SPARSE LATELY!

I go into the site so I can sit here and slowly move my head from side to side in amazed disbelief . . . then occasionally I watch Siegfried on TV TRYING to understand . . . maybe there is something wrong with me in that I don't tremble at the sight of ageing actors . . . and I happen to be Lottie's sister, and what's sad is that we do agree on almost everything else and sigh over the same men . . . oh well, can't win 'em all!

Original Connie

UnEarthly Connie

UNEARTHLY BARB

24 November 1998

Hi Connie, this one's for you!

Barb's thoroughbred, full-gloss black Arabian stallion raced on into the night. At full pelt it passed beneath a low branch of a Flergen-gerberlergen tree (well, how should I know what kind of trees they have in Iceland, besides Christmas trees?) Since Siegfried was draped across the saddlebow, the overhanging bough did not affect him, however Barb had been sitting up straight. The branch slammed her across the chest and swiped her backwards off the horse. She landed with a bone-crunching thud, fortunately missing a dangerous rocky outcrop and ending up in a thicket of rare ice-tolerant cacti, which grew nowhere else on earth. The horse galloped on without her, carrying Siegfried away.

How swiftly our fortunes can change! thought Barb, plucking out clumps of needle-like spines from her backside. As she climbed out of the cactus patch, she heard hoofbeats returning. Siegfried, now freed from Barb's iron grip, had deftly managed to get astride the bolting horse and turn it around. He was coming back!

With consummate skill he dismounted and kneeled beside her. Heedless of the pain, she was sitting disconsolately on the rocky outcrop. The expression on her Paper Bag was unreadable.

"Vait a minute," said Siegfried, not without tenderness. "Zere is somesing I vould like to do . . ."

The Paper Bag nodded sullenly. Siegfried fished in his pocket and brought out a felt-tip marker.

175

"Zere!" he proclaimed triumphantly, having quickly drawn a smiling mouth on Barb's Paper Bag. "Don't you feel better now?"

The Paper Bag smiled at him. He produced a mirror so that Barb could view his artistic efforts through the eye-slits. Barb remained silent. "Not evil enough?" asked Siegfried helpfully, "Vat about zis?" He twisted the top corners of the Paper Bag into two miniature horns. Barb viewed herself first from one eye-slit and then the other.

"No!" she burst out at last, "Too evil! I'm sick and tired of being evil. It's someone else's turn. Why can't Donna be evil? Or Lottie, or Juliana, or Emily, or Tess? The novelty has worn off. What have I got to show for it, besides a sore backside, a smashed nose and a second-hand Paper Bag that smells as though it had a meat pie in it?"

"Oh come on, it cannot be all that bad," soothed Siegfried comfortingly.

"Oh yeah? Check this out!" With one swift movement, Barb flung the Paper Bag off her head.

Siegfried stared.

A strange look crept over his chiselled and magnetic features. "You are, you are . . ." he stammered.

"What?" Barb snapped testily, "How do I look?"

"Häßlich," he blurted out.

"What does that mean?"

"Er—BEAUTIFUL," Siegfried lied, hastily cramming the Paper Bag back on her head. "Anyway," he amended, "you are a very goot rider."

"Got you fooled too, have I?" she shot back. "I was hanging on to that horse with my teeth. Why do you think the Paper Bag is so chewed-looking? I started to fall off but luckily the horse was passing you at the time. As I tilted sideways I grabbed hold of you for support. Then the horse tipped the other way and as I went over I inadvertently brought you with me."

"Himmel!" exclaimed Siegfried. "Zis is incredible!"

"I have decided to reform," said Barb piously. "I shall buy a pair of fake angel's wings and go and dwell with the fish-stinking villagers, distributing my good works amongst them. I shall give you up, Siegfried my love. I do not deserve you. Farewell!"

Awkwardly, she rose to her feet and stumbled off, back towards the fisherfolk's cottages by the lake. The glossy black stallion started nibbling cautiously at the shoots of a Christmas tree, while Siegfried mournfully stood beside it watching Barb disappear into the distance.

P.S. Connie, if you don't watch out you may get WRITTEN INTO THE STORY!!!! (Warning!)

ORIGINAL BARB
24 November 1998
By the way Donna, I love your idea of the author's biographies. Wish I'd thought of the Tibetan monk idea first!

ORIGINAL EMILY
24 November 1998
OK ... I've been looking at too many "bodice-ripper" book covers these past two days. But it has given me the chance to write a background chapter for TOATS ... Here goes!

UNEARTHLY EMILY

24 November 1998

Barb, with a heavy sigh, slowly walked back towards that fish-stinking village.

How did I end up the villain in so many episodes? she wondered. *What went wrong? Why did all my love scenes end in unrequited passion?*

She paused for a moment.

Suddenly overwhelmed with the realization she will forever answer "paper" to that burning question, "Would you like paper or plastic?" she screamed, "Where do I go from here?!" here!…here!…here!…here!… her echo resonated through the forest. Little cute, furry, cartoonish animals scurried for cover.

"Do you have to YELL? I'm trying to read!"

"Who said that?" Barb looked around anxiously, not knowing if it might be lions, tigers or bears.

"Up here."

Barb looked up into the branches of the biggest Flergen-gerberlergen tree she has ever seen. "Emily, you scared the babelfish out of me! What are you doing up there?"

Emily swung her feet over the edge of a branch. "Well, after the melee started I ducked into the Frosty Halibut to get a drink. After it got quiet, I noticed everyone was gone, so I started walking this way following all the horse tracks. I nearly broke a toe when I tripped over this."

Emily patted a thick volume of pages bound in rich Corinthian leather embossed with the TOATS logo on the cover.

"It's the TOATS Rule Book on Etiquette that hit Juliana. You know I've never read it all the way through. There's some really interesting stuff in here. Come on up."

Barb started to climb the tree. "Really? You know, I'm trying to change my image," she said as she adjusted her Paper Bag." I was thinking of buying those Vicki's Whisper® angels' wings, think that will help?"

"I think we first need to get rid of this." In one swift movement Emily reached down and removed Barb's Paper Bag, tossing it to the forest floor. "You look like the Unknown Comic® with that thing. It had to go."

"Fine, but you didn't have to be rude about it." Barb reached the branch Emily is sitting on.

"Yeeeewwwwww your nose is...."

"I know..it's...it's..."Barb mournfully replied. "It's *Häßlich*. I've got to do something."

"Let's work on your image first." Emily opened the book to the Table of Contents. "Ah! Here is just the chapter!"

She began to read. "There are two major archetypes of women appropriate for TOATS. The Damsel in Distress and The Warrior Woman. Which do you want to hear about?"

Barb thought for a moment. "Read them both."

"Okay, in order to be a certified DID (Damsel In Distress) the following ten criteria must be met:

"1. Her style; Bosomy. perfectly proportioned. with delicate features.

"2. Her wardrobe: Much given to plunging necklines and long hemlines. Multiple ensembles, flowing sheer material, harem pants and long fluid skirts of silk, silk velvet and other rare and costly material.

"3. Her hair: Long, curling tresses a must. Possibly caught up in a jewelled net.

"4. She lives in... a castle.

"5. She is greeted with: 'Demoiselle! My Lady! Flee! Run for your life!'

"6. She rides: Side-saddle on a gentle dappled mare.

"7. Her idea of a good time: Swept up in the embrace of that handsome rogue sitting next to her at the palace banquet.

"8. Dreaming, she: Sleeps naked between silken sheets with her true love's talisman under her pillow.

"9. Her definition of sacrifice: She encourages her one true love to marry another to save his land.

"And finally, 10. Parting words after a final night of passion: My heart is yours until the stars melt from the sky and the moon breaks into a million pieces."

"Wow! What does the other one say?" Barb was entranced.

Emily began to read again.

"'The Warrior Woman.'

"1. Her style: Bosomy, perfectly proportioned, Tall, willowy and graceful.

"2. Her wardrobe: Much given to plunging necklines and short hemlines. She owns just the one outfit which she wears until it's worn out, heavy leather, metal, lots of buckles and tabs.

"3. Her hair: Sleek black or dark red hair. Possibly braided.

"4. She lives... anywhere from a pirate ship to above a tavern.

"5. She is greeted with, 'Help! Help! The Vikings are looting the village!'

"6. She rides: Alone astride a dark, blooded charger.

"7. Her idea of a good time: Plunging her sword into the heart of that handsome villain on the tavern stool next to her.

"8. Dreaming, she: Sleeps on the ground, wrapped naked, in her cloak with her sword just a heartbeat away.

"9. Her definition of sacrifice: Gives up her own chances of happiness to save her land.

"And 10. Parting words after a final night of passion: 'I'll look you up next time I'm in the Realm.'"

Barb was deep in thought absorbing this new and wondrous information like a Mediterranean sea sponge. "What else does it say?"

Emily turned the page. "It gives a sample plot and the description of the Romantic Hero too. The sample plot is 'You are suddenly transported from your humdrum job making cold calls for a large marketing research firm to a sailing ship in the middle of the Atlantic. Before you have a chance to really blow your hastily assumed role of a well-bred Victorian governess, you find that the ship is under siege. You are captured and taken aboard a pirate ship.

"Despite your corsets, hoops and numerous hairpins you are still able to draw on your skills with civil war weaponry, which just happens to have been your hobby in the modern era. When the exotic and handsome pirate captain teases your gentle comrades, you draw your saber and attempt to run him through.

"Despite the slight wound which you visit upon his very masculine body, the captain throws back his handsome, and amazingly enough for this time in history, louse-free, head and laughs deep in his throat. He is drawn to your feminine, yet liberated, charms and works hard to convince you that the respect he has for you has nothing to do with your curvaceous figure, lustrous red hair and luminescent complexion.

"You give it a while before you succumb to his lures. You hang out on the pirate ship with your new lover and fight regular battles. All of your victims are bad guys who deserve to die. You institute modern ideas of nutrition and proper eating habits. Despite the lack of dental hygiene and modern medicine you remain eternally young and vigorous.'"

Emily turned over yet another well-worn parchment page. "The Romantic Hero: The hero must excel in all thing manly: boxing, shooting, riding, drinking, gambling, etc. He must have nerves of steel and tremendous self-control. A modern romance hero must, above all things, be every woman's dream of a perfect lover and be able to prove it in bed. He must also be man enough to keep his passions in check for at least three chapters.

"Physical Characteristics and Background. Age: early thirties or older. Height: at least six foot Physical condition: Excellent. Muscular but not muscle bound. Complexion: Tanned. Hair: Blond OK in historicals, Dark in Modern. Eyes: To match Voice: Deep and sensuous. Education: Very well educated and excels in his endeavours. Knows a lot about everything.

"Overall: Our hero is wealthy. He has an aura about him that draws women to him. Victorian women dream and wonder what it would be like to be kissed by him. They find out. Modern women wonder what he would be like in bed. They find out. In both instances he is wonderful.

"He must not be cruel in any way to females, and have great respect for his parents and elders, puppies and other cute animals regardless of his background. He must kill spiders, and open jars.

"And last but not least the ideal male hero also has a good sense of humor."

KRISTA

25 November 1998

Wishing everyone a wonderful Thanksgiving!

ORIGINAL BARB

25 November 1998

And the same to you, Krista. Not that we actually celebrate Thanksgiving here in the wilds of Australia. But we do get a holiday for the Queen's Birthday.

I've got to force myself to stop visiting this site. It gives people too many far-fetched literary ideas. Just one more, just one more chapter before I retrieve my squashed paper bag and slouch into the halibut-scented retirement village after all . . .

UNEARTHLY BARB

25 November 1998

Meanwhile, (my favorite, always-reliable word to begin with), back at the battle-site on the shores of the Blue Lagoon, nothing is happening. The night is empty. The place is deserted.

This is because the battle, as Emily has already reported, is over. Nobody is quite sure what they were fighting about or who won, but Juliana thinks she was the victor, and she's celebrating back at the "Frosty Halibut".

In fact, there was a wild party going on. It was so big, it had spilled out the doors of the "Frosty Halibut", into the neighbouring tavern, the "Jolly Codpiece", and subsequently out the doors of the "Jolly Codpiece" into the streets. That was where you could find Juliana partying, with a young, heartstoppingly handsome Siegfried clone on her arm and a bottle of Baksmälla® Vodka in each hand. She was surrounded by her loyal but feral gang of Latter-Day Vikings and a few Scandinavian trolls, all singing lustily.

Nobody felt the biting cold of the Icelandic night, because they were warmed by the red glare of a thundering great bonfire. This inferno was fueled by a huge pile of TOATS Rule Books on Etiquette. Juliana, as part of her victory celebrations, had sacked the local library, where thousands of dusty copies of this work could be found lining the shelves. Above the door of the "Frosty Halibut", someone had scrawled, (rather paradoxically), "ANARCHY RULES".

"We don't need no ed-yoo-cay-shun!" chorused Juliana along with the Vikings and trolls, "We don't need no thought control! No dark sarcasm in the classroom—"®[14]

"Hang on, that's copyright!" shouted somebody. "You can't publish that on the Net!"

"Oops," said Juliana, her eyes darting from side to side as though she expected to spot a lawyer pouncing on her straight away.

At this point allow me to digress. Juliana looked splendid, as usual. She was wearing a horned helmet. A piece of silver tinsel was caught haphazardly between the horns. Her vibrant, curly hair spilled out from beneath the glimmering bronze of the helm. Her perfect figure was bedecked with leather and bronze. She looked like a cross between a Valkyrie and Xenophobia, Warrior Princess®.

---

14 © Roger Waters. Lyrics from "Another Brick in the Wall," a song by Pink Floyd bassist Roger Waters.

The attendant Vikings and trolls adored her. The young "Norwegian" Siegfried clone was dazzled by her brilliance. Just as she was about to look more striking than ever, a messenger rushed up, panting.

"Your Ineffableness!" he exclaimed, dropping on one knee before Juliana, "I bear tidings!"

"Huh?" Juliana squinted at him, leaning more heavily on the delectable Jörgen Petersen, "Do I know you?"

"No, Your Majesty," said the messenger. "I bear tidings that your distant uncle has just passed away. Lo and behold, he was the secret heir to a title and great wealth, which he has now bequeathed to you. Yes, Queen Juliana, all these years thou didst think thou wert descended from scum, but thou hast royal blood in thy veins!"

With that, the messenger threw himself to the ground and began kissing her feet. Juliana's eyes opened wide as she tried to digest this astounding information. The bonfire leaped higher. By its flickering light Donna, Lottie, Tess and (Inse) could be seen dancing with some Vulgarian sailors.

"Can this be true?" cried Juliana, dropping the two bottles of vodka with a crash and ripping the tinsel out of her horns. "Is this going to be the new me, rich and noble?"

At that precise moment, there was a movement at the edge of the firelight. A black horse appeared, and on its back a tall rider whose hair glinted like fallow gold.

Yes, Siegfried—the real one—had returned at last.

ORIGINAL BARB
25 November 1998
With apologies to all SPH fans for this utter silliness—I think you will all be glad when TOATS is removed to another place!

ORIGINAL EMILY
25 November 1998
Barb—retirement? Ha! That'll last for what? A day or two? I think it's all a ruse.

ORIGINAL BARB
26 November 1998
Emily, it's the deafening silence from the rest of the SPH fans that's making me think I ought to retire! I mean, I know you and Donna and Juliana are TOATSians, and the other Australian fans are twisted enough to appreciate it, but there's very little feedback from anyone else.

A niggling doubt gnaws at me—what if they're all just sitting back in quiet disgust at our verbal antics, too polite to say anything, just counting the days till we move off the feedback page?

I feel like Tinkerbell in "Peter Pan", gradually fading due to lack of belief in fairies. "All those who believe in fairies, clap your hands!" shouts Peter (or was it Wendy?) Tinkerbell hears the sound of hands clapping, and it swells into thunderous applause. Barb, on the other hand (no pun intended) cocks an ear in the general direction of SPH fandom and hears nothing beyond a small squeak.

Are there millions of people lurking out there in silent disapproval? Am I simply getting paranoid? Where's everybody gone? Are all the newcomers being scared off? Has TOATS ruined Donna's once-sane feedback page?

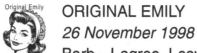

ORIGINAL EMILY
26 November 1998

Barb—I agree. I saw in one of the Kevin Spacey web sites awhile back a separate page called Fan Fics (Something like that). And that's where they post their own stories. I agree there has been a lack of outside comments. Come to think of it TOATS is a bit scary, isn't it?

Donna, is there a way to set up a separate feedback where we can post our chapters? That will free up the real SPH feedback page for the rest of the world. Then every so often clean it out and paste at the end of the TOATS page. I'm not up on web pages so you are the technical support on whether or not it's possible. What do you think?

ORIGINAL JULIANA
Friday 27 November 1998

Been gone a week and look what's happened! Donna, our technical super smart computer wizard has been working flat out again to make our smallest wishes come true! Our own little literary corner . . . that is a BRILLIANT idea. Now we just have to get rid of that tiresome California-based thespian and his blonde sidekick. We could glue our own glam pics on top of his in that Images section for a start, make and star in our own very bad (very bad) action flicks and drink copious quantities of alcohol and SMIRK to our heart's contents.

I'll be jumping into that weird and wacky world of TOATS during the weekend but it seems I have a lot of catching up to do. So au revoir everyone!
Juliana

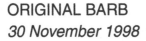 **ORIGINAL BARB**
30 November 1998
What the heck Emily, I'm getting TOATS with-
drawal symptoms. Let's just write!!! We could
preface each episode with the words FAN FICTION—NEXT
EPISODE so's not to scare people away . . . What's your
opinion?

 ORIGINAL DONNA
30 November 1998
Happy after Thanksgiving (burppp) Oh! Excuse
me! How rude. Well, is there a consensus? I was
going to allow the TOATS posts to go both places in the
future, I mean, leave them on the feedback page and also
direct those posts to the epic novel page.

But maybe you are right, and it's a tad scary for normal
people. So perhaps TOATS will migrate itself off of here
leaving the feedback page to collect nice un-scary Siegfried
info from normal people who have extremely good taste.

 **ORIGINAL EMILY**
30 November 1998
Let's preface it with 'Fan Fiction—Next Episode'. I
see we are getting a trickle of comments back so
that's a good sign. We haven't scared everyone off! I'll pick
up the pen tomorrow and write.

 ORIGINAL BARB
30 November 1998
Donna, I would love to see TOATS in both places—
right here (in a different color, with a warning not

to take it too seriously) and also on the epic novel page. Otherwise it might lose "freshness".

Looking forward with TOATS-deprived eagerness to Emily's NEXT EPISODE—and Juliana, where's your contribution? We can't expect Donna to write too much at the moment as we are keeping her busy with web-site technological stuff.

Emily I love every one of your pictures!

ORIGINAL EMILY

30 November 1998

Thanks Barb! I had fun creating them. But, for me they took forever to load. Donna you may want to cut the sizes down so it won't take so long to load. Let me know if you want me to do anything. I'm writing my (avatar's) bio . . . I'll get to a chapter next.

UNEARTHLY LOTTIE

2 December 1998

Lottie huddled—all goosebumps and chattering teeth—by the bonfire. She was still clad in that scanty gold bikini found floating in the lagoon.

But then Siegfried rode into the firelight with a little bemused smile on his face, thinking: *Why the hell have I come back to these demented women?* The massive black stallion danced nervously; reflected flames leapt in its dark eyes and firelight played across the muscular arch of its neck and the long, tangled fall of its mane. (You got the breed wrong, Barb—it's not an Arabian; it's a Friesian—horse for heroes—like the one Rutger Hauer® rides in *Ladyhawk.*®)

Astride its back sat our hero; relaxed, cool and faintly

amused. Lottie saw on TV recently how scientists had disproved the possibility of Spontaneous Human Combustion and this is absolutely the only thing that's stopping her doing just that.

Suddenly an ugly little voice spoke from the darkness.

"The horse is a good move, but it's come too late." A man in a rumpled suit, eating some smelly sandwiches from a paper bag, stepped into the firelight. "I regret to inform you, Herr P. Hinkelheimer, that you are no longer part of TOATS; you are, in a nutshell, out of the story."

"Fantastic," said Siegfried. "Does this mean I can go home?"

"Noooo!" shrieked Donna, Tess, Lottie and (Inse).

"Who the hell do you think you are, scum?" said Juliana, plucking the little man up by the scruff of his neck and dangling him over the flames.

"Yes, that's right," he gasped, "Herr Schumm at your service madam—just flown in from Geneva . . ."

Juliana threw him to the ground. "Your Majesty to you, Scum."

He picked himself up, dusting off his suit. "Beg pardon, Your Majesty; just doing my job. Herr Hinkelheimer is to accompany me to Geneva to explain his failure as a hero to the First Advisory Committee on TOATS Rules and Etiquette."

"Failure as a hero??" shouted Lottie. "But—but look at him! He's the perfect hero!"

"No he's not", said Herr Schumm, "the only heroic thing he's done this whole saga is to put up with you hideous women."

"If he goes, I go," said Donna.

"Me too, me too!!" screamed several women.

"Yeah, so clear off, creep," said Juliana, giving him a kick.

"Not so fast . . . Tinfingers!" cried Schumm.

"Here, sir," said Tinfingers, appearing out of the darkness.

"Ah, my faithful agent—good man—go and get those other females."

Tinfingers scuttled off while Schumm finished off his sandwiches. Juliana gave him a wink—could she be secretly in league with him?? Surprisingly, Siegfried looked happy at the prospect of leaving TOATS—he couldn't keep the smirk off his face.

Tinfingers returned, dragging Barb and Emily by the hair. Barb spotted Schumm's paper bag.

"Ooh, can I have that?" she said, grabbing it from him and putting it on her head. It was much nicer than her old one, with "Steingrimur Thorsteinsson's Gourmet Sandwiches" printed across it.

"You look lovely", said Siegfried. "That illegible Gothic printing gives you such a mysterious and exotic air."

"Air . . . I need some air," mumbled Barb.

Siegfried leaned from the horse, scooped her up to give her a kiss, but then dropped her in horror.

"What did you have in those sandwiches, Schumm?"

"Just babelfishpaste . . . and lettuce. My favorite," said Schumm, smacking his lips.

"I can't breathe in here," said Barb in a muffled voice, flailing her arms wildly. But the Paper Bag had wrapped itself tightly around her head and refused to come off.

"Well, I have a plane to catch," said Schumm. "Out of the goodness of my heart I have decided to give Herr Hinkelheimer an extra week. I have horses for you all—Tinfingers, bring the horses! I would suggest to you ladies that you ride off to look for situations conducive to turning this man into a true TOATS hero. You've got one week."

He turned to get into a taxi-cab just as the sun peeped over the horizon.

"What about me?" said Lottie. "There's no horse for me."

"Oh you," said Schumm. "You're out of it . . . you haven't contributed for far too long. Go swimming with Tammie." He slammed the car door and hurtled off into the sunrise.

"It's not my fault!" wailed Lottie. "Damned computers!"

The others (including clones, Vikings and trolls) rode away, chattering and making a few stupid Wagnerian type noises.

"I've read the TOATS Rule Book on Etiquette," someone said. "It said a TOATS hero must kill spiders and open jars. Perhaps if we go to a supermarket and buy some jars . . ." Their voices faded in the distance as a blizzard set in.

Amongst the howling sleet and snow Lottie trembled in her gold bikini. She suddenly remembered the warning note pinned to Tess.

"Aaagh, they've got Tess and me mixed up AGAIN!" she screamed. "Why do people always get us mixed up??! And what about (Inse)? She hasn't written ANYTHING!"

Suddenly a dark shadow loomed through the snow. A great black stallion skidded to a halt before her, and on its back was . . .

Lottie fell to her knees. "Oh, my beloved hero . . . you've come to rescue me . . . and to read my script . . ."

"Here, you must be a bit cold," said Siegfried, tossing her his jacket. He wheeled the horse around and thundered off into the swirling blizzard. A clod of snow from one of the horse's huge hooves flew through the air and hit Lottie in the face.

High on a ridge above, Connie stood with a man who looked rather like Nicolas Birdhouse (perhaps it was?). She couldn't keep her hands off those lovely muscles.

"I saw something really disgusting before," she said to him, "coming out of The Jolly Codpiece. A man, and he had all these gorgeous, nubile women hanging off him. Reminds me of my sister. I'm worried about her—she's fallen in love with . . . Good gracious!!"

Connie was looking down through her binoculars at a forlorn figure stumbling through the blizzard. "That looks like her . . . but it can't be. I had a postcard from Greece, then outback Oz; surely she couldn't be in Iceland! Well, let's get out of here; this cold is unnatural—must be the Fimbul Winter."

"What's that?" her companion asked.

"You know; Ragnarok; doom of the Gods; end of the world and all that stuff. Where's the airport?"

Somewhere across the mountains a huge wolf howled . . .

ORIGINAL LOTTIE
2 December 1998
Emily, I just love your TOATS covers!! Very clever!
I plan to do some black & white illustrations when
I get the time.

ORIGINAL EMILY
2 December 1998
Lott—brilliant chapter! Now you've got me thinking
. . . P.S. I LOVED *Ladyhawk.®*

ORIGINAL DONNA
2 December 1998
yikes, watch out, the site might behave oddly while
i test out the changes. hang onto your hats & I'll
post again when the dust is all settled . . .

ORIGINAL DONNA
2 December 1998
AAAAAAAAAHHHHH!! BEG YOUR MILLION
PARDONS. THE BOOK WILL BE BACK ONLINE
LATER, WHEN MY oops didn't mean to yell, when my brain
stops hurting . . .

ORIGINAL DONNA
2 December 1998
oops i had made a little error before . . .
donna is insane

ORIGINAL DONNA

2 December 1998

Please pardon this test of the Emergency TOATS Interruption Service. This is only a test. And now, back to the story . . .

ORIGINAL DONNA

2 December 1998

Well, not another one!! Yes, it's me again. It's safe to send TOATS and normal posts. If your post is for TOATS, just enter it normally and check the little box on the form, and voila! I have to add something to the intro on this screen so that people visiting the site have some clue what the heck's going on, but other than that I think it's all set . . .

UNEARTHLY EMILY

2 December 1998

. . . the howling dissolved into a high-pitched whine . . . "Omelette or mixed grill? Omelette or mixed grill?"

The next moment Siegfried woke up on the plane to Fiji. A pointy-nosed air hostess hovered over him.

"What?" he said, rubbing the sleep from his eyes.

"Sir, your entree—would you care for the omelette or the mixed grill?"

Siegfried focused, trying to remember the bizarre dream he'd just had. "Omelette," he replied without thinking. The air hostess placed a tray in front of him.

These long flights are murder he thought. "Excuse me. How long till we arrive in Fiji?"

"Three hours."

Several rows back, Barb overcome by an intense feeling of déjà vu, stopped reading her Thrills and Spoons® novel.

Could it be? she thought. No—impossible. What are the odds? Still a nagging feeling crept up her spine . . . that voice, it was so—familiar . . .

Barb looked around the cabin. She spied the drink cart approaching. Biding her time, she waited until the air hostess went in search of a few more Diet Kolas®. Barb nonchalantly got up and pushed the drink cart down the aisle, bumping into a few headrests along the way.

"Oops, sorry," she offered.

As she neared the front row her heart began to beat faster. She was sure everyone in First Class could hear it. Barb took a deep breath and looked to her right.

There he was.

Magnificent. Tousled curly hair. Black jeans and white shirt.

"C . . . c . . . c . . . coffee? T . . . t . . . t . . . tea? Orange Juice? She inquired as he looked at her with his dazzling blue eyes.

"Orange juice, thank you."

She poured him a glass. As she passed it to him, their momentarily touched[15]. He cocked his head a little to study her face. Barb, while entranced, realized the air hostess was starting up the aisle.

"Do I know you?" Siegfried inquired.

"Uh.. I don't think so . . . " Barb said, her voice trailing off as she saw the hostess approaching.

Siegfried noticed Barb's furtive looks down the isle and smiled. "You're not a flight attendant are you?" he said with an amused look on his face.

---

15 We have deliberately left this typo in the story. Read on . . .

"What? No . . . actually it's kind of funny . . . you see I thought you were someone I knew, and I was going to play a joke on you.. heh.. heh.. but my mistake.. sorry for the interruption," she replied as she scooted back to her seat, trying not to just die right there in front of everyone.

Barb buried her head back in her book 'Stupid . . . stupid . . . stupid.' she berated herself.

"If I was to have anyone play a prank on me, I could not have asked for a lovelier prankster."

Barb froze. Her body went completely liquid. She dared not look anticipating that she would melt right before his eyes. She managed to get enough control over herself to look up.

With all the poise and finesse she could muster, she said, "What? Did you say something?"

He smiled. "Allow me to introduce myself. My name is Siegfried." He extended his hand towards Barb.

"Barb. Is this your first trip to Fiji?". . .

On Original Earth, Barb stared perplexedly at her computer's monitor. What was going on? How had the story jumped from Inauthentic Iceland right back to the very beginning, a repeat of the scenes on board the Air Banana flight from Fictitious Fiji? It was a mystery. In the next chapter she'd better take matters into her own hands and get the tale back on track . . .

ORIGINAL EMILY
2 December 1998
I made a typo in my story. Their HANDS momentarily touched . . . get your minds out of the gutter! :)

ORIGINAL DONNA
2 December 1998
THAT WAS NO TYPO! Emily you did that deliberately, confess. Okay, I updated the online TOATS with Barb's spell-checked and etc. version, thank you thank you Barb the scribe for saving all the TOATS related entries for posterity (which has apparently arrived?)

Now remember everyone you don't want me writing your author bios (how subtle) and congratulations to Connie for getting herself written into the story!

Ha! Now to go and ponder how to get MYSELF back into an upcoming episode!

ORIGINAL CONNIE
2 December 1998
After all this time as a closet TOATS reader I cannot believe I have somehow materialised into it! Barb merely threatened, but Lottie . . . well what can I say?

I was deeply shocked but somehow also deeply amused . . . I don't mind how often you have me fawning all over Nicolas Birdhouse . . . how could any red-blooded female possibly keep their hands off those muscles (and yes, my sister and I DO agree on this one)—I might just see if there is a Nic Birdhouse Web Site . . . although it is EXCEEDINGLY DOUBTFUL it would come anywhere near the complete depravity of this site (nor would I want it to)! And don't expect me to write any episodes, your collective imaginations are way ahead of mine!

ORIGINAL BARB
2 December 1998
I would urge all visitors to the Siegfried P. Hinkel-heimer Fan Site to take a look at Emily's amazing Jacket Art for our SPH Fan-Fiction. These covers are to be found at the link, or click on "TOATS" as shown above. In particular, look at some of the backgrounds . . . they will appear significant to regular readers.

ORIGINAL EMILY
2 December 1998
Barb—I tried to find the most attractive crocodile to be Nigel . . .

ORIGINAL DONNA
3 December 1998
Oh, yes, I had a good laugh at the clever back-grounds on the TOATS covers, hearty applause for Emily's creations! By the way the red-head is me, but that was before I went back to my natural shade. Haha!

BELINDA
5 December 1998
On my search to discover a web site devoted to Siegfried P. Hinkelheimer I arrived here. Haha, you guys are crazy—but I'm just as insane because for me Siegfried is among the hottest of the hot, even if he's not as young as he used to be.

Your FanFic is a blast, I've been looking through it and laughing my head off. Love the book cover pictures, too!

11

ABOARD
AN AIR BANANA
FLIGHT

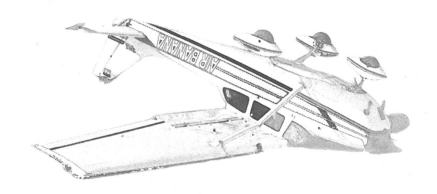

UNEARTHLY BARB

8 December 1998

A voice came crackling over the aircraft's P.A. system—"Um, er, dis your Capiten speaking…" the voice was suddenly submerged by ear-splitting microphone feedback. "Hey Umbala," said the voice in muffled tones, "how you work dis ting?" A moment later the feedback subsided, to the passengers' relief, and the voice resumed. "Sorry 'bout dat, ladies and gentlemens, dis your Capiten speaking again. Fasten seat belts please, we got some bad wedder ahead. We in for some wild ride."

As Siegfried hastened to his seat and clicked his seat belt buckle into place he wondered (not for the first time) whether he had been wise in opting for the cheap ticket with Air Banana, sole airline of the tiny island republic of Bananawana. It had been surprisingly easy to obtain the ticket, considering the airline consisted of only one operating plane and a wooden gyro-copter.

As he waited for the turbulence to set in he glanced about to see how the other passengers were handling the situation. He could not see Barb from where he sat but he was slightly unnerved at the sight of so many burly, thick-set passengers wearing balaclavas and carrying violin cases.

It occurred to Siegfried that before he had boarded the plane, he could not recall having walked through one of those metal-detecting doorframes usually seen at airports. This was glaringly obvious now that he thought about it. What normally happened when he passed through the metal-detector was complete silence as the alarms failed to go off and all the female airport staff stopped talking simultaneously, their jaws hanging ajar. This was inevitably, followed by a large lady official ordering him to stop and be thoroughly frisked, while the rest of the female staff lined up behind her to have their turn. Siegfried muttered a curse to himself. How could he have forgotten this familiar routine? "Too late now," he murmured.

An air hostess hurried up the aisle towards the cock-pit, carrying a shoe-box filled with elastic-bands. Alarmed, Siegfried leaned down and fumbled beneath his seat, feeling for the reassuring shape of a life-jacket. His hand meeting something, he pulled it out. It was an inflatable rubber duck, yellow with an orange beak. Hastily stuffing the rubber duck back under the seat, Siegfried unclipped his seat-belt and strode off to the cockpit, intending to find out exactly what was going on. Thrusting the beaded leather curtain aside, he stood a moment irresolute.

There before him was a lucky rabbit's foot dangling from a coat-hanger attached to the cockpit ceiling. To one side, a battered transistor radio was jangling out "Those Magnificent Men in their Flying Machines", while the man seated in the pilot's chair was busily thumbing through a battered and ancient copy of "How to Flye Ye Aeroplane". On the floor, the co-pilot was kneeling. He had ripped up one of the floorboards and was fiddling with some exposed machinery (presumably vital to the plane's remaining airborne), while the flight attendant passed him extra elastic-bands to fix it with.

Without uttering a word, Siegfried drew the curtain and returned to his seat, bestowing a kindly glance on Barb along the way. He portrayed a confidence he did not feel. In fact he was feeling distinctly nervous.

Compared to zis, it vas looking good back zere in Iceland, he thought to himself in English with a German accent, *I vonder—if I try to get some sleep now, maybe I can return to zat same dream . . . or is zis za dream? If I go to sleep in zis dream vill I vake up in ze real world?*

Closing those gorgeous baby-blues, Siegfried lay back against the plaited raffia upholstery of his seat and began to doze.

12

IN THE
SNORING SQUID
SUPERMARKET

UNEARTHLY BARB

8 December 1998

While Siegfried was dreaming about airplanes—presumably having fallen off his horse during the blizzard and hit his head on an icicle—in the Fish Department of an Icelandic supermarket, Barb wandered lost among icy shelves of cod, groper, mullet and deep-sea bass.

A petrified babelfish had fallen off its perch and frozen onto her left foot, while a putrefied squid adhered to her shoulder. A dead electric eel had wound itself about her neck like a worn-out tire and was staring blankly ahead with vacant eyes.

At the corner of Barb's vision she spied a figure standing outside the cold window pane, in a howling blizzard. It was Lottie in a gold bikini, hammering on the glass with a desperate expression on her face.

"What?" mumbled Barb vaguely. "What are you shouting?"

But Lottie could not be heard above the feral screaming of the wind, so Barb nodded politely at Lottie and moved on.

"How did I get here?" she sighed through the crinkled fabric of her Paper Bag. "I was looking for the Cosmetics Department, or failing that, the False Nose Department—"

She broke off, as a furtive figure peered around a gondola-end. (Yes, a gondola-end! That's actually big-business jargon for the ends of the rows in supermarkets.)

"Tinfingers!" cried Barb distastefully. "What are you doing here? I thought you were with the others, looking for hard-to-open jars on the Hard-To-Open Jar Department, and giant tarantulas in the Pets Department."

"Cannot leave you, Mistress," replied Tinfingers dolefully, loping towards her with a twisted limp. "Your servant. Your employee."

"What? So I'm stuck with you, am I?" cried Barb tactlessly. "If I were not a reformed character and devoted to doing good works amongst the poor, I would say to you Get Thee Hence, Scoundrel, and don't call me 'Mistress'. But unfortunately," she amended with regret, "I am no longer evil and cruel enough to say such things."

The misshapen gnome sidled up to her. Barb was, of course, still wearing that rather fetching black leather outfit, close-fitting and exceptionally flattering to her superb figure.

Tinfingers pointed to the alien equipment dangling from her waist-belt. "Use Medical Kit, Mistress," he said.

About an hour later, Barb (never renowned for alertness) caught on and said, "Oh yes, the Medical Kit from the Planet Splinge. What a good idea!"

Unzipping the alien Medical Kit, she started tossing out a multitude of small packets, marked with such titles as "Morphing Pills" and "U-Gro Wings". Finally snatching up a package marked "Instant Nose Job", she laughed, tore the Paper Bag from her head and jammed the contents of the package onto her derelict nose. Five seconds later her nose emerged, smooth and new-looking. She admired it in her handy alien mirror, patting her hair back and pouting smugly.

"Now I look even better than my face-model Cloudy Chiffon®," she simpered. "How irresistible!"

As Barb fondly stroked her reborn nose, Tinfingers was gathering up the discarded remnant of the Medical Kit. Surreptitiously he opened the packet of Morphing Pills and looked through the tiny boxes inside. They were labelled with such interesting names as "Gabriel Yearn," "Lance Boyle", "Ray Fiends," "Nicolas Birdhouse" and "D.D.L." Reflectively, Tinfingers broke the seal on one box and swallowed the contents. Behind Barb's back, his form heaved and distorted. He was turning into a delectable, utterly mouth-watering shape familiar to movie-goers.

Who could it be? And where are the others? The girls, the Vikings, the trolls? (It's question time.) And what are they doing? Have they found any hard-to-open jars? Is Juliana enjoying being Queen of Vikings? Is Lottie destined to become an ice statue on display outside the supermarket? Will Siegfried wake up before he freezes to death in the blizzard? Will the Air Banana aircraft in his dream reach its destination in one piece? Is this story getting hard to follow? Has Emily found any more copies of the TOATS Rule Book on Etiquette? Am I confused? Yes!!!

ORIGINAL DONNA
9 December 1998
FAN FICTION—Next episode: BLAST! and DAMN!

ORIGINAL DONNA
9 December 1998
Forgive my outburst, I just realized that when I replaced the text in TOATS with the set Barb sent me, I left off the little trigger that tells the program where the next instalment goes. So, duh. I put it back and added the two new EXCITING instalments!

Barb can I be in that supermarket? I want to hand out those little morphing pills all over the place! God, to fill the world with desirable men! Wait—do they keep their old personalities???

ORIGINAL CONNIE
9 December 1998

PLEASE don't keep me in suspense . . . has Tinfingers turned into Nicolas Birdhouse? Can I be there fawning all over him? I'd even ignore my sister outside in the blizzard wearing a bikini, with hypothermia setting in.

ORIGINAL EMILY
9 December 1998

In regards to the TOATS Rule Book on Etiquette there is a one in a million chance that whatever Tinfingers turns into can fall in the "Frog Prince" category (section 12 paragraph 9)—you kiss him—he turns back into a frog. Let's just say I warned you all in advance :)

UNEARTHLY EMILY
9 December 1998

Tinfingers writhed and contorted, as his transformation was complete. Barb's jaw hit the floor. "Oh—my—gods! There before her in all his morphing splendour was a TOTALLY naked . . . Tinfingers.

Quickly he ran to look at his reflection in the glass door of the Frozen Fish section. As stunned Icelandic shoppers scattered, screaming Tinfingers dropped to his knees and started to sob.

"No! No! No! I've done everything... everything!" he moaned.

Barb, still stunned, experienced a flashback. She remembered what Emily told her about in the TOATS Rule Book on Etiquette. She thought: If he morphed and I kissed him he would return to be an ugly misshapen toad. ("That's frog Barb," Emily whispered, out of writing view.)

"Whatever." Barb waved a perfectly manicured hand in the air and placed it under her chin, thinking some more. "That means if he's already a toa.. er.. frog—"

Barb approached the sobbing naked Tinfingers. She gently (and hesitantly) sat beside him with an obvious grimace on her face. She placed one hand under his chin and lifted his face to hers.

I can't believe I'm doing this, she thought to herself.

"What?" Tinfingers managed to articulate.

"Trust me, it's in the book," said Barb as she closed her eyes and planted a kiss on his warty lips.

Blackness. Nothing. No feeling whatsoever, she thought, afraid to open her eyes.

Slowly the lips pressed against her began to respond and she was in a serious lip lock. (Ewwwwww gross) But wait! ...the lips that were now kissing hers were soft and tender and somehow familiar. Barb slowly opened her eyes. Staring straight back at her with the sexiest, happiest grin was the gorgeous DDL-lookalike.

"Daniel! Daniel!" Barb flung herself into his arms. "Daniel, what happened? Is it really you or are you really Tinfingers?" Laughing, he pulled her close (hmmm... any closer and she would be in back of him).

"It's really me," explained the handsome avatar whose hair, to Barb's delight, was in character as the long, black locks of "Sparrowfoot". "I accidentally fell asleep in a fairy circle back in Implausible Ireland and the Fairy Queen put a spell on me. But now you've broken it."

"Why didn't you tell me? I would have kissed you sooner!"

"I couldn't. That's in the Rule Book too."

"I'm going to have to have a talk with Emily the next time I run into her."

A small crowd was starting to gather to gawk at Barb and the naked DDL-lookalike.

"We'd better go. Hey haven't you seen a naked celebrity before!" Barb barked at the crowd. "Move along! Move along!"

Daniel gratefully wrapped Barb's rich velvet cape around himself. As they walked outside into the howling wind, a frozen Lottie posed immobile, peering in the window at the slowly turning rotisserie chickens. Looks like they forgot to bring in one of the summer sale mannequins, Daniel thought to himself as he hailed a taxi.

They sped away towards the Interglacial Hotel where a hot bath and a fresh set of clothes awaited him. Although Barb suspected he would not need the clothes till tomorrow ...

13

THE STUNNED MULLET DUDE RANCH

 UNEARTHLY EMILY

9 December 1998

Meanwhile back at the ranch. What ranch? You ask. Well, don't interrupt and I'll tell you. Ahem... as I was saying, meanwhile back at the ranch Donna, Tammie, Emily and Tess were sitting around the lodge playing poker and drinking some of Emily's spectacular coffee concoctions.

"Can you believe Barb's wandering around a supermarket right about now? I'll take two."

Donna passed Tammie two cards. "I know! She's reformed and all, but I question her Siegfried loyalty just a tad. She REALLY likes 'DDL' if you ask me. I'll hold."

Tess guarded her cards close to her chest.

"You know I was thinking the same thing. But we're all guilty of other passions aren't we?" Donna replied.

"That's true. I'll take four, please." Emily tossed four cards on the table.

Donna passed Emily four new cards. "Dealer holds." Donna waited for Tammie to make the next move.

"You know that weirdo Her Schumm only gave Siegfried one week to be a hero." Tammie said as she threw two chips in the pot.

"He has been dragged all over the place, hasn't he? I'll see the two and raise you one." Tess added a chip to the pot.

Just then Siegfried walked into the room with an ice pack on his forehead.

Emily saw him first. "How's the head?"

"Ach, it's killing me I've been hallucinating for hours. For a while there I was on an airplane headed for some island. I have to be more careful on Friesians, I forget how spirited they are. Or it could have been the Bananas Foster I ate for dessert."

"It wouldn't have happened if (Inse) hadn't scared the horse half to death." Tammie replied, trying to sneak a look at Tess's cards.

Siegfried frowned. "Where's Lottie?"

The women looked around. "Come to think of it none of us know."

Siegfried looked worried. "You mean she could still be out in the cold? Freezing in that howling blizzard? I must go and find her! I still haven't read her script!"

He grabbed his suede coat with lambswool collar and dashed for the door. In his haste, he didn't shut it all the way and snow swirled about on the wooden floor.

Diana, Tess, Emily and Tammie sat silently watching the door for a moment. They simultaneously jumped up with raised hands and did a group Hi-Five "YES! Now we can get on with the game!"

Donna walked over and closed the door. She shivered as she headed back to the poker table. "I only hope Barb remembered to give Lottie that velvet cape. I'd hate to think she was outside in this weather wearing that tacky bikini…"

ORIGINAL BARB
10 December 1998
Ooh, yum.

ORIGINAL CONNIE
10 December 1998
Something's got me wondering … if Siegfried finds Lottie in the blizzard, assuming she is still alive, and he gives her his suede coat with the lambswool collar, is she going to lose it like she did the other one he has already given her in a previous episode? Or is Lottie a masochist who would rather stand around in blizzards wearing a teeny-weeny gold bikini than accept Siegfried's nice warm coat? Why am I worrying about this? Haven't I got something better to do? (No … as it's about 110 degrees Fahrenheit outdoors, I'll stay inside and look at silly websites instead.)

ORIGINAL BARB
10 December 1998
This site's got you hooked, eh Connie? Happens to the best of us, eventually.

Something's got ME wondering. Is Siegfried actually on an aeroplane dreaming about Iceland or is he in Iceland having just finished a hallucination about being on a plane dreaming about Iceland?

UNEARTHLY BARB
10 December 1998

Barb knows full well that Tinfingers was lying to her, back there in the Fish Department of the Snoring Squid Supermarket.

Although not renowned for her astuteness, she is not stupid enough to believe he is the original Daniel de Licious-lookalike cursed by some leprechaun's spell and now returned to his former masculine glory. After all, she left the real one back on Planet Splinge.

Why then is she cavorting in the Interglacial with this re-modelled misfit? Well, wouldn't any hot-blooded babe, if he looked exactly like six feet two of DDL, right down to the sculpted cheekbones, the taut musculature and the long black hair falling softly across the broad, strong shoulders? Who cares what kind of personality is living in a body like that?

Besides, she has a suspicion that Emily the Irish Fairy Queen is going to slyly remove this likeness in a forthcoming chapter, so she's determined to make the most of this DDL effigy before he morphs back into a lopsided, drooling excuse for a henchman.

UNEARTHLY BARB

10 December 1998

SCENE CHANGE: Back in the cosy warmth of Inauthentic Iceland's famous Stunned Mullet Dude Ranch, Connie had joined the poker game and the players were placing bets.

"I'll lay odds," said Donna energetically, "someone will mention aliens, alien artefacts, magic spells or something else supernatural within the next five episodes of TOATS."

"Nah!" Emily demurred. "We've gone past all that stuff. We're moving towards realism. I can feel it in the air!"

"That's not realism in the air, that's frost," said Tess, swigging on another bottle of vodka to keep out the cold, "And by the way, what's SHE doing here?" Tess pointed accusingly at Tammie. "I thought she floated down the river as a direct result of never contributing to TOATS any more!"

Tammie started guiltily. "I just sneaked back to see what was happening," she mumbled, departing in a hurry.

"TOATS Rule Book on Etiquette, Rule 49.164," stated Tess, "You get written out if you don't write in."

Just then the door banged open and Juliana entered in a swirl of snow. Icicles were hanging like crystal chandeliers from her eyebrows.

"It's cool out there!" she understated, stamping her feet and blowing on her fingers. "Oh good, an empty seat."

Queen Juliana of the Latter-Day Vikings settled into Tammie's recently vacated chair, doffed her horned helmet and grabbed a spare bottle of vodka. "Who's that?" Juliana demanded, staring flintily at Connie.

"She's here on probation," silkily smiled Donna. Donna was feeling secure in the knowledge that as the creator of the entire TOATS SubUniverse she could never be written off. Connie adjusted her Nicolas Birdhouse charm bracelet, fanned out her hand of cards and prepared to get back to some serious poker.

We now leave our heroines to their gambling, swigging and cavorting while we swing to another SCENE CHANGE.

UNEARTHLY BARB
11 December 1998

Back to Siegfried. Yes, Siegfried—remember him? Our idol, our heart's desire, our reason for visiting here in the first place? "Where is he now?" I hear you cry.

He's out in a blizzard looking for Lottie, who's been frozen solid outside the Snoring Squid Supermarket, wearing only a gold bikini. She lost the first jacket Siegfried gave her because she thought it was too precious to be exposed to the biting air of Inauthentic Iceland. There stands true fan. Or at least— there STOOD a true fan. Lottie no longer adorns the front of the supermarket because she has been carted away on a sled by the mayor and the town councillors.

Siegfried arrived at the spot and was aghast to find no Lottie. A be-shawled and cod-stinking passer-by informed him of her whereabouts. "Erb ge-flergen gerder der-en," said this local villager, wrapped to the gills in seal-fur. Translated from the original Inauthentic Icelandic, this meant "They've taken her to the museum."

And this was indeed a fact—it had occurred to the mayor that such a perfectly cryogenically frozen specimen of gorgeous babe-hood ought to be placed on display at the local museum. For security reasons, the frozen Lottie had been enclosed in a gigantic glass jar with a tight-fitting lid, which sat on a pedestal, perpetually guarded by six giant tarantulas. Now, don't tell me you've guessed what's going to happen next!

Yes, our hero Siegfried arrived waving his suede coat with lambswool collar. He saw the delectable Lottie in distress, cryogenically frozen inside a glass jar.

With alacrity and a good deal of bravery he approached the six tarantulas, flapping the suede coat with lambswool collar as though it were a red cape before six hairy bulls. The spiders charged, Siegfried deftly stepped aside and the spiders, driven by momentum, rushed headlong into the Egyptian exhibit next door. Swiftly, before they could change direction, Siegfried leapt lightly onto the pedestal and seized the lid of the gargantuan jar. It refused to budge at first, but with an almost superhuman effort, he gripped it hard with his lean, long hands and gave a stupendous heave.

The lid budged. The strain was beginning to show on Siegfried's face, but he did not give in. Panting, he continued to pull hard at the lid until at last it turned fully and unscrewed. Throwing the lid off, Siegfried fished out the petrified girl, her skin as pale as alabaster (for want of a better cliché). He took her in the warm sweatiness of his arms and kissed her hotly. Needless to say, his kiss was so passionate it melted the ice and Lottie woke up to find herself in her hero's embrace.

And he IS a hero! He has passed the hero test!

"What about the spiders?" I hear you cry. "He didn't kill them!"

"Ah," I respond wisely, "That is because a true hero doesn't actually kill them, he takes them outside with extraordinary tenderness and releases them in the (preferably the neighbor's) garden."

Siegfried wrapped Lottie in his suede coat with lambswool collar and asked her to marry him. (She said yes—of course—what else would she say? Come on, it's time to get realistic.) So they became betrothed and Lottie is no longer Lottie the Loser.

NOTE: According to the TOATS Rule Book, you can get engaged as many times as you like but you cannot actually get married in TOATS. The institution of marriage is too solemn and serious and (did someone say boring?) for a saga such as this—besides, Rule 15.765 states that every character has to be single.

MEANWHILE, somewhere in the Interglacial Hotel, Barb is getting writer's cramp. Time to stop and turn to other exploits . . .

UNEARTHLY EMILY
11 December 1998

Emily, feeling slightly dizzy from the Irish coffees she'd been drinking, excused herself from the poker game at the Stunned Mullet Dude Ranch and headed upstairs. Out of sight, she locked her bedroom door and started to pace the floor.

"How perceptive Barb is," she cursed. She stopped in front of a full-length mirror framed in fish hooks and reels.

Her true self appeared in the glass. The Irish Fairy Queen contemplated her next move. *Obviously Barb is smarter than I thought . . . my realism ploy isn't working and that Connie person . . . she keeps asking questions. I can't believe she's read TOATS all the way through and remembers the other coat incident! I'll have to be more careful. Maybe if I distract her with a Nic look-alike . . .*

. . . Meanwhile somewhere in Implausible Ireland . . . the real Emily is bound and gagged in an old Irish castle struggling against her restraints as a bored elfin guard drinks morphing potion after morphing potion asking, "What about this one?" Poof! "Ok, Ok, how about this one?" . . .

UNEARTHLY BARB

11 December 1998

Back in the overheated gaming-room of the Stunned Mullet Dude Ranch with its cowboy Icelandic ambience of timber-lined walls, fireplace the size of a pizza oven and a stuffed swordfish over the mantelpiece, Donna tapped the side of her nose with a knowing wink.

"Told you," she said sagely to the other gambling females sitting around the table. "Not an episode has gone by without someone mentioning the supernatural." She sighed. "TOATS just can't seem to Get Real."

"Whadya mean?" demanded (Insert Your Name Here) from under the table.

"Emily's just gone upstairs and turned into the Fairy Queen or something," replied Donna, "which means that everybody owes me fifty bucks."

(P.S. That's $50 Australian, which is equivalent to about four cents in US$)

ORIGINAL LOTTIE
13 December 1998

Hurry up, Donna—I've got all these ideas for another TOATS episode churning around in my brain (even though it's difficult imagining Iceland when we're experiencing one of the hottest Decembers in living memory) . . . but I'll try to be patient and wait for your instalment.

In occasional spare moments I'm working on an illustration for TOATS as well, but I'm finding Siegfried about the hardest person in the world to draw—so apologies (in advance) if it looks nothing like him!! By the way—has anyone any news about NEW Siegfried films? How long can we keep playing our old videos before they disintegrate?

ORIGINAL DONNA
14 December 1998

RE: "Is Siegfried actually on an aeroplane dreaming about Iceland or is he in Iceland having just finished a hallucination about being on a plane dreaming about Iceland?" . . . and if he's on a plane dreaming about Iceland, does his heroic rescue of Lottie count, or are we still ticking away at Herr Schumm's countdown??

UNEARTHLY DONNA
15 December 1998

When we last saw our Hero, a euphoric Lottie was seated behind him on the proud back of the magnificent Friesian stallion Brian. As they galloped along her brain was pleasantly numbed by the memory of his kiss (Siegfried's, not Brian's)

[Ed's NOTE: he did NOT turn into a frog/toad (trog? froad?) after that kiss!]

And now . . . Lottie's contented stupor was rudely interrupted as Siegfried drew their mount to a halt, listening.

"What is it?" mumbled Lottie, her mind fogged by reverie.

"Sshh . . . I hear zomezing . . ."

Lottie forced herself upright, emulating something like concentration. "I don't," she replied, settling down and molding herself contentedly against Siegfried's back. "Except for your heart, beating, " she mooned senselessly.

"Klemmen Sie Ihre Lippen," shushed Our Hero. "It is coming closer!"

As the rumbling drone became a thunderous roar in his ears, Siegfried wildly searched the skies, the horizon—"Vat iz it?! Nossing is zere!" he shouted in growing frustration—but his surroundings were becoming less distinct, and Lottie's voice, crying "No! no! You hear nuss-ing! noooooo..!! You haven't read my scriiiiiiiiipt!!" began to fade as the rumbling sound grew ever louder, closing in and surrounding him, until . . .

. . . he opened his eyes amidst the deafening roar of an Air Banana passenger compartment.

"Mein Gott! Ein was für Traum!"[16] he babelfished, attempting to stretch his cramped limbs in the child-sized air banana seat. Disturbed by the intensity of his dream and an uncomfortably over-full bladder, he headed to the head, seeking a place to hide and compose himself. Ominous sounds from behind the restroom's bead curtain suggested it may be some time before the air on the other side became fit to breathe.

---

16 My God! What a dream!

"Damn," he muttered, reluctant to return to his painful seat. Suddenly recalling the dazzlingly attractive, shy young woman he'd met on the plane earlier, he wandered instead down the aisle to her location. *I hope she won't be annoyed by my interrupting her,* he thought.

"Entschuldigen Sie mich junge Dame[17]—" he said aloud as he reached her seat, but stopped abruptly as he found himself gazing down into the face of a horribly ancient and ugly woman. The crone smiled at him toothlessly and mouthed something unintelligible. Her greasy, frizzled hair was tied back in a severe bun and she had not recently bathed. The aroma of long-dead cod wafted from her clothing, reminding Siegfried forcefully of his recent nocturnal trip to Inauthentic Iceland.

Her mumbling became clearer, "Stellen Sie sich in meinem Honigtopf vor[18] . . . " she was crowing, her breath filling his nostrils with the stench of decomposing flounder.

Horrified, Siegfried hurriedly backed away, up the aisle back toward the bathroom. But it was still extremely occupied.

I have to get out of here, he thought desperately. *But vat has become of Barb? Vas she too only a dream? I must find her. She vas so . . . compelling.*

With a sigh, and resolving never to opt for a cheap and easy way out of a TOATS predicament again, Siegfried entered the cockpit—just in time to see the last of the Air Banana crew exiting through the open hatch. The man who happened

---

17 Excuse me, young lady
18 Imagine yourself in my honeypot.

to be the pilot (you could tell by his pointy head) shrugged and said "Ick beh <snort> hic popo"—which of course means "Time to disembark" in Bananawana. He flicked a finger briefly at an open chest on the floor of the cabin and leapt from the plane.

Siegfried rushed to peer into the open chest, which contained three large rubber bands, a single parachute, and a lump of something unidentifiable.

"Männlicher Welpe des weiblichen Hundes!![19]" cried the hero, with less than a week to save himself from the clutches of Herr Schumm. Siegfried's gaze shifted rapidly from the hatchway, to the single parachute, to the array of flashing lights, dials, switches, gauges, cardboard and duct tape of the control panel, then back again to the parachute. "No!! I can not leave Barb behind to perish!" He sat down in the pilot's seat, leaving everyone wondering why Donna's chapters always involve air disasters . . .

UnEarthly Lottie **UNEARTHLY LOTTIE**
15 December 1998
After Siegfried's short snooze in the Icelandic snow (during which he entered the parallel world of Bananawana), he leapt up, thankful it was all another nightmare, vaulted back onto his horse Brian, lifted Lottie in his strong, jar-opening arms and galloped back through the swirling snowflakes.

Lottie thought that at any moment she would wake up and find herself on a plane bound for Bananawana, but no . . . here

---

19 Male dog of female dog!

they are, arrived at the Stunned Mullet. As Siegfried carried Lottie inside, she had eyes only for him and so completely missed the ghastly green-tinged sneers on the faces of Emily, Donna, Juliana and Tess , and the look of horror on the face of her sister, Connie.

Nic Birdhouse put his face in at the door. "Here you are, Connie! Been looking for you everywhere. We were headed for the airport, remember? Then you vanished and now I find you playing poker. Come on."

Connie headed for the door with a last glance at her demented sister. "I hope you know what you're doing!"

"Oh yes", breathed Lottie. "We're getting married . . . we're going to the little church down the lane, by the birch grove. Siegfried in black—he looks so nice in black, don't you think— will ride big black Brian and I'll sit behind him, all in purest white, with a train so long it will trail behind us through the snow. And the birds will sing and the birch trees sigh in a gentle breeze under a cloudless sky. Then he'll carry me down to the ocean and our honeymoon ship will be there, anchored and restless in the bay—a huge sailing ship with a sleek black and white hull. She'll spread her dark canvas wings to the wind . . . "

"Lottie, please; calm down," said Siegfried, but Lottie waffled on, oblivious of Tess sticking a finger down her throat and pulling faces, and the other women looking really ill.

"We'll sail with dolphins leaping in our bow-wave and albatrosses soaring majestically above our long wake as it stretches away behind us across all the oceans of the world. And then off Cape Horn, as the seas tower, wind-lashed, around us, we'll embrace—passionately, violently—while the wind shrieks in the rigging and our strong ship shudders as the waves crash across her steel hull . . . "

A loud voice butted in on Lottie's ecstasy. "You ain't goin' nowhere just yet."

A huge man in a ten-gallon hat, puffing away on a cigar and with hundred-dollar bills falling out of his bulging pockets, had just walked in, grinning broadly. "I've read yer script, girl, and I love it! I'm ready to make you an offer, right here and now; five million bucks. If that's not enough, double it . . . treble it! As for you, Siegfried, this is the role of a lifetime; ya might as well start writin' yer Best Actor Academy Award speech right now!"

Lottie gaped, lost for words; all her fairytales had suddenly come true. If it were not for Siegfried's heroic arms enfolding her still, she'd probably have fallen over and died.

"Well, here's m' check book—how 'bout I jus' write ya out a blank one and ya can fill in the amount yerself. What's yer name . . . Emily what?"

"Emily?" said Lottie. "My name's not Emily."

Emily's ears pricked up and she strolled over with the beginnings of a gloat on her face.

"Oh, must'a got the wrong girl," said the big producer. "Where's Emily?"

"Here I am," said Emily, her gloat now fully formed. "A blank check will be fine—just make it out to Emily Fairy Queen."

"Look Lottie," said Siegfried, withdrawing his heroic arms, "I wouldn't like you to think I've changed my mind about this wedding, but how about we wait till after Emily's film is made? That'll give us plenty of time to think about it, eh?" He gave her a gently encouraging pat on the shoulder, which knocked her senseless to the floor, then turned and followed Emily and the big man out to discuss business.

Outside the door he stopped by some quivering snow-covered shrubbery and looked in. "Hello Tammie; I'm glad you're still around. I was worried when I saw you drifting out to sea."

"Ssh, don't tell anyone I'm here—I'm not supposed to be."

"I won't tell," he said, chivalrously kissing her icy little hand. "You know, it's easy to get back in . . . just a sentence or two . . . I miss you."

Suddenly a vast horde of Vulgarian sailors appeared on the horizon. The horde paused momentarily then came stampeding down the hill, throwing up huge clouds of snow from countless hob-nailed boots, its collective hot breath misting the air for miles around. As one, the sailors spotted Tess staggering from the Stunned Mullet.

"Tessss! Tessss!" they cried (a piercing, haunting cry—never to be forgotten); "Ve need you! You must help us make child!"

"Sure fellas. No worries," said Tess as they picked her up and carried her off. Her gleeful giggles—interspersed with hiccups —could just be heard above the mighty thunder of their boots crunching away through the snow.

(Unfortunately for Tess, the Vulgarians are in the middle of a really absorbing and difficult jigsaw puzzle of a Bananawanan child. They just didn't know the English word for "jigsaw".)

14

IMPLAUSIBLE IRELAND

ORIGINAL BARB
16 December 1998

'Twas a night before Christmas. I dialled up the Net,
And sent a few emails—to whom, I forget.
As usual I ended up (to my delight),
At THE One And Only Herr P. Hinkelheimer Web Site.
A heart-stopping vision arrived on my screen—
A hero whose eyes had an amethyst gleam.
I stared at the graphics as you would stare too.
Those cheekbones like sculpture! That gaze, icy blue!
A shiver ran through me on sighting that face—
Charisma was oozing all over the place.
But next to the old Feedback Page I moved on,

To see what had happened while I had been gone.
(For TOATS is a milestone in literature,
Destined to be showered with praises, be sure.)
Our Emily had written a new episode
In which Daniel D-L. turns into a toad.
Or maybe it's really the other way round—
Things get quite confusing in TOATS, I have found.
When Tammie and Juliana had added a word
The plot was becoming completely absurd.
We'd like some more authors to make it complete,
So newbies, feel welcome—please don't get
cold feet!!!!
Sit down to your keyboard and sort out this mess—
It's fun to be writing for TOATS, I confess!
I'm off now to visit the babelfish site.
To all, "Frohe Weihnachten," and a good night!

 ORIGINAL BARB
16 December 1998
Great chapters Donna and Lottie! BTW Emily, I
meant to say I loved your last episode and laughed
myself silly, particularly at the last line.

 ORIGINAL CONNIE
16 December 1998
Barb, just LOVE your poem! You really are quite
the cleverest person I have ever met. Loved your
episodes Lottie and Donna . . . I'm thinking, I'm thinking . . .
it's a confidence thing with me, I just don't think I can do it . .
. one of these days I'll just go for it anyway . . . it'll be like me

changing the car wheel the other day. I didn't think I could do it, but I sure felt good when I did! Is that what it's like? I could become another world famous TOATS author!

By the way, Lottie told me that the bit about the Vulgarian sailors calling out for Tess to "Help them make child" is true! It actually happened while they were on a Vulgarian sailing ship, and it was shouted right down the deck for all & sundry to hear . . . what a blast!

ORIGINAL DONNA
16 December 1998
Barb your poem is wonderful, perfect. (applause, applause). I think it should be included in the story!

UNEARTHLY BARB
16 December 1998
Little do Siegfried and the Hollywood producer suspect, but the Emily with whom they are discussing business outside the Stunned Mullet Dude Ranch in temperatures of 45 degrees below zero is not the Real Emily. She is in fact, the Irish Fairy Queen in disguise.
This is why, while the two men are shivering, she is nonchalantly clad in a slinky, ankle-length off-the-shoulder Verbose® number, jade green to set off her long chestnut hair and emerald tiara.

While this is happening (note the clever dodge around the word "meanwhile"), The Fairy Queen suddenly remembers that Barb is having a fantastic time at the Reykjavik Interglacial Hotel® with Tinfingers, who is disguised as

Daniel de Licious-as-Sparrowfoot. With a snap of her pretty fingers, the F.Q. returns Tinfingers (at long distance) to his previous shape. Her supernatural hearing detects a faint and far-off scream from the direction of the Reykjavik Interglacial Hotel®.

The F.Q., still disguised as Emily, links her smooth, warm arms through the arms of Siegfried and the Hollywood producer. She smiles seductively up at Siegfried. Having ruined Barb's day (Licious), Lottie's wedding plans and the Real Emily's physical comfort (as you may recall, she has been lying bound and gagged in an old Irish castle watching a bored elfin guard drink morphing potion after morphing potion), the F.Q. is feeling rather pleased with herself.

However, unbeknownst to the F. Q., the bored elfin guard has finally struck on the right morphing potion. In the guise of Gabriel Yearn, he has freed Emily and run off with her to a neighbouring old Irish edifice, Ballykissmefoot Castle, which enjoys the latest amenities including central heating and Guinness on tap.

A small bell tinkled in the F.Q.'s left ear. She snatched her magic pager out of her pocket and consulted it, a frown furrowing her Emily-like features. The message, written in light, flowed across the LED display. A jealous elfin guard in Implausible Ireland had just informed the F.Q. of what had happened.

"Gotta go to Implausible Ireland," the F.Q. interrupted the discussion. She whistled for a taxi and one appeared instantly out of the snowbound landscape. It was bright yellow, with "TOATS Taxi Service" printed (redundantly) on the side and a complicated radar apparatus adorning the roof.

"Not the TOATS Taxi Service!" cried the F.Q. angrily, "I want a decent cab and a believable driver, who will get us to the airport without any disturbing detours."

A New York cab appeared.

The F.Q. stamped her foot. "You idiot!" she screamed at the air, "I said—"

The two taxis roared off into the distance and disappeared under a snowdrift. A large golden pumpkin on skis materialised, drawn by six white horses. It had "Cinderella" painted on the side. The F.Q. ripped out a handful of her own hair. The coach-sleigh quivered in fear and started to turn vaguely transparent.

"No, leave it here!" screeched the F.Q. in exasperation. "That'll do!" To Siegfried and the Hollywood film producer she said, "Quick, get in, you two. We're off to the airport. If we hurry we'll be in time to catch the same plane as Nicolas Birdhouse and that Connie person.

"No, wait!" cried Siegfried. He was distinctly suspicious of the F.Q. He had never seen Emily acting like this. "I'm not coming unless Lottie comes too," he declared determinedly.

"Oh, all right," muttered the F.Q. bundling the senseless Lottie into the pumpkin coach. "If you insist."

"Don't leave us behind!" shouted Donna, Juliana and the insane (Insert Your Name Here). Rudely, the F.Q. ignored them.

The rat-like coachman whipped up the horses and the coach-sleigh was off, sliding swiftly over the sugary snow on its golden runners, heading for Reykjavik airport. As it passed out of sight, the TOATS Taxi turned up again and skidded to a halt, ever hopeful of a fare. (A TOATS Taxi driver never gives up.)

Seeing the cab, Donna and Juliana looked at one another.

"Do we dare?" asked Donna in trepidation, remembering the last time they took a ride in a TOATS Taxi.

"Sure we do!" yelled Juliana, throwing open the door and jumping in.

Donna and (Insert Your Name Here) crammed themselves in alongside her. With a scream of bald tires and a rattle of chains the TOATS taxi surged out across the icy sludge in pursuit of everyone else. On the way to the airport it stopped at the Reykjavik Interglacial Hotel to pick up Barb and her misshapen henchman, Tinfingers.

They all reached the airport okay, flew to Implausible Ireland without mishap and landed safely on the private airstrip of Ballykissmefoot Castle. Everyone immediately headed off towards the Hard Shamrock Cafe, where the irate Fairy Queen, still disguised as Emily, prepared to confront the Real Emily and her mutinous elfin guard who looked exactly like Gabriel Yearn.

What will happen next?

15

THE HARD SHAMROCK CAFÉ

Original Emily

ORIGINAL EMILY
17 December 1998
THANK YOU Barb! Gabriel is the perfect Christmas present. Too bad it's TOATS and we all know what that means… it won't last more than a couple of episodes, if that. But it's the thought that counts! The AODHI (Admirers of Dark Haired Irishmen) lives on!
I also loved the poem.

So there I was, working under three deadlines, little sleep over the past couple of days thinking to myself, "I need to see if anyone's posted a TOATS episode". I innocently wander to the Feedback Page see a bunch of postings —I scroll down and start to read… Suddenly I am laughing uncontrollably and Susan is looking at me like I've totally lost my mind. I now realize that TOATS needs a warning label if you are at work.

UNEARTHLY EMILY

17 December 1998

Emily (really the Fairy Queen) ordered another overpriced appetizer at the Hard Shamrock Café. *What to do, what to do? But whatever I do—will Barb spoil it again? Or will someone else?* She methodically tapped her fingers on the table to a tune from *Quiverdance®*. Looking around, she noticed a TOATS Rule Book on Etiquette was poking out of Barb's carryon bag.

Quickly, she assessed everyone's whereabouts. Lottie was trying to convince the Hollywood film producer her script was much more interesting than Emily's, while Siegfried was ordering another Guinebeer Stout®. Juliana and Donna were admiring the Me2® Gravel and Crumb Display and Tess was nowhere to be seen. Off in a quiet corner Connie was snuggling with Nic and (Inse) was flirting with the busboy.

Tinfingers was trying to convince Barb he was really DDL. "Ok remember this line?" he was saying. "'You're strong. You stay alive. I will find you . . . no matter how long it takes, no matter how far . . . '" Barb regarded him disbelievingly over her Irish coffee and sighed.

Emily (The FQ) seized her opportunity and grabbed the book. Hurriedly she flipped through the pages until she reached the chapter on Implausible Ireland, then began to read the introduction.

"Inhabitants: Some indigenous life, but mostly Germanic, American, and Australian tourists. Implausible Ireland is a small island with a population of roughly 3.2 million, and by an extraordinary coincidence, a landmass of 32 thousand square miles. Further extending the disbelief, is that it's divided up into 32 counties.

'Implausible Irish people have no aversions to leaving Implausible Ireland since the farther away they get the more Implausibly Irish they become. This has caused the situation where the external population of Implausible Ireland seems to go into the hundreds of millions, as opposed to the previously stated internal population. (However, this does make for big St. Hat-trick's day celebrations on the 17th of March.)"

"Emily", keeping an eye on the rest of the company, flipped pages and paused to read some more...

"Gourmet Implausible Ireland—From pubs to palaces, Implausible Ireland is a gourmet's odyssey. Journey into the heart of Implausible Ireland. Walk the countryside in search of mushrooms, talk to the local cheesemakers, learn the ancient process of smoking salmon, tour the herb gardens...."

Who writes this drivel! Where is the pub directory?! Where is the chapter on Fairies! "Emily" turned a page and the next chapter was, "Alcohol in Implausible Ireland—A Way of Life."

She smiled. This was more like it! "Implausible Ireland is famous for its pubs. Anyone who looks the least bit alive will be dragged into a friendly conversation with at least one surrounding table of people. The only way to prevent this is to become drunker than them, and hence not care what happens."

She turned the page, which contained a footnote: "In general, any pub you happen to walk into will be friendly, so long as it is not called the Hard Shamrock Café or the Faud Shaughran (Stray Sod). The latter are tourist traps, and places to send people if they wish to end it all quickly."

"Emily" faked a sneeze. "Ahhh ... AhhhAhhh...Chooooo!" while simultaneously ripping this very important piece of information from the book.

"Gesundheit!" Siegfried replied. Startled, "Emily" quickly slipped the book back in Barb's bag.

"Danke," she returned.

Siegfried went back to his conversation with the Hollywood producer and Lottie. Then he suddenly realized that "Emily" had spoken her first German word in this whole story!

"Vait a minute!" He turned around, but "Emily" was gone. "Did anyone see vere Emily vent?"

ORIGINAL EMILY
17December 1998
Connie, once you start writing you realize you may need therapy but counsellors usually want you to keep a journal, so in a way this IS therapy and it's free. Besides TOATS is so much fun. Go ahead give it a whirl even if it's only a couple of lines. We're waiting!

ORIGINAL BARB
19 December 1998
Donna—glad you liked the poem—please feel free to include it in the story or anywhere else you see fit :)
Nice chapter on Ireland, Emily!

Connie, (encourage, encourage), you could maybe start contributing to TOATS with a brief description of what everyone is wearing and how their hair is done. That would be a good way to "break the ice".

Note from TOATS Rule Book: costumes (in general) are usually exotic and/or sophisticated, and/or barbarian, and/or freakish and above all, sexy. Only the "sexy" adjective applies to Siegfried, who looks so great simply in jeans and a white or black T-shirt and does not have to look flamboyant to melt our hearts.

Since you're still in TOATS, snogging in the Hard Shamrock Cafe with Nic, it seems you owe us a chapter (pressure, pressure).

ORIGINAL EMILY

19 December 1998

A little background always helps . . . I had an idea. Actually more than one, but I'll only burden you with one of them.

Does anyone know what episode we're on? I mean if we reach the 100th mark we should create a commemorative album for the art page with those classic hits: "Omelette or Mixed Grill?" or who could ever forget Nigel's cover of Lionel Ritchie's "You Look So Beautiful . . . To Me" and "Crocodile Rock". How about Tammie's classic hit "I left my chapter in San Francisco" but wait there's more! Tess singing "99 Bottles" or Lottie singing "Baby, It's Cold Outside" . . . one more, hmmm . . . Emily singing "If You Believe in Fairies, Then Clap Your Hands."

UNEARTHLY BARB

Christmas Special, 21 December 1998

"Did anyone see vere Emily vent?" asked Siegfried again, raising his voice. Outside the antique mullioned windows of the Hard Shamrock Café, "Emily" returned to her natural shape—that of the Irish Fairy Queen. Elfin were her features, her shamrock-green eyes upswept at the outer corners, her small nose tilted roguishly. Wildflowers were entwined through the carefree tangles of her hair.

Her gown was woven from forest leaves, owl's feathers and moonlight.

Springing upon a Faerie Steed she galloped away in the direction of Ballykissmefoot Castle to confront the rebellious elfin guard who had disobeyed her orders and liberated the Real Emily from captivity.

Sparks flew, struck from the glinting hooves of the eldritch horse. They burned like incandescent needles into the snow. Snow, you ask? But we left Inauthentic Iceland behind . . . Yes, (I reply), but it is winter in Implausible Ireland, and the weather's obviously building up towards a white Christmas.

Glittering white powderings, like sugar-crystals, dust the gently sloping fields and the thatched rooves of the emerald isle. The village ponds are starting to freeze over, capturing dark vistas of snow-laden clouds beneath their mirrored panes. Scarlet as holly-berries glow the frost-bitten noses of the inhabitants, who have been doing some hard drinking to keep out the cold.

In the cosy warmth of the Hard Shamrock Cafe, with its silver plastic Christmas tree and its shady characters lurking in the corners, the electric glare of fairy lights illuminated a postcard from Australia which someone had pinned to the wall. Siegfried gazed reflectively at it. It depicted a sunny beach heaped with acres of white sand. Bronze-tinted svelte babes and iron-men in skimpy swimsuits were sunbathing around a tinsel-bedecked pine tree stuck in the sand.

"Christmas in Oz" read the caption.

"Hmm," said Siegfried, his eyes lighting up, but before he could elaborate further, Lottie tapped him on the shoulder.

"Liebling," she said, her voice syrupy with emotion, "Emily seems to have walked out on the film deal. This means we won't have to postpone our wedding!"

"What?" roared the Hollywood film producer (Author's incidental note: will someone please think of a name for this guy?), "Emily's walked out?" he blared. "I must go get her back!"

He grabbed his hat (or what he thought was his hat—in his haste he accidentally picked up a red and white Santa cap which has been left lying around) and burst out the cafe door like a frantic bull through a gate. His words drifted back over his shoulder—"It will be easy to follow her trail in the snow . . ."

Donna and Juliana peered out of the cafe window.

"Looks as though that Hollywood guy is making for that old castle on the hill," said Juliana with a shrug.

Something bright yellow shot past the window and pulled up by the door with a squeal of brakes and a rattle of chains. A short, balding figure stepped out of the TOATS Taxi and brushed off the sleeves of its smart business suit.

"Damn, it's that awful Herr Schumm!" cried Donna, ducking behind the Christmas tree. Connie and Nic escaped out the back door.

Barb gave Tinfingers a hard shove and he collided with (Inse) in the middle of the floor. As soon as these two clapped eyes on each other it was love at first sight. They began kissing under the mistletoe.

Barb breathed a sigh of relief and started flirting with the busboy, oblivious to the fact that Herr Schumm had entered the Hard Shamrock Cafe, very businesslike, flicking open his notebook and tapping his teeth with his pencil.

"Now then, Herr Hinkelheimer," bleated Herr Schumm, "haf you proved yourself a hero? Or are you going to be written right out of this saga?"

Lottie dramatically flung herself between Siegfried and the boring bureaucrat. Rapidly, the words tumbling from her mouth, she began explaining Siegfried's heroic deeds with the hard-to-open jar and the six giant tarantulas. "And we are going to be married!" she concluded, wide-eyed and breathless.

Herr Schumm scribbled notes in his black book.

"You know," said Juliana in a loud voice, "I think a really heroic deed would be to throw out that geek in the penguin suit."

"An excellent suggestion," said Siegfried, picking up Herr Schumm and tossing him bodily through the door (fortunately open), out into the snow.

Gallantly, Siegfried then ordered Irish Stew and Christmas pudding all round, as nobody had eaten anything since chapter 15 or thereabouts, and they all sat down to dine, eating quickly before a fight erupted among the shady characters in the corners.

Through the window they saw the Real Emily skiing down Ballykissmefoot Hill, followed by a Gabriel Yearn look-alike. They all raised their glasses towards her in a toast—"Merry Christmas Emily! Merry Christmas to all!"

UNEARTHLY LOTTIE

28 December 1998

In a rare fit of practicality (brought on by the food) Barb decided they'd better all find somewhere to stay the night.

"A nice hotel . . ." suggested Donna.

"No, no", interrupted Lottie, "let's find a romantic little Bed & Breakfast."

The sly barman pricked up his pointy ears. "I know just the place; you'll love it. Mary O'Really?'s B & B at Ballykildamessenger Hall—a mile or two in the other direction, half way up Ballyeatmeshorts Hill . . . rambling old place . . . can't miss it."

"Sounds perfect," said Siegfried. "Let's go, ladies . . . where's (Inse)?"

"Who cares?" said Donna, Barb and Juliana. They grabbed Siegfried's arms and headed for the door in a crowd of jabbing elbows, slamming the door on Lottie's nose.

Fending off several shady characters, Lottie got the door open again, staggered out into the snow clutching her nose and wobbled along the road after the others. Following a ragged trail of footprints the belles and Siegfried eventually arrived at the hill. At the foot of the slope they found a snow-dusted haystack, from which emerged several pairs of wriggling feet and lots of soft sighs, murmurings, moans and giggles.

"They're my sister's feet; I'd recognise her bunions anywhere," said Lottie, "so I suppose these feet must be Nic's," she added, tickling them with a straw.

"These are (Inse)'s—you can tell by the crocodile tooth-marks and the scalpel scars," said Donna. "So these hairy gnome-feet must belong to Tinfingers."

"These two are easy; they've still got their skis on," said Barb. "Happy Christmas, Emily."

"Go away, Barb," said Emily.

"This looks fun," said Siegfried, "How about we join them Lottie ... du lieber Gott, what happened to your nose?"

"Nothing happened to her nose," snapped Juliana. "It always looks like that."

"Does not," said Lottie. "Anyway, you just wait till I sell my script and can afford a nose job; you won't ... "

"Nose Job?? Sell your script? Ha ha ha," laughed Juliana. "You're a loser, Lottie; that's the only reason we haven't killed you."

"Now, now, ladies . . . " began Siegfried, but Juliana interrupted.

"As for you, you tiresome man, I don't know what I'm doing hanging round here. I must be mad. I've left a perfectly adequate clone back in Inauthentic Iceland—he may be dense, but at least he doesn't criticise."

"Well go back to Inauthentic Iceland then," said Barb. "We won't miss you."

"Yes, and take your insults with you," said Donna. "We won't miss them either, will we?" She gave Siegfried's arm a squeeze and looked up at him, fluttering her eyelashes.

"I've got to experience some of this famous Implausible Irish hospitality first," said Juliana. Effortlessly she sprinted to the hill's summit, where she opened a rickety gate and walked up the path to an ancient sprawling edifice;

the "Ballykildamessenger Hall B & B". Leafless ivy clawed up its crumbling stone walls, wind whistled round its decaying eaves and drifts of soot-blackened snow settled across its sagging slate roof.

Juliana rang the doorbell, which howled like a banshee. By the time the bell was answered the others had caught up with her.

Mrs O'Really? opened the door and looked at the scantily-clad women through narrowed eyes. "Beds? A double and three singles you say? I'll have you know we're God-fearin' folk around here! You women come with me!"

"But what about him . . . he's my fiancé!" warbled Lottie.

"NOT MARRIED THEN?" bellowed Mrs O'Really?. Lottie cringed behind Juliana.

The landlady herded the luscious damsels into a little room with four single beds and slammed the door. The floor sloped badly and all the beds were in the slow process of sliding down towards the small barred window at the lowest part of the room. Judging by the grooves worn in the sludge-green linoleum, they had done this every day for several decades. They were covered in attractive orange chenille bedspreads (over pilled nylon sheets) which clashed nicely with the pink-patterned sixties wallpaper. To complete the happy scene, crucifixes and gilt-framed prints of bleeding hearts and Leonardo's "Last Supper" with glittery bits sprinkled on hung about the walls while a collection of plastic Marys and assorted saints jostled for position on the window ledge.

"Hey, the old bag's locked the door!" cried Juliana, attempting to kick it in whilst hurling abuse (in Icelandic).

UNEARTHLY LOTTIE

28 December 1998

The door flew open once more to reveal Mrs O'Really?, She silenced Juliana with a narrow steely gaze. "You can go enjoy the sights now, but be sure to back by nine. I lock the doors then and if you're not back in time you'll sleep in the snow. Breakfast's at six sharp. If you're not there you miss out. Happy Christmas."

"But where's our friend?" squeaked Barb.

"That man? I sent him packing . . . we don't want his sort round here! Foreigner!!"

"But we're foreigners too," squawked Lottie.

"Not as foreign as him!" snapped Mary O'Really?, holding out a hand; "That'll be seventy-five pounds each, thank you ladies."

"For a ghastly room without a bath?" said Donna. "Anyway, we haven't found a foreign exchange agency open yet, so we can't pay you!"

"Very well," said Mrs O'Really?, "but to make sure you're back here, by nine, with my money, I'm taking a hostage . . . you'll do," she said, grabbing Donna. Donna struggled, but the old woman had arms of steel.

"I'm the Queen of Inauthentic Iceland!" shouted Juliana. "I command you to release her!"

"And I'm the Empress of Bananawana," snapped Mrs O'Really? sarcastically.

"Save me!" screamed Donna as the dreaded Irishwoman dragged her off down a gloomy corridor.

"We'll find Siegfried! He'll save you!" shouted Barb and Lottie as they dashed to the door.

"Why don't we just leave her there?" asked Juliana.

"We can't do that," argued Barb, as they scuttled down the path. "Without her, TOATS will come crashing down around our ears and we'll be marooned here forever . . . what a pity she didn't grab Lottie instead."

Halfway down Ballyeatmeshorts Hill they shot past the haystack, now empty of residents but still steaming.

"Well, why don't we get Nic, or that Gabriel type person, to rescue her," panted Juliana. "They're close by!"

"No!" said Lottie indignantly, "If they want to be heroes they can do it on their own web-sites! This is Siegfried's!"

UNEARTHLY EMILY

28 December 1998

Through the semi-frosted window of the Hard Shamrock Café the real Emily saw the haystack they had occupied moments ago burst into flames. Two men were rolling around in the snow trying to put themselves out.

"Look at that," she remarked. "You know, the short one in the elf suit almost looks like Herr Schumm."

(Inse) and Tinfingers snuggling in the next booth turned around to look. "It is Herr Schumm and that Hollywood Producer!" Tinfingers exclaimed.

Emily felt a slight tug in her stomach "If Herr Schumm is here then Siegfried can't be too far away." She looked at the elfin guard (in the shape of Gabriel Yearn) walking towards her with two steaming cups of wassail, and heaved a deep sigh. "Well, it was fun while it lasted but I should really get back to the others before the Fairy Queen tries anything. Connie, do you know where the girls went?"

"They're headed to the Ballykildamessenger Bed and Breakfast," Connie replied.

Emily slid out of the booth and approached the elf. "Deasmumhnach Mac Aodhagáin, you have been the best faux Gabriel—" She paused to wipe his now spittle-flecked face with her handkerchief, and untangle her tongue— "but the magic is waning and I really have to get back in the story. After all, this is SPH's fanpage."

"I... understand," Des said heartbrokenly in his Irish brogue. Fairy light surrounded him and transformed him back into his true self. "Begorrah, here is somet'in' to be rememberin' me by, me sweet colleen," he said, handing Emily a small velvet pouch. "'Tis a charm to be protectin' ye from da Fairy Queen herself, to be sure."

Emily took the pouch, put it in her pocket and kissed the unpronounceable elf. "Thank you."

Forlornly, her erstwhile lover watched her walk out into the softly falling snow in the direction of Mrs. O'Really?'s run-down B & B where Donna languished as a hostage. How brave Emily was! How beautiful and self-sacrificing!

"Come here often?"

The elfin guard turned to see a cute woodland fairy leaning on the jukebox.

"Well hello there..." he replied, instantly forgetting Emily.

UNEARTHLY EMILY

28 December 1998

Barb, Lottie and Juliana, having scuttled down the slippery path from Mrs. O'Really?'s B & B, were following the indistinct outline of a snow-covered road between leafless blackthorn hedges decorated with icicles.

Siegfried's footprints had been obliterated by a light snowfall, and darkness had fallen, but the courageous femmes fatale optimistically plodded along under the wan light of the stars. The indistinct outline of a road began to climb towards a craggy hill topped by a castle faintly silhouetted against the stars.

Juliana pushed past Lottie. "What are you stopping for! Lead, follow or just get out of the bloody way!"

Lottie, standing in a snowdrift, looked at the castle looming in the distance. "I was just thinking."

Barb started to laugh. "Now, that's a first."

"I'm serious. That castle looks vaguely familiar. Barb, do you still have the TOATS Rule Book?" Lottie asked.

"No, it's back at the Ballykildamessenger B & B."

"Never mind that!" Juliana pulled the hood of her Clawed Alabama® original closer to her face. "This wind is horrible for my complexion. Let's just find Siegfried, visit a foreign exchange booth and get back to the Ballykildamessenger to ransom Donna."

They nodded in agreement and started back up the hill, this time with Juliana striding confidently in the lead. Lottie started humming "Walking in a Winter Wonderland" as the snow crunched under her boots.

16

NEW YEAR'S EVE AT BALLYKISSMEFOOT CASTLE

UNEARTHLY EMILY

28 December 1998

Meanwhile in Ballykissmefoot Castle an ornate goblet was being hurled into a roaring fire. Flames exploded as the contents spill onto the burning logs.

"I will not be made a fool of—do you hear me?" The Fairy Queen picked up another goblet off the dining room table and several of her shadowy minions cowered in the corner of the room. "Troll!"

A large elf entered the room and bowed.

The FQ straightened her many layers of taffeta. "Troll, how could you let that stupid elf get out with Emily?"

"Well . . ." The henchtroll looked down at the floor.

"Well? I should throw you down a well! Now send out some men and find her!" The Fairy Queen raised the goblet and was poised to throw it. "I could just bash your..." She stopped in mid swing. You could almost see the light bulb go on in her head. "Brilliant. Simple genius. Troll, no need to go out. They will all come here on their own."

"How do you plan on doing that, Your Majesty?"

"A New Year's Eve party of course! Those women won't be able to resist bottomless champagne® and Siegfried in a tuxedo. It's perfect!"

Troll smiled. "You are diabolical, Your Supremeness."

"I am, aren't I, Troll. Now there's work to be done! We only have a few days. Call the sprites and arrange a band, then there are the decorations and catering of course; do we have Betsy Bakealot® in the Rotolist®?"

Just then the doorbell played a merry Irish jig. The Fairy Queen looked out of the turret to see a half-frozen Siegfried standing at the door. A smile spread across her elfin face. "Troll, let Mr. Hinkelheimer in if you please. Have him wait in the library."

The FQ waved her arm and was transformed into a stunning blonde beauty with a slight resemblance to a Siegfried P. Hinkelheimer girlfriend now long forgotten in this story. At the same time, all the creatures in the castle instantly became enchanted and looked like typical Irish servants and maids. The fairy Queen checked her reflection in the mirror. Satisfied, she started downstairs to greet her guest.

UNEARTHLY EMILY
28 December 1998

Troll escorted Siegfried into the library. "Madam will be with you shortly."

Siegfried sank into an oversized chair near the fuel-efficient gas fireplace. Presently with a swish of green silk a blonde beauty entered the room, beaming hospitably.

"Welcome to my home Mr. P. Hinkelheimer. My name is Brunhilde O'Doom ... er Dool ... O'Dool."

Siegfried stood and kissed the back of his hostess's hand. "Pleasure to meet you."

"The pleasure will be all mine I assure you," the blonde demurely replied. "What can I do for you?"

"Vell, I vas travelling with some friends of mine only ve ver separated and I could use a place to stay the night."

"Brunhilde" looped her arm through his and led him into the hallway. "But of course! You must stay! I'm throwing a New Year's Party for some friends and I would be delighted if you could attend. I even think we have time to phone Paddy O'Shoulder's Tuxedo Hire. What do you say?"

"I think it's ze best offer I've had in ze past sree or four chapters."

"Marvellous! Trollman will show you to your room."

UNEARTHLY EMILY

31 December 1998

. . . Hours later the sun was starting to rise.

It appeared over the eastern horizon, sending golden rays across the snowbound wastelands where three small figures plodded . . .

"In the meadow we can build a snowman . . ."

"Lottie, stop!" Juliana hurled a snowball at Lottie.

"What? Are we there?" Lottie looked around and saw nothing but snow and stones for miles.

"No, I mean stop singing! I can't concentrate and I think we're lost."

"Lost!" everyone exclaimed in unison.

"I never said I had a good sense of direction!" said Juliana. "Besides as Queen of Inauthentic Iceland I employ people to do things like asking for directions!"

Barb leaned against a standing stone and icily gazed at Juliana, which was easy to do with icicles dangling from her eyelashes. "We've been walking all night. If this wasn't UnEarth we'd have frostbyte by now." She added as an afterthought, "Is that how you spell it?"

"Nerd!"

"Okay, 'frostbite', then. Why don't you call 'your people' and get us out of this mess?"

"I would, but I forgot to recharge the cell phone," Juliana replied sheepishly. Just as Barb poised to smack Juliana, a bright yellow TOATS taxi with tire chains came flying over a hill and stopped in front of them. The window rolled down and Donna popped her head out.

"There you are! We've been looking for you for hours!"

"Donna! How did you get away from that witch?" Lottie asked as she got in the taxi with the others.

"Emily threw a bucket of water on her and she melted."

"Where's Emily now?"

"She's gone off somewhere in another taxi. She mentioned buying a black leather outfit and visiting a swordsmith."

"And Tess? And (Inse)?"

"Still at the Hard Shamrock Café. By now they'll be completely written off—written out, I mean. Buckle up. I'll tell you the rest on the way."

Juliana looked puzzled "On the way where?"

"To tonight's New Year's Eve Party! But first, to BallyRodeo drive. We, too, have some shopping to do, and if we're quick we'll get it done by sunset!"

 UNEARTHLY EMILY
31 December 1998 New Year's Eve . . .
. . . Strains of Glenn O'Millerghnaghobhughghan's "Stardust" filled the crisp night air as the TOATS taxi pulled up in front of Ballykissmefoot Castle.

The TOATS women exited the taxi; Donna in a silk Charles Lagerpint®. Juliana in sequined Rob Tacky®, Barb in elegant Hailstone®, and Lottie in a gold lamé creation by Goatee® (it's festive).

Connie, wearing a purple dress she had made herself (Nic's favorite color) was waiting for her gorgeous escort to park the car.

"Lottie!"

"Connie!"

"Donna!"

"Barb!"

"Connie!"

"Juliana!"

Juliana checked her makeup in her compact mirror.

"Great. Now that we all know each other, can we go inside?" Juliana walked past everyone and entered the castle.

"Apparently, they'll let anyone in," Connie commented as they followed Juliana inside.

Gold and silver woven pennants hung from the rafters and the ballroom was bathed in shimmering candlelight. Bubbles floated in the air and a big band played on the stage. Merry revellers seemed to float across the dance floor.

Standing in amazement, Lottie leaned over the railing to get a better view. "Wow. Get a load of that buffet! I'm famished."

As Lottie headed off for some hors d'oeuvres, Barb spied Siegfried waltzing with "Brunhilde". "Oh my gosh! It can't be!" she cried. "She's not allowed in this story!"

Barb manoeuvred with the grace of a jungle cat to get a better view of the mysterious blonde. She spied Nic and Connie dancing and an idea occurred to her...

 UNEARTHLY EMILY

31 December 1998

...A roguishly handsome man approached Juliana.

"Care to dance, my dear? The name's Bond."

Juliana gave him the once over. "James Bond?" she replied sarcastically.

"No, Kevin."

"Do you dance as good as you look, Kevin?"

"Let's find out." The roguishly handsome man grabbed

Juliana and whirled her onto the dance floor.

Back at the buffet, a meatball rolled off of Lottie's plate and bounced towards the wall. Looking around to make sure no one was watching her, she bent over to pick it up. Troll saw a window of opportunity and unceremoniously pushed Lottie through a secret passage.

"Brunhilde" winked at Troll as he gave her the thumbs up from across the ballroom. "One down, three to go," she muttered.

"Vat was that?" Siegfried asked as he spun the dizzy blonde across the floor.

"Nothing darling, I was just saying, 'That tree has to go.'"

Barb, snagging Nic away from Connie, was waltzing towards Siegfried. "I really don't want to get involved any more than necessary Barb," Nic protested. "Can't you find someone else to dance with?"

Barb stopped dancing for a second. "Listen, if Connie's not going to write anything, you're fair game. Now shut up and keep dancing."

Nic shrugged his shoulders and dipped Barb.

"Perfect," Barb replied as he pulled her back up close to his chest.

"You know, you are quite stunning," he said.

Barb smiled. "I know."

UNEARTHLY EMILY

31 December 1998

. . . Donna was sitting alone at a table wondering who had done the decorations.

"Is this seat taken?" said a voice.

"Lance!" Donna threw herself into her idol's arms, knocking over her chair and kissed him passionately. They rolled under the table and he chuckled as she came up for air. "Why are you laughing?" a surprised Donna asked.

"Because I know something you don't."

"What's that?"

Suddenly "Lance" pushed down on one of the floor's stone pavers and a trapdoor opened beneath a startled Donna. "Oh no not agaiiiiiiiiinnnnnnnn!" Donna's cries faded as she rapidly descended out of sight.

The trapdoor closed and "Lance" transformed back into Troll. He poked his head out from under the table cloth and held up two fingers (the polite ones) for his mistress to see. Over Siegfried's shoulder, "Brunhilde" smiled.

Oblivious of these goings-on, Juliana was waiting out on the balcony. Kevin appeared, holding two full glasses. "Champagne?"

Taking a glass, Juliana sipped the fizzing liquor. She ran her fingers under the lapel of Kevin's tuxedo jacket, seductively purring. "You're a marvellous dancer. What else do you do?" He leaned close to her as he slid his arm around her waist.

Her expression changed from delight to horror as he whispered in her ear. "No!"

She tried to break free from him. The glass fell to the floor and shattered as a now unconscious Juliana was picked up and tossed over the edge of the balcony to a waiting Troll.

Kevin drank his glass of champagne and returned to the party.

UNEARTHLY BARB

12 February 2009

After mingling with the guests for a while and sculling a few champagnes to drown out a gnawing sense of guilt, Kevin remembered that he ought to report the success of his mission to the Fairy Queen. He searched the ballroom for the green-clad beauty, but she was nowhere to be found.

The band had finished playing a number and the musicians were indulging in a few tankards of Guinebeer® before the next set.

"Beg pardon," said Kevin Bond, tapping the shoulder of the harpist, who was groping about for his tankard, which was right in front of him. "Have you seen the Fairy Queen?"

"Who?"

"The Fairy Queen. You know, our employer. The party's hostess."

"What is she after lookin' loike?" the harpist asked, adjusting his sunglasses. His other hand chanced to alight on his tankard of Guinebeer® and he seized it.

"Well, you know, she's a—" Kevin deliberated for a moment. The FQ was certainly very hot-looking, but with a definite supernatural quality. "—babe. Elfish."

259

"Babelfish?" the harpist repeated, wiping Guinebeer® froth off his lips with the back of his hand. He shook his head. "Sorry. Can't say dat oi've seen her."

"Okay. Thanks anyway." Kevin wandered off, just before the harpist accidentally put down his drink on the head of a passing leprechaun.

The bandmaster called out to the musicians, "Roight boys, We'll be after startin' the next set wit' 'Da Rare Auld Cheap Pun on da Foggy Mountain'."

UNEARTHLY EMILY
31 December 1998

. . . Ignorant of the fact that her companions were being picked off one by one, Barb excused herself to go and powder her nose.

Nic gazed longingly after her. "I'll count the minutes," he murmured romantically.

Paying scant attention to the Ladies' Powder Room attendant, Barb entered the "accessible" stall (her dress was too wide to fit in a regular stall). We will now take a short pause . . . we do not do toilet scenes.

Next moment Connie exploded into the Ladies' Powder Room, yelling "Where are you, you Nic-stealing bitch!"

When she received no reply she dropped to her hands and knees to look for Barb's shoes under the doors. On spotting them she burst into the stall, just as Barb turned around to flush. The door swung shut and the sound of rushing water filled the air. The alarmed Powder Room attendant heard a collective gasp, followed by silence.

She waited.

At length, unable to bear the suspense, she went over and tentatively prodded open the stall door. The cubicle was empty, save for the gently swirling water in the porcelain bowl. . .

UNEARTHLY EMILY

31 December 1998

. . . *One left,* thought "Brunhilde" the Fairy Queen.

She looked at Siegfried, who was poking at the food on his plate. They had finished dancing and were seated together at one of the tables. The massive grandfather clock in the hall struck eleven—there was only one hour left till midnight.

"I wonder where Emily is," said the FQ.

Siegfried once again became interested in the conversation. "Emily? You invited her?"

"She and I are very close—like twins, you might say."

"Really? She never mentioned you before."

"No matter, I was hoping I'd see her before midnight."

"So vas I."

"You like Emily do you?"

Had Siegfried not recently downed a couple of glasses of champagne he might have noticed a certain hard edge creeping into his fair companion's tone. "We are working on this script," he answered, "but for some reason I must have upset her, and she ran out. She took up with this Irishman and I haven't seen her since."

"You poor thing," sympathised "Brunhilde". "I'm sure it was nothing you did. Why don't you take the limo and see if she is at the Ballykildamessenger B & B?"

"That won't be necessary!" A loud voice sliced through the background music and babble of conversation. The guests fell silent. The bandsmen stopped playing in mid-toot and looked up in surprise.

Emily, standing on one of the rafters (looking spectacular dressed all in black, may I add) grabbed a pennant and swung across the hall, landing with precision in front of the Fairy Queen-as-Brunhilde. As she drew her sword, the crowd hurriedly dispersed.

The Fairy-Queen-as-Brunhilde looked terribly amused. "Watched a few too many Errol Flynn movies have we?" She snapped her fingers and Emily was surrounded by elfin guards. "Throw her in the dungeon with the rest of them!"

Siegfried, completely confused but always heroic, rushed to Emily's side. "Vat ze hell is going on!"

"It's too complicated to explain now," Emily gasped, "just fight!" She managed to dodge as the guards attacked.

Valiantly, the two of them fought off the Fairy Queen's guards for about an hour, but in the end all Emily's pirating experience was not enough and she was captured. Siegfried stepped forward to help her, but a guard knocked him unconscious.

"Looks like there's no more swash left in your buckle, Emily," sneered the Fairy Queen. "Guards, take her away!"

"Think again, Your Rottenness!" Triumphantly, Emily pulled out the small velvet pouch that the elf Deasmumhnichnach Mac Aodhagáinandagain (or whatever his name was) had given her back at the Hard Shamrock Cafe. She opened it and shook the contents into her hand.

Her eyes widened. *Damn*, she thought, as she found herself staring at a 'Get Out of Jail Free' card from a Monopoly game. *Stupid elf.*

"Erm," she cleared her throat, "Look, Your Majesty, I'm sorry if I was out of line with that comment—" As the guards dragged her away she managed to shove the card into Siegfried's pocket.

The clock began to strike midnight and, smirking with satisfaction, the Fairy Queen popped open a bottle of champagne.

Unfortunately for her, she never had a chance to drink it.

Clouds of fairy light surrounded the entire castle as her magic came to an end, returning the castle and its inhabitants to their pre-festivity state.

On Original Earth—*Wow. Why wouldn't the FQ have known this was going to happen?* thought Barb as she finished reading Emily's last chapter. Perhaps being previously disguised in Emily's shape and then Brunhilde's had made the Fairy Queen somewhat absent minded; for example, throughout the whole episode she seemed to have forgotten how to speak with an Irish accent.

Besides, the queen had been smitten by Siegfried, and her passion must have driven all thoughts from her mind other than the desire to rid herself of rivals. Now the scheming sprite had paid the price for her forgetfulness . . . all her machinations had come to nothing. At midnight she had been drawn back to Fairyland without the man of her dreams. . .

. . .As so often happened in this particular corner of cyberspace.

By now the thwarted Fairy Queen would be sitting glumly on an embankment where the wild thyme blew, where oxlips and the nodding violet grew, making a mental note to herself: *Next time make sure it's not a TOATS story you're getting mixed up in. . .*

UNEARTHLY EMILY

31 December 1998

. . . Drip . . . Drip . . . Drip . . . Drip . . .

"This incessant dripping is driving me crazy. Will someone please call a plumber?" Juliana complained as she paced the stone-flagged floor of her damp and dreary cell.

A heavy door burst open and two elfin guards dragged Emily into the dungeon. They shackled her arms and suspended her from an iron chain next to Lottie. The rest of the seductive TOATS sirens peered out from behind bars in cells on the other side of the chamber.

"Hi Emily! Happy New Year!"

"Hi Lottie! Happy New Year!"

Donna, still in shock at the thought that Lance had thrown her down a trapdoor, surveyed her dismal surroundings. "You know, they say whatever you are doing when the New Year comes. you'll be doing all year."

Connie and Barb, who inhabited the adjoining cell, paid no attention to these goings-on. "He can't help being attracted to me. All men are," Barb tried to explain as she wrung out her dress.

Connie ignored her, and the fact that she was also soaking wet, as she frantically tried to complete a TOATS episode on the back of a cocktail napkin to ensure that Nic stayed firmly in love with her . . .

UNEARTHLY CONNIE

1 January 1999

The next day, Siegfried awoke in a daze. "Vat has happened?" he asked himself sleepily, getting no reply. He looked around, but no-one else was to be seen. The Fairy Queen's magic had ended at midnight . . . it was now two o'clock in the morning and as he surveyed his surroundings, all he could see was the dim darkness of a somewhat uninhabited castle. He shook his head. I must get out of here—and fast! After picking himself up he staggered along the dark, dimly lit corridor, which seemed to go on and on.

He wondered what had happened to that beautiful blonde woman who invited him to her party only yesterday . . . or was it yesterday? Time seemed to have become a blur in his mind. In fact he was beginning to wonder why his life had been so odd during the past few months—all those strange bewitching women chasing him, throwing themselves and TOATS Rule Books at him, strange countries and stranger castles . . .

"Vill my life ever return to normal?" he wondered aloud, as he made his way along the corridor which now seemed to be heading downwards and getting colder and darker.

He reached a huge oak panelled door, and as he stared at it he could hear faint voices on the other side. Noticing an old rusted bolt on the outside, he heaved it aside, straining and grunting with the effort. Peering warily inside, he spied all those women he'd just been wondering about, locked up in cells!

His first reaction was, I *think I'll leave them here ... maybe I can go home and live a normal life in Hollywood.* (Of course everyone in Hollywood leads a normal life.) But somehow the words of that scoundrel Herr Schumm rang in his ears, reminding him that he was supposed to be a hero. He supposed that meant rescuing the damsels in distress.

Therefore he entered the dungeon.

"Oh, thank goodness you're here!" feminine voices cried in unison, temporarily forgetting their differences. Even Connie looked up from her mad scribblings.

"Emily," said Siegfried, "there you are at last. Vere have you been? We need to discuss that script! Barb, why are you soaking wet?"

He then noticed that all the cells were locked using swipe card readers. As he was fumbling in his pocket for something—anything—he felt his fingers close around something made of cardboard. "Vat's this?" he asked, confused. Having pulled the object from his pocket he stared at it and exclaimed, "It's a 'Get Out of Jail Free' card from a Monopoly game!"

Just as Siegfried was about to toss away the card Donna said, "What's that, a 'Get Out of Jail Free' card? I read somewhere that they have magical properties when used in the right circumstances . . . run it through the swipe card reader!"

With a shrug of his shoulders Siegfried did as she suggested, and hey presto, Donna's cell door slid open!

May as vell set ze whole horde free now zat one's out, Siegfried thought resignedly, opening the doors to all the cells. Since the last gentleman to have worn the outfit from Paddy O'Shoulder's Tuxedo Hire had accidentally left a hammer and chisel in one pocket, he was also able to unshackle Emily.

Connie said, "Right, I'm off to find Nic, and don't anyone try to stop me!" She disappeared out the door, hoping against hope that Nic hadn't fallen too hard for that bitch Barb, and forgetting in her haste to even thank Siegfried, who had got her out of that pickle.

Meanwhile the others, who had been gracious enough to express their gratitude, left the dungeon and began walking up the sloping corridor, led by Siegfried. The guards had disappeared, along with the magic of the night before, so the freed prisoners made their way unhindered to the outside world, and the relentless frost and ice of an Implausible Irish winter.

The sky was clear, dark blue and brilliant with stars. Further downhill, Connie could be seen stomping through the snow muttering something about finding that big yellow taxi and getting to the airport, get me out of this gods-forsaken, frozen hole . . . where's that two-timing Hollywood hunk, I thought he only had eyes for me . . .

In the valley below, the distant windows of the Hard Shamrock Café glimmered like amber jewellery and multitudinous voices could be heard raised in song; "Hi the dithery al the dal, dal the dal the dithery al, dal the dal, dal dithery al dee. . ."

In the absence of public transport everyone (except Connie who, in the hope of finding a taxi rank, kept stubbornly walking down the frozen road in her purple evening dress and matching stilettos) made a bee-line for that inviting haven.

On their arrival they were dismayed to find that Herr Schumm had turned up again. Still in his fancy-dress elf costume (with bell on hat), he was sitting at the packed bar drinking shots of whiskey and occasionally joining in a chorus of "Lanigan's Other Ball," which most of the patrons were belting out uproariously.

Unnoticed, Tess had long since absconded from the café with a group of Vulgarian sailors and headed for the local port, where they boarded their four-masted barque for a joy-ride. Desmond Egan had disappeared, drawn back to Fairyland when his queen's magic failed, and the cute woodland fairy, for lack of space elsewhere, was dancing an Irish jig on the jukebox. (Inse) and Tinfingers were nowhere to be seen, having rented a room together at the nearby 'Crock o' Leprechauns' Motel.

"Oh good, I'm glad you're here," said Herr Schumm, immediately buttonholing Siegfried, "I was just saying to all and sundry that you are not a real hero, 'cos the FQ's guards all disappeared, and you didn't have to fight any of them off to rescue the damsels in distress!"

"Vat?" spluttered Siegfried. "How dare you—and how did you know vat has just happened at ze castle?"

"You scoundrel, Schumm!" cried Juliana.

Donna thrust her face close to the little man's false pointy elf-ear. "I suspected you're really only saying that," she said hotly, "because Siegfried threw you out into the snow." The other delectable beauties loudly agreed with her.

In fact Lottie was beginning to think that she was fed up with all this ice and snow—she was dreaming of Morocco. During the confusion caused by the TOATS belles fiercely admonishing Herr Schumm, and the other café patrons breaking into a boisterous rendition of "Paddy McGinty's TOAT", she grabbed Siegfried by the arm and raced off with him, whispering "Come on, let's catch that big yellow taxi to the airport and escape to More-or-Less Morocco! Forget those other trollops! We can get married in Morocco, where it's warm and sunny!"

Lottie and Siegfried swiftly made their exit into the snowy night and they slithered off down the road. Due to the fact that even when they stopped running they were still sliding forward, they rapidly overtook Connie. As she slammed into her sister, Lottie was unaware that the others had noticed the pair's absence and were already in hot pursuit, struggling to push through the café crowd and reach the door.

As for Siegfried, he was only thinking of ways that he could improve his standing as a hero in More-or-Less Morocco ...

ORIGINAL EMILY

1 January 1999

Hooray! Connie wrote an episode! It's amazing how much you can write on the back of a napkin! Loved it! (insert song by Bing Crosby/Bob Hope here) "We're off on the Road to Morocco . . . "

UNEARTHLY LOTTIE

3 January 1999

A TOATS taxi suddenly overtook the trio of Siegfried, Lottie and Connie, skidding sideways on the icy road and coming to a halt facing the wrong way. Connie coughed her way through clouds of exhaust fumes and jumped in, only to find a rather sheepish Nic already inside.

As she was hitting him, Lottie and Siegfried climbed in and cuddled up together. "I can't believe I haven't passed out or died yet," whispered Lottie.

"Meine kleine schwarmerisch Idiot; du sollten besser zum Psychiatrist gehen," murmured Siegfried lovingly in her ear.

As the taxi driver tried to turn the cab around the other TOATS heroines caught up with them and flung open the doors.

"Okay, move over everyone!" shouted Juliana. "Lottie, there's no room for you—get on the floor or get out."

Lottie lay on the floor as Juliana flung herself onto Siegfried's lap. Donna (who had started weeping for Lance) and Emily climbed in after her.

Barb got in beside the driver where there was more room for her elegant Hailstone® dress (though that had lost a little of its shape since its voyage through the castle's sewage pipes).

"All here?" she asked.

"Not quite," said Donna, "we seem to have mislaid (Inse) somewhere."

"Good riddance," said Barb. "Okay driver, take us to the airport". She glanced at him and moaned. "Oh my gosh, not another alien . . . why on earth did we use this stupid taxi?"

The driver chuckled wickedly as he turned to squint at them through hideous white eyes. The passengers made a dive for the doors, but then noticed the driver was removing some contact lenses. "Just my little joke," he said with a handsome grin, "It's me, Bond. Kevin Bond . . . remember?"

Juliana got her talons out and lunged for him. He ducked. "What are you doing driving our taxi?" she screamed.

"Calm down," Kevin said, putting the vehicle into gear and starting down the slippery road. "Herr Schumm gave me this job because your last driver unexpectedly ran away and my last employer unexpectedly vanished at midnight . . ."

"I don't get that," said Connie contentedly, her voice muffled from within Nic's arms. "Why did she bother with that big party and locking us up and all . . . just to go and vanish? Seems stupid".

"Yes, it was stupid," said Kevin, "a rare lapse that unfortunately for her proved fatal. You see, despite her outward appearance of icy cruelty, she had fallen hopelessly, desperately, in love with that guy in the back seat . . . what's your name, mate?"

"Nicolas."

"No, not you; the other one, the German guy . . . Siegfried is it? Pleased to meet you," Kevin said, reaching into the back seat to shake hands. Backing the taxi out of the ditch he'd just driven into, he continued, "She forgot the old rhyme, you see— centuries old—that all fairy queens must NEVER forget. Goes like this:

"Dread Faery Queen, heed our warning,
Take good care at New Year's dawning,
Be thou sure as Old Year dies
To lust not after azure eyes
For New Year's waxing shall be dire
If sexy German hath kindled thy fire.
So as the spent year doth dwindle and wane,
Chasten thy yearning woman's brain
Lest darkest midnight's very last stroke
Sendeth thy magic up in smoke."

"Ooh, that's truly awful," moaned Lottie from under six pairs of feet. "Who wrote that crap?"

Kevin took a rather roundabout route, stopping off to sample about forty-six pubs on the way. They all reeled merrily into the airport, bought their tickets, replenished lost and mislaid TOATS Rule Books on Etiquette at the bookshop (so they could read up on More-or-Less Morocco during the flight) and ate some takeaway meat pies.

"Interesting flavour. I wonder what sort of meat this is," observed Donna, who had failed—like the others—to notice the small print on the packaging: "Imported meat, cooked in Implausible Ireland by Mrs O'Really? of Ballykildamessenger Hall."

They boarded the plane for More-or-Less Morocco, but Siegfried stopped, aghast, in the aisle. "Verdammt noch mal! This is an Air Banana plane!"

Sure enough, "Safety fly with Air Banana into the New Millennium!" proclaimed the sign tacked to the bulkhead; "Worry not over no nasty Bug—we have none Computers!"

"Scheisse!" gasped Siegfried. "Du lieber Gott, I'm getting confused . . ."

As the decrepit plane laboured into an ominous winter sky, leaving one of its wheels rolling despondently along the runway, Kevin Bond stood in the snow outside the palm-thatched Air Banana terminal and waved his white hanky, occasionally mopping at the copious tears streaming down his ruggedly good-looking face.

"What wonderful people," he sobbed. "What scintillatingly fabulous women; what magnificently charismatic heroes! Especially Siegfried . . . Yes!!" he shouted excitedly, punching the air. "He will be my role model! I will strive always to be like Him!" He jumped into his taxi to begin practising sexy smirks in the mirror, just as a limousine screeched to a halt beside him.

Two rather singed men leaped out, one waving a fistful of hundred-dollar bills.

"G'dammit, we've missed 'em, Woolfie!"

"Don't fret, Isambard—an Air Banana plane leaves here every ten minutes for More-or-Less Morocco[20,] so we'll be hot on their heels!"

The first speaker was none other than Isambard the Hollywood film producer, who'd finally received a name from his inventor. He was last seen in a red and white Santa cap purposefully heading up the hill to Ballykissmefoot Castle in search of his favorite scriptwriter, Emily. What had happened to him on that fateful New Year's Eve only the Fairy Queen could tell, and she wasn't admitting to anything. Accompanying Isambard was a new, freshly named sidekick he had apparently picked up at the castle, who was wearing a matching Santa hat.

Meanwhile, at a pebbly beach nearby, another Siegfried supporter staggered from the sea, water streaming from his black coat. Yes, it was Brian the horse, who had just swum all the way from Inauthentic Iceland. And around his neck clung a tattered remnant of a woman—Tammie; storm-tossed, sodden and salty. "I'm looking for Siegfried P. Hinkelheimer," she gasped to a local character out walking his wolfhound.

"Beggorrah, to be sure now, poor wet colleen," said the character, "ye've just missed de man. He flew out—dat bunch o' banshees wit him—bout five minutes ago, bound for Morocco."

"Thanks," said Tammie. "Come on Brian, let's go."

They sadly turned and headed out to sea again just as a great four-masted barque glided into the bay, folding her wings from the sea.

---

20 This has gotta be a lie, considering the size and condition of the Air Banana fleet.

Thousands of Vulgarian sailors clambered aloft to peer landwards. "Where is our glorious Kapitan?" they yelled.

A voice floated up from the waves. The sailors were surprised to see a woman and a horse swimming strongly to the south-east. "You've missed him," yelled Tammie. "He's gone to Morocco!"

The helm was spun, the yards braced, halliards and sheets hauled home and the ship bounded to sea again with a bone in her teeth. "Trreesh; we're going to More-or-Less Morocco!" shouted the handsomest of the Vulgarians, a sailor named Mishka. Tess looked up from where she was kneeling on the deck, hopelessly lost amongst vast mounds of jigsaw pieces.

"Huh . . . what?" she said.

On Original Earth: "Gosh, this story is certainly action-packed," Barb said to Lottie as they sipped coffee and idled in front of Tess's computer.

"Yeah," said Lottie. "Nobody has slept since I can't remember when—except Siegfried, who was actually unconscious and hallucinating—and as for food, we must be starving. When was the last time anyone ate anything? "

"I can't remember. That's probably why we cyberchicks have all got such great figures," mused Barb.

Lottie added, "Or went to the toilet?"

"Well as for that," said Barb, "it's not safe to do anything in the TOATS universe."

"Your computer fixed yet?"

"It's supposed to be ready today..."

275

ORIGINAL CONNIE

Monday 4 January 1999

Barb sends her apologies that she hasn't contributed to the site for so long . . . her computer has been sick, plus she's in holiday mode so hasn't managed to get it fixed yet. My, won't she have a lot of reading to catch up on! Lucky thing!

ORIGINAL BARB

4 January 1999

'Tis I. The Fake Red-Head and Erstwhile Evil Person From Australia is back. My server collapsed or something over the last few days, isolating me from the SPH site for many chapters.

Gone for a handful of days and look what happens, Emily flushes me down the toilet in a really nice dress. You can't turn your back on this site for five minutes.

Emily, I loved all your episodes. Lottie —excellent poem! Connie—congratulations on your maiden chapter. Keep up the good work.

Donna, it is impossible for you to be written out of TOATS since you are the Webmistress of TOATS Cyberspace and therefore you possess god-like qualities.

ORIGINAL BARB

4 January 1999

If anyone else out there is reading TOATS, please feel free to contribute. It's not a closed group of authors and we'd love to have chapters from new contributors.

Siegfried's Favorite Girlfriend (Barb)

ORIGINAL EMILY
4 January 1999
Excellent poem Lottie! I must look up More-or-Less-Morocco in the TOATS Rule Book on Etiquette . . . By the way Barb, all dresses worn in TOATS episodes can be sold on consignment at *Isambard's Shabby Chic Clothing and Juice Bar*. (However, they will charge you extra for dry cleaning).

17

MORE-OR-LESS MOROCCO

UNEARTHLY EMILY

5 January 1999

Mishka the good-looking Vulgarian sailor shouted at Tess above the pounding waves of the North Sea: "Morocco!"

"No thank you, I've had enough cocoa!" Tess replied, resuming her puzzle. With a shrug, Mishka returned to the helm...

...Meanwhile, in the barren desert landscape of More-or-Less-Morocco, a lone camel spotted the Air Banana flight on the horizon. Streams of black smoke were pouring out of the engines. From his vantage point, the camel saw several passengers parachuting out the side of the plane.

Moments later the plane spiralled into the dunes, creating a fantastic explosion. The camel, being an inquisitive creature, decided to investigate.

Siegfried disconnected himself from the harness of his parachute. "Everyone okay?"

"I think I broke a nail," Juliana said, inspecting her manicure.

Lottie looked around and saw nothing but undulating sand for miles. "Oh my gosh, we're in the middle of the desert! We're doomed!"

Siegfried put his arms around her comfortingly. Softly he told her, "Don't worry. Before you know it you'll hear the sounds of the Casbah, the music of the snake charmers, the lonely call to prayer from the minaret of the mosque, the dogs of Tangier howling as the moon becomes full . . ."

Emily, shaking the sand out of her hiking boots, overheard them. "I think I'm going to throw up."

Barb, who was trying to figure out how to convert the parachute silks into a nice harem outfit, looked at Emily. "As nauseating as that display is, don't do it. You might get dehydrated in this heat."

UnEarthly Lottie

UNEARTHLY LOTTIE
10 January 1999
Siegfried shaded his eyes with a lean, tanned hand as he gazed across the desert to where pieces of Air Banana plane lay strewn across the sand-dunes. "Shouldn't we go and investigate?" he said. "There might be some more survivors."

"Total waste of time," answered Juliana. "We got the only parachutes."

"Yeah, those poor little Bananawanans didn't stand a chance against you, did they Juliana?" snapped Donna. "You and your berserk Viking act."

"So? You would have given them the para . . ."

"I don't think it matters," interrupted Barb. "Bananawanans always bounce—they're indestructible."

"Anyway, I think one of them caused the crash," said Juliana. "I'm sure it started when something highly combustible exploded in the toilet—and someone was in there at the time."

"Talking about toilets," said Emily, head deep inside her copy of the TOATS Rule Book on Etiquette, "it says here that the most treasured memories some tourists take with them from More-or-Less Morocco are of the toilets." She read in silence for a moment, then said, "Ugh, gross! Why the hell did you choose More-or-Less Morocco, Lottie? Let's go somewhere else."

"And how do you propose we do that?" asked Connie, looking up from whatever engrossing business she and Nic had been involved in.

"Here comes a speedy-looking camel," said Lottie hopefully.

"Look," said Siegfried, pointing, "over that sand-dune . . . I can see a bus-stop."

"I think we should avoid buses," said Emily, her nose still in the TOATS Rule Book. "Says here, 'When catching a bus in More-or-Less Morocco you will invariably find yourself sitting next to someone carrying an animal—usually dead, often smelly—wrapped in newspa . . .'"

Her voice was drowned out by the sudden pounding of hooves as, unexpectedly, hundreds of terrifyingly fearsome Barbie tribesmen, whooping a blood-curdling war-cry, came charging over the nearest dune to swoop down upon our hero and his women.

All the women leaped behind Siegfried for protection (except Connie, who made do with her poor substitute). Kicking up plumes of sand, the fiery Arabian stallions slithered down the dune to circle the group in a terrifying merry-go-round of flashing hooves, sweat-streaked hides, blood-red nostrils and rolling eyes. With voluminous robes flying, the riders stood in their stirrups, firing rifles into the air and brandishing wicked, curved scimitars that matched the grinning gleam of their white teeth. They dragged their horses to a halt in a snorting, prancing circle and their leader rode forward. With a lustful leer on his fat, oily face and drool trickling down several chins, he ogled the cringing women through blood-shot eyes.

"Save us Siegfried," whimpered Barb, Donna, Emily and Lottie. (Not Juliana though—she was busy sharpening her fingernails.)

Siegfried shrugged, very calm and oh so cool behind those dark glasses. "Sorry ladies; I'm slightly outnumbered," he said.

"Save us Nic," whimpered Connie.

"I'd overpower them all with my bare hands, Connie darling, but I can't—this is not my website," he replied.

"You are almost welcome to my land, sir who brings beauteous women," said the leader to Siegfried. "Please, allow me introduce myself . . . I am chieftain Ibn Hourrid Oyliman el Fatifata, Scourge of the Desert! Your *jamil* women each with two eyebrows will make very excellent gift to the illustrious Sultan Siliman for his harem. He will love his servant Oyliman forever! But I will keep a couple—oh fortunate ones!—for myself." Gesturing to his followers he cried, "Take them!"

The Barbie chief's men grabbed the women and threw them, kicking and screaming, face down across their saddles.

"Bind this man hand and foot," said Oyliman, looking Nic up and down. "He will fetch big price at the slave market. As for this one," he said, eyeing Siegfried disdainfully, "no conceivable use for him ... leave him to the merciless desert ... to die!"

Oyliman and his grinning followers turned to depart.

"But what about my wedding ... ?" wailed Lottie, bouncing around a horse's neck like a wet rag.

"Hey, Oily, haven't you forgotten something?" said Juliana. "What about that bus-stop, hey?"

"Ha ha ha!" Oyliman and his men laughed riotously.

"The bus-stop!" shouted Oyliman, "Oh silly me—it had escaped my notice. Better give you a bus timetable, dear sir." He hunted round in his robes, found one and handed it to Siegfried. "Here you are, sir ... and look—I've found a menu too—you can have that as well—it's my cousin's place—the Baib-el-Fish Cafe in Casablanca! Happy eating ... if you make it there! Ha ha ha ha!"

They all galloped off, showering Siegfried with sand. He dusted himself down and checked out the timetable to discover that the last bus had left half an hour earlier and the next one was due in two years' time.

Siegfried stood alone in the vast desert. Even the camel had wandered off. Around him the pitiless sun beat down on endless sand. Something caught his eye on the distant western horizon and he narrowed his gaze to watch it; a mere dark speck, appearing, disappearing—a mirage, surely. But no, the shadow gained size until suddenly, as if emerging from a shimmering curtain, it took shape . . . a great black horse, muscles gleaming as he ran, his tangled mane floating in pennants on the sky. He gave a trumpeting neigh and slid down the last dune to stand, nostrils quivering and flanks heaving, before Siegfried.

Yes, it's Brian, horse for heroes—returned (having left Tammie white, waterlogged and wrinkly, drying out on a beach somewhere) just in time to help our hero save his doting ladies from a fate worse than death!

UNEARTHLY EMILY
10 January 1999
Siegfried broke into a smile. "Brian old friend, I know little café in Conjectural Casablanca—if we're lucky, we can make it in time for dinner." Brian neighed and shook his mane in agreement as he and our hero galloped off towards the coast.

Someplace else in the desert, multi-colored caravan tents stood in the shade of palm trees. The oasis hideaway of the scourge of the desert, Oyliman, was in a flurry of activity preparing for the Sultan's arrival. The heavily-guarded harem tent lay on the edge of the camp, and inside it . . .

"You know this outfit is a lot more comfortable than I thought," Emily commented as she admired herself in the mirror. "I look good in jade."

284

Connie, now firmly trapped in TOATS, held up a sequin-edged top and matching pants. "What do you think of this one, Emily?"

"Very Sheherezade—I love it!"

Juliana, trying to cut a hole in the tent wall with her newly sharpened nails, was getting annoyed "Do you mind? I'm trying to escape here!"

Lottie was crying on top of a mountain of silk pillows. "I'll never get married . . . sniff . . . and Siegfried will never read my script . . . waaaaaaa!"

Donna walked over and smacked Lottie across the face. "Get a hold of yourself woman!"

Just then Oyliman entered the tent. "Ah . . . most beautiful desert flowers, the Sultan has arrived. Which two of you shall I keep? The decision is a most difficult one."

"Let me make it easy for you." Emily walked over to Oyliman defiantly. "Surrender now and I won't have to kill you."

Oyliman burst out laughing and left the tent. "That's a good one . . . surrender now . . . ha . . . ha . . . ha . . . kill me . . . ha . . . ha . . . Guards! Bring them all to my tent."

UNEARTHLY EMILY

12 January 1999

Only the turrets and rooftops were visible against the evening sky as Siegfried on horseback approached the city. The facades of the Moorish buildings gave way to narrow twisting streets crowded with merchants and people in the native section. Siegfried spotted a neon sign displaying the name "Rick's Café Amerikanisch".®

"No that's not it Brian, keep going."

A few twists and turns later another more decrepit café came into view. "There it is! The 'Baib-el-Fish Café.'" Brian stopped, allowing Siegfried to gracefully dismount.

Within the dimly lit interior of the establishment bamboo ceiling fans spun lazily. Colorful carpets hung on the adobe walls. The occupants of the café were a mixed bunch of Europeans, Moroccans in silk robes and a woman—sitting alone. Taking off his sunglasses for a better look, Siegfried approached her. "Hello Tammie."

Tammie looked up from her cup of iced qahwā. "Siegfried, It's been a long time." He sat down next to her. "The last time I saw you was—"

"Inauthentic Iceland." Siegfried finished her sentence as Tammie slowly stirred her drink with a camel-shaped swizzle stick.

"You remembered," she replied, finishing her drink in one gulp.

"But of course I remember. That was the day you floated away. It wasn't an easy day to forget." Siegfried took her hand.

Tammie sighed deeply. "I remember every detail. I wore a gold bikini and you wore black."

"Tammie, I need to ask you a question."

"What is it?" Tammie answered, running out of dialogue because she hadn't written anything in forever.

"I need to find out where the Oyliman's camp is."

Tammie smiled. "He's at—"

Just then a TOATS taxi driver entered the café and grabbed Tammie. "Sorry Siegfried," Tammie said regretfully, "looks like its time for me to go. I'm out of text." She paid for the *qahwā* and as she was being hauled off she yelled. "Here's looking at you, kid."

UNEARTHLY BARB
13 January 1999
Where have I been for the last four chapters?

UNEARTHLY EMILY
13 January 1999
We did forget Barb... out of site out of mind? You must be back at the plane crash . . .

. . . I met Barb in an antique land, who said: "Two vast and trunkless legs of stone Stand in the desert. Near them, on the sand, Half sunk, a shattered visage lies, whose frown, And wrinkled lip, and sneer of cold command, Tell that its sculptor well those passions read Which yet survive, stamped on these lifeless things, The hand that mocked them and the heart that fed. And on the pedestal these words appear— 'My name is Ozymandias, king of kings: Look upon my works, ye Mighty, and despair!' Nothing beside remains. Round the decay Of that colossal wreck, boundless and bare, The lone and level sands stretch far away."[21]

My homage to Barb lost in the desert . . .

---

21 From the poem "Ozymandias" by Percy Bysshe Shelley.

UNEARTHLY BARB

14 January 1999

"Three forms of travel," mused Barb, seated in the throbbing shade of the ruined statue of King Ozymandias, "and each from a vastly different era."

She had just witnessed, across the shimmering desert horizon, a rider galloping. Small spurts of sand tossed up like feathers behind him. The horse had seemed made of polished ebony. Its mane and tail streamed out like the war-banners of some barbarian tribe of nomads, black against the sun's fierce glare.

Barb wiped the perspiration from her brow. The second traveller to pass across the distant dunes had been a wheeled vehicle, bright yellow, topped with unimaginable mechanical devices and the silver dish of a gigantic radar. (A TOATS taxi, in case you hadn't guessed, carrying the textless Tammie.) It left crazy, winding tire-marks in the sand.

Some hours later, as the sun was beginning to slide like a broken egg down the impossibly brilliant blue enamel plate of the sky, the third mode of transport had appeared. The flying saucer had hovered briefly above Barb as she reclined dehydratedly in the lengthening shadow of King Ozymandias's left foot. (Note: the TOATS Rule Book clearly states Left Feet must be mentioned as often as possible).

Underneath the alien vehicle's whirring bulk, a small door had slid open with a click. A crate had dropped out, landing perilously close to Barb's elbow and tossing up sand all over her. Subsequently, the spaceship had slammed its door and risen vertically, from its hovering position, into skies now painted with the honey and carnelian of a desert sunset.

In the blink of a sand-encrusted eye, it was gone.

"Legs, fossil fuel, antigravity," said Barb deliriously to the air. As parched as a withered leaf, she was beginning to hold conversations with herself, like a madwoman. The pupils of her eyes rolled disconnectedly. She was trying to focus on the myriad mirages which appeared to be swimming among the dunes.

Blearily, Barb squinted at the crate half-buried beside her. Reaching in, she pulled out a glass bottle. "Thank the powers of the Goddess Donna," she bleated. "Some kind alien has sent me water." Unscrewing the lid, she tipped the bottle to her blistered lips. Alas, not a drop slithered forth.

Feverishly, Barb tried all twelve bottles, one by one, strewing the lids across the beach-like ripples of powdered silicone surrounding her (otherwise known as sand.) At last, with a cry of despair she flung the final container as far as she could. It struck the stone face of King Oz, chipping his front teeth, and shattered into shards which caught the red rays of the dying sun, reflecting them back like rubies.

"Oh, the cruelty," sobbed Barb, too dry for tears, "Who could have sent me a crate of empty bottles?"

Rummaging around the crate she found a harem outfit, which she immediately changed into (before stuffing her ruined evening dress down an ant-lion's burrow), and a note. The note read, "#&*^@!!+>" Fortunately, Barb recognised this language at once. Not yet available on the Babelfish Translation Website, it was Splingian—the native tongue of the planet whereon she had dwelt and prolifically bred with a Daniel de Licious® lookalike in earlier chapters.

Shaking sugary granules from the long tresses of her henna'ed hair, Barb translated aloud for the benefit of King Oz's statue. (She was delirious enough by now to imagine those ears of granite were listening.)

"My darling Barb," (she read), "love of my life, siren of my dreams. I hope you are enjoying your holiday back on UnEarth. Thought you might be missing the rarefied and ethereal airs of Planet Splinge, so am sending you a dozen bottles of it.

"Think of me as you breathe. Recall the taut planes of my face, my strong chin and straight, dark eyebrows, my long, lean thighs and the way I stride across the mountains gracefully, like a young lion. Remember the way my waist-length hair falls like a cascade of dark silk across the musculature of my wide shoulders. Visualise the heady wine of my kisses.

"Alas, never can I return to UnEarth, so beware— anyone you happen to see who resembles me is not the original DDL-lookalike but some fake cooked up by Emily or Lottie. I miss you—come back soon. All my love, Daniel. XXX OOO."

Ecstatic, Barb raised her lovely head towards the painted glory of the desert sunset. In her madness, it seemed to her that the frozen lips of King Oz began to writhe. A sonorous voice issued from the ruined, royal mask.

"Alack, the winds of the red planet have been sniffed into the nostrils of the lost damsel," he intoned mysteriously. "Beware the winds of the perilous world."

"Wha—?" stammered Barb thickly. Through her mists of lunacy, an idea clicked into place. "Oh yes, I remember now — the air of the planet Splinge induces a terrifying wickedness in whoever breathes it . . ."

Barb took a deep breath. She felt foul villainy, appalling devilry and a lot of bitchiness flooding through her veins. She rose to her satin-slippered feet. All at once the feeling of thirst deserted her, if you'll excuse the pun. She felt strong, free and utterly bad.

Throwing up her slim, lightly-tanned arms in exultation, this young beauty uttered a feral cry which echoed like a wolf's howl across the rapidly darkening dunes, curdled the blood of whoever heard it and made camels jam their heads into the sand. The left foot of King Oz cracked in two pieces and cumbersomely fell apart. "Aha!" shouted Barb in triumph.

Immediately she took a copy of the "TOATS Rule Book on Etiquette" out of her harem-pants pocket, sat down and began looking through the index. "A, B, C, D," she muttered, "Ah, here's what I'm looking for—R." Turning to the chapter headed "Revenge", she ran her finger down the table of contents. "People whose names start with A, B, C—here we are. 'Revenge on People Whose Names Begin With E or I.'" Interestedly, she began to read.

Night fell.

Around midnight, another wild howl could be heard resounding across the dunes. Scorpions and jackals fled. The starlight silvered the lithely voluptuous form of a girl striding across the landscape with a book in her hand. At her back, a crumbling statue loomed ominously on the horizon.

Barb's last words resounded up into the glittering vault of night—"She'll pay for this! First she casts me into the cesspits of an Implausible Irish Castle, then abandons me in the Moroccan desert! Emily will pay, oh yes, she will suffer. Sweet revenge shall be mine!"

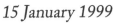

UNEARTHLY EMILY

15 January 1999

Emily (ignoring the fact that she was about to be taken to Sultan Siliman at that very moment) had a funny feeling that SOMEONE possessed an over-developed sense of revenge.

She flipped to the end of the TOATS Rule Book. "T ... U ... V ... ah here it is; 'Villains. When a villain seems dead, she never is. She will always be allowed one, possibly two resurrections. The hero will frequently see her coming, even if her back is turned. If she doesn't, a friend will finish the villain off. The villain usually kills her henchman for failing, yet doesn't seem to run out of loyal henchmen. Villains lurk until a flash of lightning reveals their presence. The villain, having finally gotten the good guy into his clutches, will usually spend a few megalomaniac minutes gloating over her victory and her opponent's downfall. This increment of time will prove just enough to allow Emily—I mean the good guy—to figure a way out of her predicament, or just long enough to allow a rescue attempt by the hero.

"'You can kill the villain by taking careful note of any object that the writer has lingered on for an unnecessarily length of time; typically this is something like a meat hook or a jagged bit of glass. A fabulously staged fight may commence, and at the appropriate time you can become inspired (usually by either an insult from the villain or a look of faith from your love interest) with strength enough to force the villain into/onto/under/in front of the aforementioned object.

Actor's Equity (Hollywood) requires that within fifteen seconds either side of the villain's demise, you utter your trademark phrase.'"

On the SPH fansite Feedback Page, Emily had mentioned a new character called Katie, so Barb thought she'd better write her in.

UNEARTHLY BARB
15 January 1999

Back at the oasis hideaway of Oyliman, the scourge of the desert, the five abducted damsels were being escorted under guard to the tent of their captor.

Juliana fluttered her eyelashes at a particularly tall and handsome guard. "Rescue me and I'm yours," she crooned, with devious intent. The guard grinned, his perfect teeth flashing white against his dark tan. However, it was likely he did not speak English.

Servants flung open the tent flap and the girls entered. Oyliman was seated fatly upon tasselled cushions. A slave waved a fan of peacock feathers above his turbaned head. A gilt dish of sweetmeats balanced at his elbow.

"Come in my desert flowers," slimily effused Oyliman. He glanced at Connie. She looked stunning in her sequin-edged top and matching pants, which (she was unaware) were made from semi-transparent fabric. "You are my first choice," greased Oyliman, ogling her from head to toe. Connie's jaw dropped. Aghast, she realized that Nic would be unable to save her from a fate worse than death, since he was currently being sold in some far-off slave-market.

"There is only one way to get out of this predicament," someone whispered in Connie's ear, "you'll have to WRITE yourself out of it."

Connie stared at the speaker. She saw a nubile girl in a purple silk genie outfit, its edges stitched with gold coins.

"Who are you?" Connie whispered in return.

"My name is Katie," replied this vision of loveliness. "I, too was abducted by Oyliman."

"Silence!" roared Oyliman.

"Oh, shut up," returned Juliana irritably. "You're really starting to get on my nerves."

"Ha ha ha!" giggled Oyliman, the spare tires around his middle bouncing in time to his laughter, "I like a mettlesome girl. You are my other choice, Vikinger woman!"

"No!" shrieked Juliana, lunging at him with her sharpened nails. The guards instantly intervened. She struggled vainly against their strength and at that moment a trumpet sounded.

"The Sultan approaches!" called a voice.

"Take away my two new brides-to-be and bring the other four to show the Sultan," commanded Oyliman.

Emily, Donna, Lottie and Katie were dragged out of Oyliman's tent. There beneath the shade of the oasis palms, Sultan Siliman and his vast retinue had already gathered.

Grovelling slaves were busy rolling out a red carpet for the Sultan. With difficulty he heaved his bulk out of his stretch limousine, which had been pulled here by a team of camels since it ran out of petrol just beyond the Algerian border.

His beady eyes lit up as he spied the four spectacular babes lined up before him. Emily pocketed her TOATS Rule Book on Etiquette, its Villain Chapter bookmarked by a dried palm frond. Sneaking a look sideways, she thought she spied a gap in the ranks of the guards. If only some sort of distraction would occur, she might break away and make a dash for freedom . . .

Just then, Lottie fainted. Donna stretched out her hand to help Lottie and a large clump of ripe dates fell from an overhanging tree right into Donna's outstretched palm. (No pun intended.)

Donna paused, surprised. She gaped at the fruit that had fallen so unexpectedly into her hand. The Sultan and his retinue drew breath in amazement. Taking advantage of this moment, Emily boldly broke away from the guards. Adroitly dodging them, she slipped through their ranks. Before they came to their senses she had disappeared behind a dune with a swiftness no-one had expected.

"Let her go!" commanded Sultan Siliman. "She will not get far. But what have we here? A girl who merely has to hold out her hand, for food to drop into it?"

295

He scrutinised Donna more closely, gasped and dropped to his knees in front of her. The color drained from his moon-like face. "Forgive me Your Worshipfulness!" exclaimed this portly Prince of the Desert, "I now see you are the living image of the ancient statue in the temple—the Goddess Donna! Come from heavenly palaces to visit us at last!" The Sultan bowed his head right down to the sand, and all his retinue followed suit.

Oyliman wailed, "Ah! What have I done? Forgive me, Goddess."

Katie whispered to Donna, "Play along. This could work out well! If they think you're a goddess there's no end to what you might do!" Bowing devoutly at Donna's feet Katie continued in low tones meant for her ears alone, "you will be able to save Connie and Juliana from Oyliman's clutches."

"Let them save themselves," responded Donna acerbically (the goddess thing was already starting to go to her head). "They can write themselves out of trouble."

"Oh wretched Siliman," Donna went on in a loud voice, "you have displeased me greatly. You must make amends for your rotten treatment of myself and my handmaidens. Shower us with riches. Make every effort to see to our comfort."

"Yes Your Worshipfulness, at once Your Worshipfulness," gabbled Siliman, reduced to a quivering wreck. At that moment a scream was heard from the dunes where Emily had disappeared.

"What's happened?" cried Donna.

"Nothing I assure you, Wonderfulness," squeaked Oyliman. "It's just that the camel dungheap lies over that hill . . ."

Will Siegfried ever find the damsels he has set out to rescue? Can he fulfil his mission to win his Hero Certificate from Herr Schumm? Will he finally get to read Lottie's script and marry her? Will Emily manage to extricate herself from the pit of camel droppings? Will the evil Barb catch up with Emily and wreak her terrible revenge? Will Connie and Juliana contribute a chapter towards their own rescue? How much will Nicolas Birdhouse fetch in the slave-markets of Conjectural Casablanca? Is there really a desert in More-or-Less Morocco or is it actually in Alleged Algeria? Will Donna demand that the Sultan builds a new temple dedicated to her? Will Katie regret becoming part of TOATS, or will she enjoy it? Tune into this site soon to find out!

ORIGINAL BARB

15 January 1999

Hi Emily, interesting Villain Chapter! I loved your Chapter 97. Visitors to this site, please note: Siegfried does actually feature in this story sometimes . . . He will doubtless soon return to the narrative.

UNEARTHLY EMILY

15 January 1999

"Finished!" Tess exclaimed, placing the last piece in her "Where's Wotsisname?"® puzzle as she knelt on the gently rocking deck of the tall ship.

Mishka walked over to her and admired her handiwork. "It said three to five years on the box and you did it in two weeks. You're a genius!"

297

Tess blushed. "Thanks, Mishka. So—how long till we arrive in More-or-Less Morocco?"

With a huge crash the ship ploughed into a pier in Casablanca Harbour, throwing Tess into the handsome sailor's arms. "We're there my little Kartoffel," he replied. (I know, I know Kartoffel is German not Vulgarian.)

At the same time two men in business suits and Santa hats were standing on the pier in front of a food vendor's stand. "I'll have the roasted goat with tabouli and a Kemi-Kola®. What would you like Woolfie?"

Woolfie was oblivious of Isambard.

"Woolfie what are you staring at?" Isambard turned around to see a HUGE Vulgarian sailing ship headed straight for the pier. "Run! Run!" he yelled, dragging Woolfie away from the path of the oncoming vessel.

As for Siegfried, having successfully intimidated the owner of the Baib-El-Fish Cafe into revealing the location of the Sultan's palace, he headed for the distant mountains. (See, those bad guy roles finally paid off!)

Meanwhile, back at the tents . . .

While wiping camel doo-doo off, Emily found herself surrounded by Oilyman's guards. Using her superior intellect she grabbed fist-fulls of the foul-smelling substance and started flinging it at the guards—who, being the obsessively clean type, recoiled in horror and ran away. Emily dashed over to the corral and grabbed the nearest Arabian stallion. Being careful to tie a handkerchief over the horse's nose so the steed would not expire of her odoriferous condition, she took off at lightning speed . . .

Tired and dusty from his long ride, Siegfried spotted a crystal blue Moroccan stream lined with green vegetation.

"That's just the spot to rest for the night!" he said. After dismounting with surpassing agility he took off Brian's saddle and let him go. Brian hesitated, his ears pricked forward as he heard the soft jingle of tiny bells coming from the bushes nearby. "Vat is it Brian?"

An Arabian stallion, his mane decorated with ribbons and tiny bells, was nibbling on the bush's succulent leaves while soap bubbles floated by his head. Intrigued, Siegfried sneaked in for a closer look. Around a rocky outcrop he saw wet clothes laid out to dry—and, to his delight, Emily bathing in the stream, her magnificent body illuminated by dappled sunlight as tiny bubbles floated in the gentle breeze!

Captivated by Emily's radiance, Siegfried roguishly leaned on the rock for a few moments and watched her wash her raven-colored hair. Presently he said, "That isn't ecologically sound, you know."

Emily was taken by surprise. She was thrilled to see Siegfried again and, realizing there wasn't another TOATS woman for miles, grinned wickedly. Gracefully she waded over to the bank. "It's biodegradable," she replied in her sexiest voice as a small rivulet of soap trailed down her forehead and landed in her eye.

"Ow! Ow! Ow! My eye!" The lovely damsel frantically splashed water on her face, knocking Siegfried off balance, and they both fell into the stream.

UnEarthly Lottie

UNEARTHLY LOTTIE

17 January 1999

At Oyliman's oasis hideaway, Sultan Siliman, Chieftain Oyliman and their complete entourages, from Barbie warrior to lowly servant, scurried around frantically in a vain attempt to fulfil the divine Goddess Donna's every whim. (New temple—air conditioned of course—shiny red Forgeroni® sports car, Lance's head on a plate, etc.)

In the handmaidens' tent Lottie, having at last come around from her swoon, sobbed in terrible despair. The mounds of silken cushions in which she buried her head had turned sodden and squelchy under the deluge of her tears.

"Cheer up, Lottie," said Katie. "Things are looking up. They all think your friend Donna's a goddess, so . . ."

"You don't understand," interrupted Lottie, raising her wet, blotchy face from the pillows. "She, Emily, everyone—except me—seems to have forgotten . . . that vile slug Oyliman left Siegfried in the desert to die . . . " (shuddering sob) " . . . miles and miles of scorching sand . . . " (gurgle, gasp, groan) ". . . vultures, hideously silhouetted against a pitilessly burning sun, circling, circling . . ." She broke off in a mournful wail of inconsolable woe.

"Siegfried?" said Katie. "Who's Siegfried?"

"My hero," whimpered Lottie. "Oh, the fathomless blue of his eyes," (pathetic sigh) "the endless fascination of his cheekbones, the lovely curls of his hair . . . " (sob, splutter, moan) "I love even the things I don't like about him . . . and we were going to get married . . . and now—oh gosh!—he'll never even get to read the script I wrote for him!"

"You surely can't mean Siegfried P. Hinkelheimer," whispered Katie incredulously. Lottie gave a sorrowful nod and put her head back in the soggy pillows. "But I love that man!" said Katie; "Even if he does have a wobbly neck. You mean to say he's out there, in the desert somewhere? I must meet him!"

She rushed to the tent-flap to wildly scan the horizon. Featureless sand stretched as far as the eye could see. (She failed to notice, in the far distance, tiny spurts of sand flung up at every furious stride as Barb pounded the warpath on her Emily-hunt.)

"Meet him? Too late!" wailed Lottie plaintively. "He'll be dead by now, his beautiful bones" (snotty snivel) "picked clean and scattered on the dunes!"

"Control yourself," said Katie, getting hold of Lottie's shoulders and shaking her till her teeth rattled. "Look, he's a hero; he'll probably come and rescue us. He can't die."

"Yes he can—I watched *A Dry White Season* the night before last and he died in that!"

"But he was a villain in that," argued Katie. "He deserved to die."

"What about *Thrill Schmooze*, eh? . . . and *The Constable and the Young Lady*? What about" (pitiful moan, choked groan, strangled whimper) *Das Rat*!! Even when he's a good guy he goes and dies!"

"Lottie, I think you're getting a bit confused," said Katie. "They're just movies . . . this is real life".

"Real life?" wailed Lottie. "You call this real life? I think you're the one who's confused . . ."

UNEARTHLY LOTTIE
17 January 1999

As we all know, Siegfried is not dying in the desert—in fact he seems to be doing remarkably well after riding that excellent horse, Brian, hundreds of miles across the Atlas Mountains to Casablanca and back. The only vulture to be seen at present is a particularly beautiful one, with long floating tresses of midnight hair and eyes to match the gorgeous jade outfit into which she is sliding her delectable body.

The vulture was, of course, Emily, sporting a look on her face that resembled that of a rapacious carnivore satiated after a particularly pleasant meal. She managed to rearrange her face into something she hoped was an expression of sweet innocence before turning to face Siegfried who sat, dry again (after his unexpected—but exceedingly pleasant—swim) and a little bit sleepy, in the dappled shade on the bank of the stream. A soft breeze from the desert ruffled the tousled curls of his hair as Emily sat down beside him, leaned her head against his shoulder and murmured, "I'm so happy".

Siegfried stifled a yawn. "Actually Emily, I feel I should confess to you—you almost didn't see me again; any of you. Back in Casablanca—in the cafe—a feeling of freedom overwhelmed me. I thought, *I need never see any of those fright . . . ah, beautiful women again. If I can somehow avoid TOATS taxis, and Air Banana planes, I could just go home . . . see the kids . . . feed the cat . . . Aah . . . Gluckseligkeit!*

"But then I thought of you poor defenceless creatures in the clutches of Oyliman . . . and, what the hell—here I am . . . bescheuert Idiot, eh?"

"Wha . . . ?" began Emily, totally confused. Had she heard aright? Did this man just imply he'd rather feed his cat than spend time with the divinely gorgeous her? (Or, for that matter, any of those other alluring females that had been hanging off him for the last few months?)

But before she could attempt to unravel this mystery, her thought processes were violently interrupted by the roar of a dozen motors and a stinging spray of sand erupting from skidding tires across them both.

UNEARTHLY LOTTIE

17 January 1999

Blinking painfully, Emily peered through smarting, sand-filled eyes at a nightmare vision; at least a dozen cars had halted before them—three in the stream, two upside down and one wrapped around a palm tree. From each of the cars an impossible number of people clambered forth and all of them, even the women, even the children, looked uncannily like Oyliman!

In one quick, catlike movement Siegfried was on his feet. Emily clung to him as one of the Oylimen, bigger than the rest, edged his way towards them with, strangely, dollar signs sparkling in his eyes.

Siegfried pushed Emily roughly aside. She glanced at him, hurt, then stepped back in confusion. My gosh! (she thought) he suddenly looks like; who? Charlie Dude, out of *Sugarcane Jones?* Michael Bogan? . . . ALL of his villains rolled into one! Really mean, really tough, really BAD.

"Followed me here, did you, Slim?" Siegfried said with a menacing voice and an ugly sneer.

Mr Slim (not his real name) clapped his hands delightedly. "Oh very good, very good, Most Excellent and Enthralling Actor! You see, when you are in my café drinking my excellent *qahwā*, I am thinking, I am thinking; I have seen this man! Oh, but my feeble brain . . . ! But it is my wife; this is she . . . this is Fatima—" (indicating a large woman who hid, blushing and trembling behind him) "—she see you leave my café. Even at a hundred paces the Great Force of your Charisma knock her to the floor! She cannot get up for an hour!

"When she regain sense, she utter the magic word, 'Hollywood'! Then I remember all your movies; *Reproductive Killers*! *Judge Mental*! *Sugarcane Smith*—my favorite; very nice girls! And I think—" (tapping his sweaty brow with a be-ringed finger) "—that is why he want my cousin, Scourge of the Desert! He want fierce Barbie warriors for big Hollywood movie! So here we are—whole family; many extras you will need! Here, jump in my car—you also, Glamorous Hollywood actress! We drive you to my Illustrious Cousin! Let's go!"

Siegfried shook his head sadly and mumbled to himself (as he squeezed into Mr Slim's car beside quivering, giggling Fatima); "I seem to have an amazing talent lately for getting myself into really stupid situations."

UNEARTHLY BARB

18 January 1999

Siegfried and Emily arrived at Oyliman's Desert Hideaway with their entourage of Oyliman's cousin's extensive family from the Baib-el-Fish Café, including his twelve strapping sons who resembled extras from the TV show *Hero-Clues®* and his ancient granny, who resembled a prune.

"Not only is this a really stupid situation," thought Siegfried breathlessly, continuing on from the last chapter, "it is also getting very crowded. Lottie is brilliant at crowd scenes. I really must read her script . . ."

His thoughts were interrupted for a moment as their vehicle swerved past a large cage made of palm-tree saplings lashed together with leather thongs. The two women inside this edifice were desperately shaking the bars, calling out pleadingly, but the car's V8 engine roared so loudly that Siegfried could not hear them. As they flashed past, it came to him that they looked familiar—that red-haired one with the horned helmet—had he seen her somewhere before? And that alluring blonde in the risqué semi-transparent harem outfit—she looked like someone he had once known . . .

But there was no time to wonder. Mr. Baib-el-Fish's car slewed to a halt, teetering on the brink of the oasis' well. Oyliman's slaves opened the doors with a flourish and the cousins embraced.

"Hey, Oyli!" bellowed Mr Fish (otherwise known as Mr. Slim), "where is the Sultan?"

"The goddess Donna has appeared before us," babbled Oyliman. "At her command, Siliman has taken her with her handmaidens to his palace in the Great Citadel." He appeared still jittery, but relieved.

"That's exactly where we are going, cousin!" smiled Mr. Fish. "To make very excellent movie with the fabulous Mr. Hinkelheimer."

"A movie?" Oyliman's eyes lit up like two TV screens. He turned to Siegfried with a bow. "You will be needing extras, sir!"

Without further ado, Oyliman packed his entire retinue onto camel-back. A massive crowd now spilled across the sand, departing from the Desert Hideaway—fifteen cars filled to bursting with passengers, forty-seven camels piled high with goods and riders. They set off in the direction of the Great Citadel.

"Cosy, isn't it!" said Emily with a sweet smile at Siegfried, pouring herself in between him and Fatima. "Oh. look!" She pointed out the window. The edge of a long dune cleanly sliced the sky. There, along the golden spine of this wind-rippled ridge, a small figure was striding relentlessly, kicking up tiny puffs of sand. It seemed to be heading in the same direction as the Oyliman caravan. Emily squinted. "That almost looks like Barb! I wonder what did happen to her."

She yawned, dismissing the thought and snuggling in under Siegfried's rather sweaty but infinitely desirable armpit.

UNEARTHLY CONNIE

18 January 1999

Back at Oyliman's desert hideaway, inside the cage made of palm-tree saplings, Connie and Juliana were close to despair. The only slightly pleasant thought they could muster was that at least Oyliman and his family and hangers-on had all sped off into the distance with Hollywood-style thoughts in their heads.

"Oh what are we to do?" wailed Connie. "Nic is about to be sold at the slave markets! He might have been bought already! With those looks, that body . . . he's bound to have been snapped up by some entitled, wealthy old princess who wants him as a sex slave! Oh dear!"

Juliana's fierce Icelandic eyes were looking a tad worried now, wondering if she could get out of this one . . . she didn't really want Oyliman to decide which way he would like to amuse himself with her on his return.

Then Connie suddenly realized that she did possess some muscles, a leftover from her body-building days. She began to pull at the saplings, causing the leather bindings to strain, and strain. Her eyes nearly popped out of her head, veins protruded from her temples, her blonde tresses were glued to her head with perspiration and her harem outfit had become more transparent to the point where she would easily win the next wet harem-outfit competition . . . except she was determined to be back in Hollywood with Nic long before that illustrious event.

Suddenly, SNAP! The saplings broke and Connie fell out of the cage!

Juliana, realising that she had regained her freedom, screamed out "I'm sick of this whole More-or-Less-Morocco thing! I'm off to Inauthentic Iceland—where's that damned TOATS taxi?" And with that she stomped off over the nearest sand dune in search of one of the ubiquitous yellow cabs whose crazed drivers from outer space were ever-hungry for a fare.

Connie was much too preoccupied with thoughts of her task at hand to worry what might become of Juliana, wandering around the desert.

She spied Brian, who had joined a group of camels happily munching hay. Remembering that she used to ride horses (even before the body-building) she leaped on to Brian's back, praying her rusty equitation abilities had not deserted her. Brian sprang away with a startled snort.

Connie whispered into his ear, "Take me to the slave markets please, Brian!" and being the magical horse that he was, he understood and obeyed!

UnEarthly Connie

UNEARTHLY CONNIE
18 January 1999

Brian galloped over the sand, his magnificent mane catching the rays of the afternoon sun and glowing gold. This of course was matched by Connie's golden tresses streaming out behind her head, set off beautifully by the semi-transparent harem outfit.

They soon reached the outskirts of a dirty, crowded town and Brian slowed to a trot. They made their way carefully through alleyways crowded with noisy stalls and loose animals. The flies and the stench of open drains rose up into Connie's nostrils, but she was oblivious of all that, so intent was she on achieving her goal.

As she neared the markets, she could hear people yelling loudly. They were bidding for a pathetic-looking slave who was standing up on a makeshift platform, hands and feet bound, wearing nothing but a grubby loincloth. She scanned the scene—this wasn't Nic—where was he? Had he been sold already? Panic began to set in.

As she desperately scanned the area she noticed a bejewelled figure waddling down an alleyway. Following the lead of her sex-slave theory, she guided Brian in the direction of that ungainly posterior. As she neared it, cautiously, she spied Nic, being led away by a wealthy slave-owning princess, by means of a rope tied around his wrists. His shirt had been ripped off and he was looking particularly dishevelled. Even in her haste Connie couldn't help but admire those muscles ... *snap out of it, woman! Rescue him, don't swoon over him!*

She spurred Brian into a gallop, and headed down the alley screaming "Nic! It's me!"

She (having gained amazing powers in her quest) leaned over and wrested a knife from a market stall owner who was busily slicing up something unimaginable, continued on her way, and, amidst the confusion created by Brian's flying hooves, cut the rope. Nic's captor had time only to look up and gabble something unintelligible, but her erstwhile slave had already leapt onto Brian's back behind Connie. They galloped away down another alleyway, and then another, leaving the outraged princess's feeble screams far behind.

UNEARTHLY CONNIE
19 January 1999

As Connie and Nic emerged into the late afternoon from the close confines of the crowded and seedy town, Brian was still galloping. Sweat was flying back and lathering his relieved riders.

They gradually brought him back to a walk. Nic could not believe his luck. He had been rescued from the clutches of that tyrannical old princess, and, being the SNAG[22] that he is, he didn't even mind that it was a woman who had rescued him.

---

22 Sensitive New Age Guy

Connie was quick to inform him that the others had all raced off with Siegfried to make a movie.

"If we arrive at their shooting location," she cried, "Oyliman will be so overawed to have TWO Hollywood greats in his movie, I'm sure he won't notice that I've escaped from his harem! Anyway, even if he does, at least I've now got you to protect me! Question is, how do we get there? The TOATS taxi has probably gone off with Juliana in it . . . maybe Brian is programmed to return to Siegfried—I'll ask him."

She whispered into Brian's glossy black ear, and sure enough, he turned and started off in (they hoped) the direction of the movie set.

Will they find the others? Will Juliana find a taxi rank and make it to Inauthentic Iceland in one piece? Will the reviewers and critics like the movie? Does anybody else at this site care two hoots that Nic has been rescued? Will anyone brush all that sweat out of Brian's coat? Stay tuned!

UNEARTHLY EMILY
19 January 1999

Isambard and the film agent Woolfie, having narrowly escaped the collision of Tess's ship with the Casablanca pier, were comfortably ensconced at "Rick's Café Amerikanisch"® drinking mai-tais when Woolfie's cell phone started ringing.

Woolfie put the phone to his ear. "It's Schumm," he said. He listened intently.

"What is it Woolfie?" Isambard asked.

Woolfie silenced the film producer with a wave of the hand

and started scribbling notes on the tablecloth. "I see. Uh huh. Yes. Right away. Of course, I'll take care of it immediately."

He put the phone away and looked at his companion. "Forget Emily's and Lottie's scripts. Have I got a story for you!"

The big man said excitedly, "What is it?"

After looking around carefully to make sure no one else was listening Woolfie leaned forward. He whispered, "TOATS."

"What?"

"TOATS! TOATS! Mares eat TOATS and does eat TOATS and little lambs eat ivy."

Isambard sniffed Woolfie's drink. "Just what did you order?"

Woolfie dragged Isambard out of the café. "Come along. I'll explain in the cab."

" . . . so you see," Woolfie was saying moments later as the taxi hurtled along spraying up sand on either side like flamboyant wings, "Tess is on that Vulgarian ship which just missed hitting us on the pier, Tammie has been dragged away by a TOATS taxi driver because she ran out of text, Barb—having turned evil from bottled air—is racing after Emily for that flushing incident, and Connie, having fulfilled her fantasy by writing four episodes of nothing but Nic is heading with him to the movie set in the desert, where Emily, Siegfried, and Lottie and Katie are in the clutches of the Oyliman family.

"Donna is a goddess and all of Oyliman's relatives are on the set too. Juliana is waiting for a taxi back to Inauthentic Iceland and Brian can miraculously travel enormous distances in the blink of an eye. Got it?"

Isambard scratched his head in confusion. "But we've already done *It's a Mad, Mad, Mad, Mad World*®[23]!"

UNEARTHLY BARB

5 February 2009

The two men stared at each other in desperate perplexity.

"Are you thinking what I'm thinking?" they said simultaneously.

"Yes!" they chorused, continuing in perfect synchronisation. "Let's just forget the whole idea and go back to where life is simple and the only worries are world financial crises, climate change and whether a meteor collision will throw the world off its axis!"

Without further ado they told the driver to make for the airport, where they caught the next flight home.

---

23 ©William Rose and Tania Rose.

18

WHAA??

Where'd everybody go?

At this point, the story gets cut in half.

If you want to read the rest you'll have to get hold of Book 2:
Cyberchicks Go Wild, subtitled with that classic clickbait line,
"What Happens Next May Shock You!" (which Barb discov-
ered on a "List of Clickbaits" website).

"Why bother with Book 2?" I hear you ask.

And I reply, "Because it's filled with wacky words of undis-
covered genius and some pretty funny scenes."

These include:

- An unfortunate episode with an Air Banana aicraft,
  followed by a parachuting scene in which UnEarthly
  Barb wears a paper bag on her head in an effort to
  remain incognito

- Another scene in which UnEarthly Emily pulls a loose thread on Siegfried's jacket only for him to unravel until he ceases to exist, leaving her holding a tiny piece of tweed thread in her hand
- The cyberchicks performing Quiverdance® in perfect unison shortly after they stumble across an outback ants' nest
- New cyberchicks including Mayra and Marjorie; and (Insert Your Name Here) assembling a crude computer out of old toenails, odd strands of hair, rats' nests, and spit, called a "Ratintosh®".

So you see, it's not to be missed.

Readers with perspicacity, sagacity, tenacity, eccentricity and all those other classy cities will read Book 2 knowing that they'll get at least some benefit out of it, even if it's only a few minutes of confusion followed by a sense of relief that they can put it down and return to "normality".

See you in Book 2!

~ Barb

In Book 2 you'll meet Mayra from Brazil . . .

Original Mayra

UnEarthly Mayra

and Marjorie from England.

Cyberchicks series

Book 1: Cyberchicks in Love

Book 2: Cyberchicks go Wild

For more books you'll love,

Visit the Leaves of Gold Press website

www.leavesofgoldpress.com

Write a review

Enjoyed frolicking with the fangirls?

Consider reviewing this book ^{with lots of stars} on Amazon

https://tinyurl.com/cyberchicks-1

and Goodreads https://tinyurl.com/nicereviews

It means the world to us!

Scan this QR code with the photo app on your smart-
phone, then tap on your phone's screen. It'll take you to

the Amazon.com page for this book!

Milton Keynes UK
Ingram Content Group UK Ltd.
UKHW040623290424
441922UK00001B/17